SINS OF EDOM
A Senior Sleuth Crime Novel

Carl Brookins

DEDICATION

To my dear, wife Jean, editor, shipmate, friend, source of constant encouragement and excellent mother of our daughters.

ACKNOWLEDGMENTS

It is often said that writing is a solitary profession. Yet few successful authors can ever say, honestly, that the books they produce are purely the result of the author's solo effort. I am pleased to acknowledge and even celebrate the interest, attention and critical efforts of fellow crime writers Karl, Susan, John, Greg, Sarah, and Amy, I am intensely grateful for their honesty, patience and forbearance.

Sins of Edom

ISBN: 978-0-9969991-3-7
Carl Brookins 2021

First Edition

Copyright Brookins Books LLC 2021

Cover photograph by Bernice Tong from Upsplash

CHAPTER 1

Alan Lockem stood in the back of the sanctuary of the church, leaning against the wall. His arms were crossed. He hadn't been in that church since his baptism seventy-plus years earlier. The sanctuary wasn't large; it held maybe 250 worshippers on a busy Sunday. He stared at the pulpit, a simple lectern of finely crafted and polished white oak. It was draped with a banner in royal blue that carried a gold representation of the traditional Protestant Christian church. Behind the pulpit was the choir loft, a series of hand-made wooden chairs in a box. Against the back wall, behind the pulpit stood the altar. In this church it was a well-designed table that could be moved about the elevated platform as appropriate for different celebrations and services. The elevated platform or stage stretched across the breadth of the space, four wooden steps above the floor of the sanctuary with its fixed rows of wooden pews Above the altar, against the wall of the building the arrangement of organ pipes, both real and false, soared in a precise arrangement of several rows, some extending to the ceiling thirty feet overhead.

As bespoke the modern church, the vaulted wood-sheathed ceiling that reached high overhead was festooned with high-intensity lights, speakers, and a network of black connecting wires. Two walls carried multiple well-crafted stained-glass windows that displayed fragments of important Christian messages from the Bible.

Between the pews and the steps to the altar, a long strip of bright yellow plastic tape hung from the railings on each side of the space and displayed a different message repeated in black block type:

CRIME SCENE DO NOT CROSS.

CHAPTER 2

It surprised the man standing in the
sanctuary that the crime scene tape remained. Alan
Lockem, former Army Lieutenant first class, assigned
to Intelligence Operations, had been told by police with
jurisdiction that the church had been examined in
detail and released back to the congregation. He
continued to visually survey the crime scene. His
religious affiliations and experiences had ended with
his long-ago introduction to the malfeasances in some
religious sects when he was first entering college.
Those experiences and observations, about which he
had never spoken publicly, had turned him toward a
more personal and heartfelt if unorganized faith.

Years later, after a medaled and successful
career in Military Intelligence, he encountered a
sensitive and sensual former chorine and star stage
performer with whom he formed an almost instant
connection. Over the intervening years he and Marjorie
"Kandy" Kane had established an enviable reputation
as a couple to go to for help in extenuating
circumstances. Erroneously accused individuals found
Lockem and Kane to be agile and valuable assistance
in extricating themselves from sometimes strange or
odd criminal activities. Even though local law
enforcement generally avoided employing the services
of private and non-licensed operatives, somehow,
through intelligent research, high ethical standards,
and careful decision-making, as well as a certain level
of luck and development of cordial relations with local
law enforcement, Lockem and Kane had developed a
reputation in the Twin Cities as help to turn to in
highly fraught situations. Local criminal defense
attorneys also found the couple's services of
considerable help.

Today, Lockem, tall, slender, still keen of eye in
his advancing years, stood in a crime scene with

appalling consequences. The pastor and a female parishioner had been brutally and viciously murdered. The woman had apparently been consulting the pastor, the Reverend Martin Elliot, on a personal matter. The woman was not well-known to church members and appeared to have only tenuous ties to the larger community.

After neighborhood talk and posts to social media surfaced with questions about the pastor, and about his relationship to the murdered woman, a group of church members had approached Marjorie Kane for advice. She was not a church member but attended a book club that met in the big meeting room in the basement of the church. And so a plea for help went from a small group of church women to Marjorie Kane She had met privately with the members of the church and after judging them to be sincere and sincerely concerned about the murders and the progress of the police in solving the crimes, Marjorie talked to Alan about the church women's questions and here he stood, a few days later, in a cool sanctuary where extensive cleaning had already taken place, and where plans were under way to alter some of the space and reconsecrate the sanctuary, a ceremony normally carried out when a church had been violated.

Until the murders were solved and the church again consecrated, all activities, even non-religious ones were suspended which had caused a scattering of the congregation and some serious schedule upheavals for groups that depended on the spaces afforded by the church building.

Lockem thought about the situation, even while he examined the area around the altar and the doorway to the robing room where the bodies had been found. It had taken him some time to find the church secretary who had the keys because Carolyn Action only now came to the office two days a week to handle the collected mail. He could smell, faintly, the cleaning solutions used by the firm that specialized in cleaning and sanitizing sites of serious trauma, like murder.

He raised his eyes again to the back wall. He was not very familiar with the kinds of pipe organs commonly found in churches but Lockem remembered reading somewhere that the array of pipes exposed to parishioners were mostly fake, just arranged there for show and that the working pipes were hidden behind. So he bent carefully under the crime scene tape, walked up the steps past the choir box to the altar table that stood against the back wall below the organ pipes. He noted that the organ keyboard was in a small separate box on his left, close behind the pulpit. His footsteps on the bare wood floor echoed through the sanctuary space until he stood before the wall.

Lockem stared at the pipes for a long moment. From an inside pocket he took a small shiny black digital camera. Expensive, with high pixel rating and a first-class lens, the camera provided superior quality and tight detail as required. Lockem also carried a phone with a built-in camera, but when he wanted fine detail, he knew he could rely on the Nikon. He recorded several views of the areas where the bodies were discovered by the choir director almost two weeks earlier, then he went closer to the wall and stared over his head at the pipes.

The sanctuary had been redecorated and largely rebuilt in the past year so surfaces were smooth and unmarred. Then he saw what appeared to be a dent or nick in the side on one of the largest pipes. The defect was located several feet above the floor and marred the pipe very near the next pipe so it would only have been seen from a particular angle and when the lighting was just right. Lockem wondered briefly if the police investigators had noticed it. He also wondered where the bullet had lodged. He was pretty confident the defect he had spotted was caused by a bullet. He believed he was looking at a bullet nick because a small caliber pistol had been the killing instrument used to take the lives of both the pastor and his parishioner. He took several pictures and then stepped into the small room behind the choir and altar where the reverend, Martin Elliot, kept a rack of robes and other clothes.

A small mirror, sink and cabinet held a glass, deodorant and hangers for robes and other accoutrements of the profession. It was a very small room, almost a closet on the back wall of the church building with a tiny window high by the ceiling. Lockem stared at the window and realized it was a fixed double pane in the opening and had no handle.

He turned from looking at the robes, casual clothes, and empty hangers on the racks when rapid footsteps sounded across the bare floor behind him. He turned to see Ms. Action coming toward him.

"I'm sorry, Mr. Lockem? Will you be much longer? I do have to lock up fairly soon."

"No problem, Ms. Action. Sorry if I've kept you too long, this afternoon. I realize it has been an imposition."

Without directly responding to him, Carolyn Action spun on her high-heeled black shoes and walked briskly back the way she had come. Lockem knew she had not approved of a civilian poking about in church business. She'd made that very clear when he arrived at her office two hours earlier. He suspected she didn't like having the police and crime scene specialists there, either.

Chapter 3

After Ms. Action's footsteps faded to silence, Lockem stood quietly, listening to the building, he would have said. He opened his mouth to breathe more softly and cocked his head. He couldn't have said why he did that—Marjorie, his boon companion, would have remarked it was his listening stance. Lockem could sometimes breathe in messages from a crime scene. It was as if the building spoke to him in an ancient and obscure language. Unfortunately, Lockem admitted, he didn't know the language, couldn't translate the sounds, and often only understood their significance after a case was completed.

He shrugged his shoulders and walked softly away from the altar, back toward the large double doors that gave exterior access to the street from the sanctuary. Lockem had been given to understand that those doors were only unlocked on Sunday mornings before traditional services and on other important occasions such as weddings, funerals, and similar regular business of this congregation. Today, the doors were locked. Lockem wondered whether or not the doors were locked on the afternoon when the dead pastor was meeting with his parishioner.

Alan Lockem awoke to a ray of sunlight in his eyes. It had found its way through a tiny space between folds of the drape that hung over the bedroom window It was a large floor to ceiling window that gave a panoramic view of their backyard patio, hedges, and the park beyond. He moved his head to the left on the pillow and his gaze encountered a return look from one lovely blue eye securely attached to his companion, retired head-line dancer, stripper and former chorus lady, Marjorie Kane.

"Good morning, love. You must have been more tired than you thought."

"Hmm, I guess you're right." He rolled his head and kissed her nose. "Huh, it's after seven," He sat up and scratched his head, further messing the thick white curls that adorned his head. He didn't have a buzz cut, but his army grooming had left him with a habit of keeping his hair fashionably short. As he aged, somehow his hair became thicker and curlier.

Swinging his long legs to the side he sat up on the edge of the bed. His thoughts went almost immediately to what he'd seen at the church where the two bodies had been discovered a few days earlier. Alan continued to process his observations while showering and dressing. Down a single half-flight of stairs he entered the dining room where Marjorie was just putting out their cold breakfast makings, along with the utensils.

"You can think and cogitate over the sounds of crunching cornflakes," she smiled at him. "But lunch and dinner are on you."

"You are out all day?"

"Yup. Three small meetings and lunch. So you decide on what you want for dinner and get things started. Plan on my getting back here around seven."

"Okay. Which car do you want?"

"Oh. The Morris if that's okay?"

"Sure, no problem." Alan sat and poured cream onto his bowl of cereal.

"You going to tell the police about the nick in the organ pipe? I thought about it some and I wonder if perhaps they already know and have dismissed it. The cops." She raised one eyebrow in the way she had.

"I'm betting they didn't see it or did and decided it wasn't important. Like, not a bullet mark. But I will mention it to the cops in charge."

After clearing the breakfast dishes and seeing Marjorie off, Lockem went to his desk and his growing file of notes on the church and called the Saint Paul police department. Once he was identified and passed on to an inspector responsible for the case, he reported his find.

10

"Tell you the truth, Mr. Lockem, I don't see anything in the file here about damage to the pipes. I expect our crime scene people would have examined it. Could it have happened after the murders?"

"That's possible. I didn't get a ladder and make a close examination of the hole."

"That's good. I doubt somebody is shooting random holes in the church organ, 'specially the site of two recent murders. I assume there's another solution. The records show we recovered bullets for each of the wounds in the two Dbs. Dead bodies. However, I thank you for the information. We'll decide if it requires another visit." The Inspector cleared his throat and said, "Mr. Lockem, I've been advised that you have been asked to look into possible church connections with this case."

"That's true, although I'm reluctant to discuss my client."

"No, no," responded the Inspector. "I've talked to an officer who knows you well. He assures me you'll come forward with information whenever you think its relevant. If it ever is. I just wanted you to be aware, as are we."

"Thanks."

"The murdered woman had a fairly interesting though not unusual past. She was an active blogger, however, and may have associated with some unusual groups."

"Is that so? Care to expand on that?"

"Not yet, Mr. Lockem. At least not now. I'd prefer that you develop that line of information on your own. I'm sure you'll know if or when we need to talk again."

Lockem agreed and he and the cop severed their connection. He wondered about the conversation. The inspector had been both cautious and open. Something appeared to be going on under the surface.

He fired up his computer and began a search. The murdered woman, Delilah Cooper, had a blog, and Lockem reserved his examination of her writings until

11

he had more background on the victim. He started
with Ms Cooper, assuming winkling out information
about her would be easier than penetrating the veils of
silence that often were in place in church
organizations.

Her web site detailed important life elements of
a young middle-aged white woman with few questions
visible in her on-line life. Married and divorced, Delilah
Cooper had grown up and gone to school in Galveston,
Texas. Her divorce had occurred a few years after
moving to Saint Paul, Minnesota. There were
apparently, no children and she seemed to have
displayed a lot of friendly, smiling pictures of a
midwestern professional woman who, at the time of
her death, had a nice apartment in the Uptown
neighborhood of Minneapolis and a job she enjoyed
with the local office of a national public relations
agency.

Lockem's initial scans through the pages of her
web site raised no questions. He took down some
information and decided a drive to her former
residence was in order. He also started an itemized
and dated event calendar, based on what she had
shared. Naturally, there were gaps, but he might be
able to fill in those as things went along.

He went to the garage and backed out, pausing
in their driveway to send Marjorie a brief voicemail
that he'd take care of dinner after a quick trip to
Minneapolis. His turn off the Boulevard onto twenty-
eighth Avenue was difficult due to heavy oncoming
traffic. He finally made the turn, tires squealing, and
noted another vehicle that followed closely. The two
vehicles cruised slowly up the street, east toward Lake
Street. Lockem spotted an open meter and abruptly
pulled to the curb. The following vehicle hesitated
briefly, then cruised by and turned right at the next
intersection. Lockem parked and stepped out of his car
into gusts of spring breeze. Bending his head against
the pressure of the wind he stepped toward the
building's door. He didn't expect anybody to be in the

12

deceased woman's apartment, but he pressed the button anyway. After a brief pause a male voice responded. "Yes?"

"I'd like to speak to Ms. Delilah Cooper."

"Sorry, she's not available." The voice was neutral, he thought, tending toward business abrupt.

"I believe I have an appointment."

"I doubt it," the voice responded. "Ms. Cooper is out of town."

Lockem wondered if the unseen male attached to the voice had been informed she was dead. Why did a male answer a page to the Cooper apartment? He'd expected a cop but this voice was possibly a building employee. Had he been given a script by the authorities? He shrugged and turned away. His gaze swept the building and the sidewalk toward Hennepin Avenue. A man stood at the corner of the block. Lockem only noticed him because he wasn't moving. Lockem couldn't tell if the man was watching him because the distance between them was too great.

Without a hitch in his movement he continued his turn and walked unhurriedly back to his car. Once strapped in and with the engine idling, he looked through the windshield to see that the man had disappeared. Lockem drove up to Hennepin and turned left, his mind now busy with the traffic and problem of getting onto the freeway toward Roseville and dinner.

Chapter 4

"**Tasty** dinner, even if it was mostly leftovers," smiled Marjorie. The couple had moved to their small living room where the music player and the big television were installed. Since they had acquired an upscale music system right after they moved in together, Alan had wired it to their cable feeds in order to have improved sound. The mammoth speaker cabinets anchored one corner of the room below the wall mounted TV.

Now comfortably ensconced in their favorite chairs, the couple relaxed with their usual after-dinner drink and talked over the day's activities. "Any new thoughts on motives?" asked Marjorie.

"Not a one," Alan responded. "I told you about finding what appears to be a bullet scar on one of the organ pipes. Saint Paul PD assured me they'd take a look and they may have. I don't really expect them to keep me in the loop."

"Even though they expect you to keep *them* in the loop."

Alan smiled and sipped his drink. "I think I mentioned the watcher."

Marjorie sat up straight. "Watcher? I don't remember any such mention."

"Oh, sorry. When I was in Uptown this afternoon, I happened to see a man who appeared to be watching me as I went up to Delilah Cooper's apartment building."

Marjorie raised her well-shaped eyebrows in a silent question.

"He was—I think it was a man--just standing at the corner of a building in the next block looking toward me. It's possible he had his attention elsewhere, maybe even had his eyes closed," Alan continued.

"We have to also realize that even if they find the slug that made the scar, it may not tell us much of significance, if anything."

"True. It could fall under the heading of useful evidence if and when a killer is apprehended."

"What will we do, going forward?"

If you have a little time, could you do some research for me?" Alan was adept at using the computer nets they regularly used, but he knew from experience that Marjorie had superior research skills. Moreover, her associative instincts were superb. Just a word or a phrase might trigger a new trickle or stream of inquiry. In the past, such trickles had often been helpful in the extreme.

"Of course." She nodded. "You have but to request."

Alan smiled. "I want to know about this pastor." He glanced at his notebook. "His name is Martin Elliot. He's been the pastor at that church for at least five years. I'm off to go back to the apartment address where our other victim supposedly lived. Minneapolis PD has given the building super the word that I'm to have access to the apartment."

Marjorie smiled and turned to her office and desk computer. It looked like an ordinary retail-available machine but the two additional monitors and more wires than usual snaking from her desk to the wall in the corner of her office gave a clue to the multiple connections and thus her reach into the bright known as well as dark and obscure reaches of the cyber world. Allen's career in intelligence had made it possible for her to have unusual Internet access.

She sat in her ergonomically designed chair and dialed in a low level of vibration that would soothe her lower back. She activated the computer and slid the keyboard into her lap, kicking off her shoes at the same moment. Her toes eased the pillow under her desk into a satisfactory position and she tapped the keys that signed her into a national alternate low-profile cyber network. This net gave her rapid access to

15

the personal data of millions of people located all over the world.

She cursored to a search window and typed in the dead pastor's name and several other characteristics: male, Caucasian, Christian, Elliot's age, and citizenship. Marjorie knew the system to which she was connected already was processing some information, including the identification of her computer and who the person was who had created the password routine. She knew that information would be recorded in a government database somewhere. Ordinarily, she didn't worry about such things. Records of her and Alan Lockem's contacts were facts of life, just as were her records of phone calls and certain other business. Modern life held very few secrets any more from those who wanted to tease them out.

Two hours later Marjorie closed her terminal and watched the laser printer spew out ten pages of print detailing the life of Pastor Michael Elliot.

"He had an interesting life, cut short," Marjorie related sometime later after Alan had returned from Minneapolis. She lifted the tidy stack of paper. "I printed it out so you can read it."

"Good, but tell me the highlights, please?"

"Michael Elliot is a home-state boy, born and raised in Austin. That's Minnesota, not Texas. He graduated high school there. Played a little basketball and ran the half-mile in track. His parents gave him a nice graduation present."

Alan raised his eyebrows.

"Yeah," she went on, "an all-expenses paid two-month trip to Europe. He left with two friends in late August and wandered around central Europe, visiting galleries, spas, nature vistas and cities and towns. They rented a car in France. Took tons of pictures, wrote journals and cards and letters home. I found it interesting that the pastor's website and his Facebook page contained so much of this information."

"I wonder if there's anything in those journals that might help."

"I didn't contact the other two boys or Elliot's parents who are still alive in Austin. Apparently, all three made extensive records of their travels. One boy, a Trevor Howland, taped his narrative and gave Pastor Elliot a copy when they got home. Again, that's based on information from the Facebook pages and the Elliot website."

"More work, perhaps." Lockem started to write a note and realized that Marjorie would have already included a self-directed indication to follow up in other sources.

"Michael Elliot graduated from high school in 1965 went to Europe and a year later, entered Divinity School in Illinois." Marjorie took a sip of her coffee. "Six years later, aged twenty-five, he was the assistant minister for a large Chicago congregation on the south side. After four years he was sent by the church to be a part-time traveling minister to five tiny congregations in West Virginia where he lasted until the Saint Paul church asked for him. I don't know why the congregation here requested him specifically, but we'll find that out. He became the Pastor four years ago."

"He gives every appearance of being a good man, you haven't mentioned any trouble that required a transfer."

"Nope, although this is just a cursory look at his trail. Lots more levels to drill into."

"Yep." Alan stretched long arms overhead. "I am particularly interested in whether any parishioners had a problem with their minister. Doesn't even have to be somebody from his last church. If anybody had a problem, they could have followed him here, right?"

"If that's what happened, it will have to be a member of one of his churches, don't you agree? I can't really see a citizen of Wheeling coming all the way to Saint Paul these many years later to kill him, can you?"

Alan shook his head. "No and now I wonder if either of them will turn out to be collateral damage." He bowed his head, contemplating what he had just said.

"Mm hmm," responded Marjorie softly. "That's really too bad. Collateral just seems so dismissive. Wrong place, wrong time? We still need to try to bring both of them some kind of justice."

"I agree. And we shall." Alan rose, patted his companion's shoulder, and walked slowly down the hall toward his office. He carried the printout Marjorie had made. "I'm going to read this and make some notes. See you later."

"Okay but remember the PBS Masterpiece series we really like is on at nine."

Alan waved and disappeared into his office.

Chapter 5

Late the next day, Alan climbed the steps from the garage to Marjorie in the kitchen and said, "I was able to get into the apartment over in Uptown. Delilah Cooper's. This time."

Marjorie handed Alan a small glass of Amorulla, one of their favorite liquors for after dinner or in late evening relaxing. "What was different?"

"I reached out to Ed Caplan at Minneapolis PD."

"Anything interesting?" Marjorie asked.

"The receptionist this time was a different person who apparently had received different instructions or had a more positive public attitude. He was pleasant, had a set of keys for me and seemed to know who I was. Maybe the church sent a message in addition. I'll find out from the board president, hopefully tomorrow.

"Anyway, Ms. Cooper has been a resident for five years, give a week or so, and leases a very nice, neat and clean if small apartment on the fifth floor. It faces the lake, but the trees along the boulevard and shoreline obscure about half of the near side of the water. Her drapes and blinds on the south side of the building are pulled so there's no chance of observation by someone in the next building. Her furniture is modern, comfortable, and not at all unusual for a single working woman. The bedroom is likewise, ordinary, expected and un-spectacular."

"No sex toys then." Marjorie smirked. Alan would not have mentioned it unless she brought it up. He well-knew her professional background as a stripper, dancer and headliner had exposed her to the franker side of life. They'd talked about her background, and his, when they first got together and both revealed they were not innocents, but never particularly promiscuous.

"No, and her small library of paperback and hard cover books didn't reveal any particular interests.

No salacious literature and no religious bent, either. There were two obvious open spaces in the bookshelves where one or two books might have been removed. I only noticed them because everything else on the bookcase was organized. In fact, the entire place was very neat. I didn't find a bible or other reading material on her bedside table. No bible on the living room shelves, either. Her kitchen was, like the other rooms, unremarkable. Bathroom, same. The apartment almost gave me the impression that nobody lived there. Then we get to her desk. A small fold-front with two drawers and five cubby holes. All empty."

"Empty?" Marjorie frowned.

"Her desk had been completely cleaned out, not a scrap of paper remaining. Hardly any dust, and the desk had obviously been well-used. I checked with the Minneapolis PD, which is coordinating with Saint Paul, I understand. They didn't take anything because they apparently didn't find anything relevant. The investigator I talked with said the desk was empty when they arrived. I called Saint Paul, but they haven't called back.

The landline telephone chimed.

Alan stood and reached to take the phone from its cradle. A twinge in his lower back reminded him he was getting older and needed to resume a regular exercise routine.

"Hello. Alan Lockem here." He and Marjorie had discussed at length how far they should go and how much they should spend in various security systems, such as cameras, lights, electronic locks and even telephone cut-outs. So far, neither felt their clients had sufficient levels of criminal or international connections to warrant heightened security until Lockem became entangled with Jason Butteridge and some intel smuggling.

Now their contract with the security company had been reduced to random daily on the ground surveys of their property. Glancing out the window he saw the big furry dark muzzle of the company dog in the window of the van parked at the curb.

"Mr. Lockem, the crime scene sergeant asked me to respond to your query." The detective coughed gently after she identified herself.

"Thank you for the call," he said.

"I'm advised to tell you the crew found nothing suspicious in the victim's apartment, except the condition of the desk. It was completely empty. A note says the tech had the impression the interior of the desk had been wiped clean. No fingerprints. In or on the desk. He essentially agrees with the Minneapolis police assessment. Anything else?" She was apparently impatient to get on to something more important.

"No. Thanks again." Lockem pressed the button to disconnect. He had barely reached to cradle the instrument when it chimed again. Lockem frowned and answered the call.

"Lockem here."

"Terse, today, aren't we?" Lockem recognized the voice of Lieutenant Vernon Gage his contact at the local police department,

"A little frustration, Lieutenant. I visited a dead woman's apartment and found zilch."

"Zilch?" Gage chuckled. "Not a word I normally associate with a homicide investigation. Maybe I can help. The dead woman, Delilah Cooper? We have a file on her."

"Really?" Taken aback for a moment, Lockem had no ready response.

"Really. Ms Cooper was arrested several months ago at a bar on Rice Street. She had become belligerent, loud, and aggressive acting. Patrol took her to jail and for reasons I won't get in to now, her friend was then allowed to take her to the friend's condo."

"Did you issue her a ticket?"

"Apparently not. And I'm not sure why she wasn't jailed, except we can assume she settled down and presented no further problem. The patrol officer is no longer employed by the department and Cooper's friend has no other recorded contact with us."

"I appreciate the information. Can I have the friend's address?"

"I can't give you that, but I know where she will be tomorrow afternoon. She will be attending a memorial service for Delilah Cooper at Roseville Lutheran Church, beginning at one p.m. Look for a woman with long flaming red hair."

Lockem thanked Lieutenant Gage, cradled the phone, and looked at Marjorie.

"What news?"

"Would you like to join me at a memorial service for Ms Cooper tomorrow afternoon?"

Marjorie raised her well-shaped eyebrows in a question. "Information from our friend Lieutenant Gage? Yes, of course I'll join you."

The rest of the day and the night passed without memorable notice and the next morning dawned with bright promise. By noon Marjorie and Alan had dressed and were just about to leave for the funeral home on the northeast side of Roseville. They drove the mile and a half in silence and found the parking lot nearly full. Inside, busy attendants directed the slowly moving crowd toward the small auditorium. Marjorie and Alan found seats in the very back row next to the double doors that connected the auditorium with the foyer. Marjorie sat and half turned toward her companion. That way she could see everyone entering after them. Lockem had scanned the people already seated looking for the red-haired woman. His task was made more difficult in that many of the women wore hats. This was not an informal gathering.

He sat after a minute and glanced at Marjorie who shook her head minimally. More people arrived. One or two clutched crumpled handkerchiefs. It appeared there were no family members in attendance, as the seats reserved for family were all empty. Lockem wondered about that. He noted two men who appeared to be police officers in civilian clothes. A tall slender woman in a long dark skirt, high heels and a dress jacket walked by. Her hat was wide brimmed and close fitting. Marjorie nudged him. He looked more closely at the woman who turned and took a seat a few rows in front of them. Her hair under the hat was flaming dark red and he could see she had curled it so her hair fell almost carelessly to her shoulders. The crowd of fewer than fifty all appeared to be dressed as he commonly saw in business offices throughout the city. There was a pause in the numbers of people entering and the music rose in volume and then stopped.

The organist for the funeral home played a soft piece that Lockem recognized as a popular hymn from his youthful times in Sunday School and a short squat man dressed in black strode to the podium. The ensuing service was undistinguished from others he had attended and a minister whom Lockem assumed was on call by the funeral director, made a few generic comments about life and humanity and the untimely loss of Ms. Cooper. Lockem wondered where and when the service for the pastor killed at the same time and place would happen.

Service concluded, Marjorie and Lockem followed the red-haired woman out and into the parking lot. She stopped abruptly and turned toward them.

"It looks like you are following me. Is that right?"

"Yes," Marjorie responded. "This is Alan Lockem. He and I have been asked to look into the unfortunate deaths of Ms. Cooper and Minister Elliot."

"I wonder if you have time to answer a few questions, Ms....?"

The woman produced the ghost of a smile and said, "do you know the Bon Pain coffee shop in the shopping mall across the highway?"

"Yes," said Marjorie.

"We can have coffee and talk. I have some time before my appointment." She turned away and opened her car door.

Lockem shrugged and led Marjorie to their vehicle. The restaurant was just a block and a half east and the two vehicles made it across the busy highway and parked beside each other outside the restaurant. Together the three walked into the place.

Chapter 6

A waiter took their order and brought the coffee for Alan and the red-haired woman and iced tea for Marjorie.

"Are you private detectives?" asked the stranger.

"No, not exactly," said Marjorie. "My partner and I do investigate things, sometimes crimes."

Alan sipped his hot coffee and eyed the woman in what he hoped would be seen as a friendly way. "We have a friend, a member of the church board, where Ms. Cooper and Pastor Elliot were killed. She has asked us to assist the police in this matter." It was an uncertain and somewhat unusual statement for Lockem, who normally went straight to the point in his interviews. That was likely because it had sometimes been necessary in his earlier career to exchange intel while under intense enemy fire. Today, he hoped he and Marjorie were disarming enough to learn something that would help them find the shooter.

"Ms Cooper, of you don't mind my asking, who do you work for?"

"I don't mind at all. I work in downtown Minneapolis. My employer has offices all over the world. It's called Worldwide." She went on to describe a Swiss-based conglomerate called Worldwide.

"I lived—live in an apartment on the other side of the building from Delilah." She drank a little coffee.

"I liked her, as a fellow renter on our floor. As you may know, it's a large building and I understand that some of the floors are home to partiers. That's not me and that's not Delilah Cooper, or the other tenants on our floor.

"We didn't socialize. Oh, occasionally an afternoon glass of wine—she liked Cab-Savs—and I prefer a good sharp white..." she stopped, sniffled and wiped one eye with a crumpled tissue.

"She dated, I guess. At least she dressed up and went out some evenings."

"Did you ever see her with this man?" Marjorie spoke so softly the redhead had to lean in. She took the small black and white photograph Marjorie held out to her and studied it closely. Alan leaned back. He knew the picture was a portrait of the dead pastor, Elliot. He casually scanned the room, looking for anybody showing more than occasional interest in the three of them. No alarms jangled in his mind.

The woman smiled a little and seemed to relax. She handed the photo back to Marjorie saying, "No, I don't know him and I don't believe I've ever seen him. Certainly not with Delilah. Is he the pastor who was killed?"

Marjorie nodded and tucked the photo back into her purse. "Have the police interviewed you?"

"Yes. Investigators from both cities talked to me, just as you two are doing. I'm afraid I haven't been much help. If any."

"Could I have your name?"

"Lorna Cooper—no relation to Delilah. At least, none I know of."

"How long have you lived at your present address?"

"Five years, give or take. Police asked the same question." Ms. Cooper stood to leave, apparently sensing the interview had reached a dead end.

"Did you ever see her working at her desk?" asked Alan.

"No. It was always closed when I was in her apartment." She turned to leave and then stopped, looked down at Marjorie and said, "There is one odd thing. She had a lot of bibles. I remember seeing at least six or seven on the shelves. I asked her about them, but I don't think she ever explained why. She seemed fond of reading from them. She quoted something from a bible once in a while. At least she said that was the source. Like a saying, you know: Honor thy father and mother."

"Was that what she said?" Alan asked.

26

"Oh, no, no. I can't remember her exact words. Just casual, in conversation."

"Thank you for talking with us, Ms. Cooper," smiled Marjorie, and she and Alan watched her walk slowly out of the restaurant.

"I didn't see any bibles in the dead woman's apartment," Alan said quietly watching as Lorna Cooper disappeared into the street. "Not a single one."

"So we have to assume somebody, probably police investigators, took them for closer examination."

"Agreed, but that's strange, isn't it? Especially since nobody's mentioning it. I'm calling the PD again." Alan fished his flip phone out of his pocket and cursored to the entry and then pressed send. When he reached one of the investigators assigned to the case, she had the case file in front of her.

"It appears from the file that it was at least an hour before the bodies were found. We found a Minnesota driver's license in her purse but it was not her correct address."

"I take it then there was a fairly long delay getting to her apartment," said Alan.

"That's correct, Mr. Lockem. In fact, the Minneapolis investigator, later assigned to her case, entered the apartment approximately two hours before we did and that happened, as I said, more than two hours after her body was discovered." She paused and said softly, "Oh. There's a note here. Minneapolis detective told our investigator he thought the desk had been emptied before he arrived."

Alan thanked the woman and slowly replaced the phone in his pocket. "Interesting. Minneapolis noted the desk looked like it had been cleaned out."

"So, somebody may have been there ahead of them," said Marjorie. "And I'll bet their inventory doesn't mention bibles."

"You are suggesting whoever carted off the contents of Ms. Cooper's desk also took some bibles?" Marjorie nodded.

"But why?" Alan frowned as he spoke.

27

She smiled. "C'mon, Alan, don't tease. You know bibles are an age-old classic medium for carrying messages."

Alan shrugged. "True enough, but I thought we'd progressed with intelligence technology beyond trying to find biblical references to carry information. On the other hand, this act of double murder is probably not attached to any secret network activity between nations. It's a lot more likely there's a personal element here."

"Except the removal of the bibles and the scrubbing of the desk, to borrow your terminology, raises several questions."

"There are frequently unexplained oddities in murder investigations," Alan pontificated with a manufactured frown on his face.

"You didn't mention Delilah's altercation at that bar and Lorna's involvement," said Marjorie.

"True, I didn't, and it bears more investigation," Alan muttered. "Sometimes, for reasons I can't readily explain, I don't ask obvious questions in an interview."

"Speaking of investigations, there's a restaurant and some stores in a small area only a couple of blocks from the church. We need a couple of things from a grocery store and I wouldn't mind a nice pastry and a cup of coffee." Marjorie smiled and rose from the table. While Alan paid their bill, she sauntered to the rest room, and they then left to get their vehicle.

** ** **

The shopping area in northwestern Saint Paul lay only a couple of easy miles from their location near the funeral home, and they arrived to park on the street midway down the block toward the Corner Restaurant, half a block from the Speedy Market. As they had suspected, the recent double murder at the nearby church still concerned neighborhood residents and they had no difficulty engaging in casual speculation which, at first blush added only fragments to the file.

28

"It's a real tragedy," a woman at the meat counter stated. "Pastor Elliot was such a gentle, soft-spoken man. I mean, I didn't go to his church, but he was active in the community so you were always running into him."

"That's right," another customer chimed in, pausing beside Marjorie in the crowded aisle. "He helped at the tables during our annual park festival. Would you hand me that box of crackers, please?" She did so and then asked, "Did you know the dead woman, Delilah Cooper?"

The woman took the box of crackers and stepped slowly away. She shook her head. "No. She didn't live in the Park. I was surprised because there was no reason for her to be there at that time. No church reason, I mean."

So, mused Marjorie, sidling deeper into the store toward the canned goods section, *apparently Ms. Cooper was at the church specifically to meet Pastor Elliot. And if there was no activity, that explains why the church secretary wasn't anywhere to be found.*

She also wondered if the murdered Pastor Elliot made a habit of meeting with parishioners or non-members with no one else present. Marjorie glanced around to see Alan coming slowly toward her along the narrow aisle.

"Anything?" He asked in a low voice.

"They have my favorite brand of canned creamed corn, and I'm gonna get two." She plucked the cans off the shelf and handed them to Alan. She winked and gently pushed him around toward the checkout counter, located in the center of the store.

An older man at the checkout register took the cans and the lamb chops and rang them up. "Find everything you need?" he asked, staring fixedly at Alan. It was apparent the man had heard some of their conversations with other customers.

"Pretty much," smiled Alan offering some cash from his pocket. "Only time will tell if it's everything."

The clerk nodded and dropped the corn and chops into a plastic bag and handed it to Alan. "Thanks for stopping. Hope you find anything else you might need." He stared at them, obviously referring to the queries the couple had made. Alan and Marjorie went their way down the street, past the big new bank building that crowded the sidewalk and dropped the package onto the passenger's seat of their car.

Chapter 7

"Let's have a doughnut and some coffee."
Marjorie indicated the corner shop a few steps farther
down the block. Alan's words were drowned out as a
city bus lumbered by and stopped at the nearby corner
with a great hissing of air brakes. They watched
several young people exit the bus and disperse up and
down the busy street.

The restaurant was crowded and noisy but they
found a small table and two chairs against the cold
window with a clear view of the sidewalk and the
service station across the street. Alan went to the
counter and placed their order for two lattes and two
small crullers. The restaurant offered no doughnuts.

The order promptly delivered, the couple sat
silently gazing out the window at the street, but alert
to conversations swirling about them. The nearest
tables were occupied, one by a couple of older women
and a man. They were intently discussing something
and at first neither Alan nor Marjorie could make out
the words.

Then there came a lull in background noises
and Alan distinctly heard a woman at the next table
say, "The reverend was such a nice man. Family man,
but what was he doing at church alone?"

His companions appeared puzzled in agreement.
The noise level rose again.

"Alan turned to Marjorie and said in a low voice,
"I think we have to find out why the pastor was at the
church that afternoon."

Marjorie nodded. "Could be a key. And we have
to assume it might have been perfectly innocuous and
ordinary."

Pastries and lattes consumed and surrounding
conversations lacking substance they sought, Alan
and Marjorie paid and left the restaurant. "I think we
need to talk to the widow, said Marjorie, sliding into
the passenger seat.

"Funeral and burial happened only yesterday," Alan responded. "Might be too soon."

"I don't think so. She's going to be distraught for a week, more. We can't wait that long. Let's drive over and see if she'll talk to us."

Alan nodded affirmatively and shifted to drive. Pastor Elliot and his family, wife and two small girl children, lived in a medium-sized bungalow on a street that overlooked Como Park and the lake. Alan wondered as he maneuvered through traffic on busy city streets whether Mrs. Elliot had arrangements now her husband was no longer of this world.

They parked, walked up the steps through the sunny day and Alan rapped on the door. It opened almost immediately and a tall man with close cropped hair looked at them. "Yes? May I help you?"

"My name is Alan Lockem. This is my partner, Marjorie Kane. We are private investigators."

"Really? I thought the police were handling things."

"They are, in both Minneapolis and Saint Paul," said Marjorie. It's just with a multiple investigation, our client requested an independent look. I wonder if Mrs. Elliot might be available for a few questions? Mr. ?

"Oh, excuse me. My name is Trevor. Trevor Howland. I'm an old high school buddy of Ell—Elliot's. Why don't you just come in out of the sun. You can wait on the porch and I'll see if Melissa is up to talking with you."

As they stepped through the door into the front porch, a vehicle that sounded muffler-less or fitted with exhaust resonators rumbled down the street in front. Howland waved them to wicker chairs and stepped back through the door into the house. Neither Alan nor Marjorie sat. They stood close together, surveying what they could see of the interior of the house.

A large picture window, blinds open, gave them a wide view of the living room and dining room beyond.

32

Two pleasant rooms, exactly what one would expect in a home of a pastor of a medium sized city church. Marjorie scanned the room, noting a long sofa, a simply designed overhead chandelier, two table lamps beside the sofa and a floor lamp beside a recliner across the room.

Trevor Howland appeared in the doorway and invited them in, He led the way down a hall next to the living room through the smallish kitchen, to a den-like room at the back of the house. It had three small windows set high on the walls near the ceiling. Two were cranked open and birds could be heard in the yard outside.

Mrs. Elliot, looking wan and out of sorts clad in a longish dark blue dress, rose from her chair to greet them.

"I'm sorry to intrude," Marjorie murmured, stepping forward to grasp the woman's extended fingers. "We are so sorry for your loss."

"Thank you," the widow whispered. "It is such a shock, and so sudden. "We really have no family close. Fortunately, Trevor was here and members of Elliot's church have of course, been most helpful, but the loss is so abrupt. Now, how can I help? I understand you are looking into the death of that young woman as well. Is that right?"

"It is Mrs. Elliot. "We, and the police are treating the deaths together, as one crime." Lockem kept his voice low. What he didn't say was that if the two murders were separated, it might be that one would be considered as an unfortunate accident, being in the wrong place at the wrong time. If that had been the choice, the investigation might have become vastly more complicated.

Without asking, Howland appeared carrying cups, saucers, and a steaming pot of tea. Melissa Elliot resumed her seat on one end of the sofa and Marjorie joined her, being careful to stay at the end of the sofa so as not to appear to intrude on the grieving widow's space. Alan sat in the one casual chair while Howland

33

leaned against the door to the kitchen after he put down the cups and saucers.

Marjorie carefully balanced her cup of tea, turned her head toward the bereft widow and gently said, "Again we are sorry to intrude on your grief, but sometimes time is important. Did you know the woman with your husband that day?"

"Delilah Cooper? No, I may have met her at a service or other church event but I don't recall her. Do you have a picture, or a good description? The police didn't tell me anything."

Alan and Marjorie exchanged glances. Marjorie leaned forward with her phone and showed Melissa Elliot the picture, a professional portrait, of the dead woman.

Melissa leaned forward and stared at the picture. Then she briefly frowned. Finally shook her head. "No. I'm afraid I've never met or even seen this woman. In she the one who—the woman who was found in the sanctuary with my husband?"

"I'm so sorry, Mrs. Elliot." Marjorie spoke softly and reached forward to take the other woman's hand. "Sorry for your loss."

A tremulous smile appeared briefly on the woman's face. "Do you have other questions?"

"Yes," said Alan. "It is certainly possible there was no connection at all between this woman, Delilah Cooper and your husband or the church. She might be a victim of bad timing. Is there anything you can think of that might help us? Any out of the ordinary happenings?"

Melissa Elliot looked down at her lap, dabbed one eye with a crumpled tissue and looked up again, at Marjorie. "I wonder if you can help me."

"We'll certainly try," Marjorie responded.

"My husband wore a bracelet. A copper bracelet. I don't know where he got it, but it was precious to him. He never took it off, except to shower. I'd like to have it back if the police are through with it."

Marjorie scribbled in her notebook, nodded. "I'll look into it, she said."

Lockem was prevented from asking more by an explosion of sound from engines rumbling and revving and raised voices all coming from the backyard of the Elliot home. Lockem rose and walked to the back wall of the room, peering through the curtain at the activity. A vehicle now parked in the yard and surrounded by motorcycles appeared similar to the vehicle he had noticed passing on the street as they entered the Elliot home.

CHAPTER 8

Lockem focused his attention on the activity in the yard as talk behind him waned. Four large individuals appeared indistinctly through the very thin curtain. Two had apparently arrived in the unmuffled van and two others from behind the van. From what he could see, it seemed logical to Lockem that those two had arrived on motorcycles he'd heard a few minutes earlier. They were dressed in typical cycle gang gear. He assumed they'd left the motorcycles behind the garage in the alley.

All four came up the concrete walk toward the door. Lockem turned his head and said, "It appears you have visitors arriving from the back yard."

"Oh, that must be Obadiah and his friends. Pastor Martin works—worked," she gulped— "with groups of youth and others. These boys—men—are a small group we've been trying to wean away from the street drugs and general violence. They're actually pretty nice people. I don't think they even have a name for their group." Melissa smiled.

"So," Lockem murmured, "no gang jackets." He thought Melissa's smile looked a little uncertain. The sound of boots tramping into the kitchen silenced conversation in the living room. Marjorie rose to her feet, facing the door. The man in dark denim, first through the door, had not removed his sunglasses. He glanced swiftly around the room and in a belligerent tone, asked, "Everything all right, Mel? Who are these people?"

Before the Pastor's widow could answer, a second man appeared and interrupted. "I know this guy. Alan Lockem. Mr. Private Detective. Right?"

Lockem eyed the speaker. "I'm sorry, I don't remember. Do I know you?"

"Probably not. But I know you. Five years ago you sent my old man to prison. About killed my ma."

"I don't have that power, only the courts send people to prison."

"Yeah, you did. Jack Hamilton. You prolly don't even remember his name."

Lockem did remember. He'd identified Jack Hamilton as the leader of a small group of auto thieves who stole vehicles and cut them up to sell the parts. Hamilton had apparently decided it was safer to sell parts of stolen vehicles than trying to move entire cars. He'd been in his illegal business for several years until Lockem came on the scene and figured out what he was doing while on a completely unrelated case. He'd called his police contact and suggested they take a close look at Hamilton's operation in the east metro, at a big junkyard on a rarely traveled side street near the freeway. Saint Paul police assigned a man and the resulting under-cover work led to arrest, charge, and conviction of the car thieves. The case had cemented Lockem's credentials with the Saint Paul PD.

"You're Jacob, Jack's son." Lockem smiled and stuck out his right hand. Hamilton sneered and ignored the proffered hand.

"Mrs. Elliot?" the second man asked. "Are you O.K.? Are these people bothering you?"

"No, Obadiah, everything is fine. Mr. Lockem and his friend are just helping the police find out who killed Martin."

Lockem didn't add the name of the woman also killed in the sanctuary, Delilah Cooper. After a few more minutes of sparring, it became evident the opportunity for any kind of informative discussion had fled. Marjorie turned to Melissa and smiled, "Mrs. Elliot, we'll be going now. Lockem nodded agreement. He handed her a business card. "Thank you for your help," she went on. "We are so sorry for your loss, and we will keep you informed. But please call if you have any questions." She reached out to take Melissa Elliot's hand. It was a relatively meaningless gesture but it brought her other hand casually to the opening of her shoulder bag and the pistol lodged inside.

Lockem smiled approvingly. His smile looked vapid and meaningless, but Marjorie knew he'd recognized her move toward her pistol. He took Melissa Elliot's other hand in a gesture of sympathy and then stepped into Jacob Hamilton's personal space, crowding him back into a corner beside the door. He didn't normally posture in such a way but Hamilton's belligerence had, surprisingly, riled him a little. Hamilton looked startled and shuffled back a step to keep his balance.

Marjorie nodded at him as she sidled by in Lockem's wake. They walked to the front door and exited to rising murmurs from behind. Outside, a tall dark-haired young man in a tight muscle shirt and low-slung jeans leaned against the front fender of their vehicle.

He looked at them, glanced toward the door to the house and then back at the advancing couple. "Nice ride," he said.

"Something we can do for you?" Lockem knew he sounded a little too assertive, just the way he was feeling at the moment.

The man threw up his hands, palms out, showing they were empty. "Hey, man, just hangin' out, waiting for my bro." He took a step aside, away from the vehicle. Lockem pressed the key release button and leaned to open the passenger door for Marjorie. She smiled her thanks, slid into her seat, and lowered the window. She fixed the young man with an unsmiling almost-glare while Lockem strode around the vehicle and entered the driver's seat.

Lockem nodded once and pressed the starter button. When the engine caught, he shifted into gear and they rolled sedately away down the street. "I think that guy has had some training. I wonder if he's undercover."

Marjorie looked at her companion in amazement. "Seriously? I didn't see that. What gave you that idea?"

Lockem shook his head. "I can't tell you. Just an impression. I'm not a hundred percent sure I did recognize him as a trained agent, either. He looked too young to be retired. Maybe he has a military background. Like National Guard. Let's go home, I need to make some calls and do a little research."

"Ah," Marjorie smiled. "Detective work, no less."

Lockem turned onto Highway 36 heading west. "What did you think of Melissa?"

"Not much. I mean, we weren't there long enough to get an in-depth feeling, but she seemed both sincere and confused about her husband's murder. I also think she has no idea one way or the other about the dead woman."

"That squares with my impressions. The arrival of the motorcycle kids cut things short and disrupted my plan."

"Motorcycle kids?" Marjorie shook her head. "I think they're more like a gang."

Lockem waved one hand. "I just mean they seemed more like they were trying for an intimidation aura, not something that just hung on them like a mantle."

"Yeah, I got that, but I do think they could be dangerous. Do you think they have something to do with the murders? At least one of them was surely armed. Unexpected and a little unsettling. I saw the outline of a pistol in Hamilton's jacket," she went on.

"I thought you handled it perfectly." Lockem risked a quick smile to the woman at his side.

He wheeled off the highway, past the Rosedale Center and took the streets to their home, a quiet, two-story split-level on a short cul de sac in northern Roseville. As Lockem turned into their driveway and tapped the remote to open the garage door, his sweeping gaze covered the front façade of their home looking for anything out of the ordinary. Everything looked normal, exactly as it had when they left a few hours earlier. They rolled slowly into the garage and the door hissed shut behind them.

CHAPTER 9

Alan disappeared into his downstairs office and activated his computer, opening his on-line contact list looking for anybody locally who could give him some insight into the motorcyclists they had just encountered. He had a feeling there was something there. It might not relate directly to the murder of Pastor Elliot and the woman, but more information might lead to other sources. He knew Marjorie would be jumping on the Internet as well. Her understanding of cyber resources and search techniques was superior to his so he almost always requested her help when deeper dives were indicated.

In her own office, a converted den off the living room, Marjorie had already fired up her laptop and started an online profile check. She had a contact with a firm that would run Internet research checks on anybody—anybody at all. Naturally, the more important, or dangerous, the subject, the higher the fee. Usually she discussed such research and fees with the client and with her partner. There were minimal risks, but there were a few. Always. Hackers, working for a fee, might be able to penetrate the business records of a detective agency to learn who and why that agency was looking at a particular person. That information could lead to interference with a case and expose Marjorie and Alan to danger.

In this case, she felt secure enough looking for public information on a woman who was probably an ordinary citizen with few secrets in her suitcase. She had Delilah Cooper's Social Security number and other relevant information from the police, so she was looking forward to gathering together the threads of the woman's life, so abruptly terminated in a Christian church.

The screen flickered and requested additional choices after Marjorie inputted name and address. Soon she was in what she sometimes referred to as thick weeds, responding to more and more requests for details and watching the number of possible hits gradually fall to a reasonable number.

She copied the final 75 hits on Cooper's name that appeared to be the Cooper she wanted, into a separate file and began to check them against her list of known facts. Two hours fled by. Marjorie had searched for casual hits, through various public records and even into city directories. Twitter, Face Book Instagram, and other social media sites came under her scrutiny. She compiled a list of most possible connections and copied their Internet addresses into a separate file. Her cautious nature led her to immediately back up the file to a flash drive which she identified with an inked symbol on one side. She tucked the drive into the lap drawer of her desk.

She switched off the computer and stretched well-toned arms overhead, groaning softly, clenched her stomach muscles and rotated her feet under her desk. Alan walked quietly into the room holding a small glass of white wine in one hand. He extended the glass to Marjorie who took it with a pleased smile.

"Any luck?" he asked.

"Oh yes." Sipped the wine. "Our Delilah is real. The information in her Social Security file is accurate. She's forty-two, grew up and went to high school in a small town on the western edge of Arkansas. Baptized by a church in the Southern Baptist Conference. Good grades in high school landed her a full-ride scholarship to Smith where she excelled in gymnastics and volleyball, as well as in her academic program."

"What was her major?"

"Middle Eastern history and World Religions. She also studied French."

"Ah."

"Yes, ah. She got a job at a medium-sized bank in Atlanta, transferred after a few years to a branch of Wells Fargo in Dallas. Five years later, aged about twenty-nine she moved to a one-bedroom condo in

Charlotte, North Carolina." Marjorie paused, sipped her wine and waited for the question."

"And?"

"I don't yet know why she moved, but I presume it was a career change or a major life change. She lived an exemplary life in both places, no police interactions, no arrests. I can't find any organizations she joined. Never seen in any street demonstrations, which doesn't mean she didn't attend some. She has an IRA and a fairly substantial retirement account consisting of stocks, bonds, a little cash, and the condo in North Carolina. Never married. Her social entanglements, if any, are unrecorded."

"Dead end, you think?" Alan was disappointed. He'd hoped the Cooper woman might give them a thread to pull or even a road to follow. Perhaps this was just a case of wrong place, wrong time.

"Consider this. Last year, in March, she rented a small apartment in a building in the Saint Anthony Park area of Saint Paul. Signed a year-long lease. The building is that yellow brick job just off Raymond on Como."

"So, why was she living in that apartment in Minneapolis over by the lake?"

"Excellent question to which, as yet, I have no answer."

"Did she sell the condo in Carolina?"

"Nope. And that's the other side of my question. I know she established a presence in North Carolina. But within a year or so the record developed a big hole."

"What?"

"Yeah. There's a gap of about fifteen years. No job, no bank, nothing but the condo. Not in the city directory. Now it's possible she just missed those dates by being out of town every time the city came around."

Alan nodded. Smiled. "Un-huh. But our natural suspicious nature says there may be something else here."

44

"Yup, not to forget a second apartment, the one in Saint Paul." Marjorie nodded. "I applied your natural suspicious nature. She could have been recruited in Dallas to join some kind of intelligence agency, foreign or domestic. She could have moved to the East Coast to train and accept undercover assignments. Oh Hell."

"Oh Hell, indeed," said Alan. He grinned. "The logical next idea is that she was here on assignment and may have been the real target, while the churchman is collateral."

"Complications," said Marjorie. "On the other hand, the more likely explanation is that she went somewhere, maybe married and lived under a different, unrecorded name. A perfectly ordinary existence for fifteen years, and then she reappears."

"More and more this case descends into the complexities of life. I'll take some of the threads from you tomorrow and we'll start plowing in the fields of our despair."

Marjorie giggled and rose to go to go to the kitchen. Divining her purpose, Alan said, "We have a film on DVD from Netflix. I propose we order in and relax for the evening."

"Is this one of your obscure spy films?" She laughed.

"Didn't look at the title, so can't remember," he said.

"Okay, I'll order some sandwiches. You get the CD and the wine and we'll be good for tonight."

The evening passed as planned, until they both dozed off during the last few scenes of the movie so the solution remained a mystery.

Chapter 10

In the morning Lockem reached out electronically to an officer from his former Intel unit. He didn't expect much definitive information; much would still be under restricted covenant, but he hoped Lieutenant Jorgenson might offer a thread or two that Lockem could pick at. A patient man anyway, Lockem's service in the military had honed and measurably increased his patience.

His sat phone jangled and he once again considered finding a tech to modify the ring tones to something softer and more musical. When he connected, he didn't recognize the voice on the other end of the line. The woman had a soft voice infused with the rhythmic nuances of a southern resident.

"Mr. Lockem?" she asked. "My name is Sara-May. Ed Smith is my husband, the man you called. He can no longer use the telephone and he asked me to give you three names in the clear." She paused and gave a low chuckle. "I'm not exactly sure what he meant by all that, but he has been in recent touch with his former colleagues from the OSS."

"That's perfectly all right, ma'am. Is he ill?"

"Well, he's had a hard life, as I'm sure you know, and he's goin' downhill pretty fast now."

"Sorry to hear that. May I write to him?"

"Well, now, Mr. Lockem, that'd be right nice. He does appreciate the occasional card or letter. He's at Eagle's Nest Veteran's Home, here in Atlanta."

"Thank you." He wrote down the mailing address. "You said he had three names for me?"

"Yes sir." The woman recited the names and spelled them for Lockem. They said their goodbyes and Lockem made a note on his desk calendar to send a card to his former commander.

"Lorna Cooper," said Marjorie, entering his office with a bright smile. "A woman with an uncertain history."

"No kidding," Alan responded. "Why am I not surprised."

"When you didn't ask her about the incident at the bar in Saint Paul, when she took care of Delilah, I assumed you had already decided there were other layers to be privately explored. I have more research to do, but this Miss Cooper appears to be a well-traveled woman. Her passport carries multiple stamps and visas from many European and Asian nations. Her resume is very sparse, and there are some questions."

"Such as?"

Marjorie consulted the printout she held. "Ms Cooper appears to currently have one full-time job. A month ago, she might have had two, or there's just some confusion on her resume."

"What's her current employment?" asked Alan.

"She's a traffic specialist for a company with offices in downtown Minneapolis at the Trade Center. The company is called International Specialties. Ostensibly they trade in calendars and cultural icons. Like, they will supply you with a list of manufacturers or trading companies that offer Christmas and religious holiday flags, banners, wall hangings and small statues and altar pieces. I'm not clear what her connections to the manufacturing and wholesale parts of the business might be. If any."

"That could offer cover for all sorts of international travel, could it not?"

Marjorie smiled and nodded. "Might even be a cover for an intelligence agency, like Mossad or Interpol or some national police force."

"I think I need to talk to the church secretary again." He called and made an appointment to see her at ten the next morning.

It was a bright and unseasonably warm morning when Lockem parked on the street outside the church. He strolled up the curved walkway toward the heavy wooden double doors. Without being too obvious he scanned the surrounding area. Several vehicles were parked at the curb on all four streets at the intersection of Fairmont and Commonwealth avenue. The church was set back on a lot only slightly larger than a typical city corner lot in this neighborhood of medium and good-sized middle-class houses. The neighborhood had been platted and developed as the northwest area of Saint Paul in the late nineteenth century.

Satisfied he probably wasn't under observation, Lockem pulled open the heavy door and entered. Directly ahead was a tiny elevator and beside the shaft, a narrow set of stairs leading to the first-floor office door. The office door was closed and he could see through the window glass the church secretary, Carolyn Action, busy at her desk. She glanced up and waved him through the door.

She rose from her chair and said, "Good morning, Mr. Lockem. Let's go into the Pastor's office. It's more comfortable." She leaned to her phone and pressed a switch. He heard a faint ping from the room beyond and followed the woman into a second office. This room held a desk and chair, two matching easy chairs and some file cabinets. Daylight streamed in from three high windows at the ceiling. He noted as he settled into the chair nearest the desk, that a large, framed painting hung on the opposite wall. On the wall behind the desk, a small wooden cross was suspended.

"So, how can I help you?" she asked, settling into the desk chair.

"I'm trying to get a better handle on the people involved, especially those around the Reverend Elliot. My information says your pastor was a graduate of White Bear Lake high school and a divinity school in Northern Illinois. His first pastoral assignment was a small rural church and then he came here." He paused. The woman seated opposite him nodded, her expression neutral.

"The other person, Delilah Cooper, is more of a mystery," he said. Carolyn Action betrayed nothing on her face except polite interest. "She moved here to the

48

Twin Cities a few years ago and worked for an investment firm in Minneapolis. What I've been so far unable to learn is how she came to be in Minneapolis and how she came to this particular church. Can you help me out with some answers?"

A ghost of a smile passed over Action's face, so unsubstantial he wasn't sure he saw it. She leaned forward and picked up a file folder already lying on the desk blotter in front of her. She opened it and looked at the single sheet of paper revealed.

"As you may know, when a church engages the voluntary services of a member, when somebody in the congregation offers, or is volunteered by a member, we get some basic information. In our case, a brief biography is requested. Recently, the board has followed national recommendations and for certain positions we have a background check performed. We just don't want any surprises. In some cases, we might persuade a parishioner to do something else for the Church. We've never had a problem here, but I don't think the Council would approve a paroled bank robber to be our treasurer." Action smiled more broadly. "On the other hand, forgiveness of past transgressions is a cornerstone of the ministry. So, Ms. Cooper filled out her formal bio. She left nothing blank. Several people read and vetted at least some of her information to be sure it was accurate.

She was raised in an evangelical Christian family in Delaware, is a high school graduate and attended a trade school which awarded her an accounting certificate."

Lockem nodded, scribbling notes as he listened.

"We don't have any information on her marriages or employment, if any, until she moved here. I also have no idea how she found our church." Carolyn flipped the page over and examined the back.

"Thank you," Lockem said quietly. He stopped and stared at his notes. "Do you have a date for her accounting certificate?"

"Yes, it was 2001. She volunteered at some of our social events, took part in an investing seminar and seemed to be quite well-liked. I had very little contact with her." She stopped and looked at Lockem. "What is it?"

Lockem looked up from his notebook and shrugged. "I don't know, but ever since I sat down an odd feeling has been growing. I can't define it, just a vague unrest, I guess."

Action nodded. "It's the painting." She gestured over her shoulder at the huge oil hanging on the wall. Others have had a similar reaction. Pastor Elliot had the picture removed for a brief period when he arrived, but then returned to this original location. Maybe it's the size, perhaps it is the subject, such very early Christians, but several people over the years have had reactions to being in the office with it. It is supposed to have been painted by Talegiease. He was a friar. It may be the painter's school. It was donated to the church right after this Congregation was formed, in 1925. Apparently, if the painting is by Taleggios or with his students, it is worth a great deal of money."

"You said if."

"That's right. Several years ago, before I arrived, there was some controversy over the provenance of the piece. I don't know the details at all, but someone accused the church of owning a stolen artwork. Then, I guess the thing was examined and determined it might be a fake and not stolen."

Chapter 11

Lockem stood and walked around the
desk to examine the painting more closely. The
vibrations he was feeling seemed to increase slightly,
but whether positive or negative, he couldn't tell. He
turned to find Ms Action also standing, observing him
closely.

Lockem glanced at the woman and then back at
the painting. It depicted a small group of robed figures
around a central subject who appeared to be gesturing
or speaking to the others. Most of the background
appeared to be sand, like a desert with indistinct rocks
trees and pale sky filling the frame. In the background,
the direction favored by the small group of figures.
They appeared to be looking toward an indistinct gap
like a pass through the mountains that form the
background. The artist's viewpoint appeared as if he
had been standing on a low hill looking down toward
the group of figures.

"I'm certainly no expert on art forgeries, but this
sure looks authentic to me."

Action smiled. "A good deal is written about art
forgeries and how paintings' provenances are
protected. All I know is that a question of ownership of
this painting came up at a board meeting and that's
how I heard there was even an examination. Then, as I
already mentioned, a question of authenticity arose
and I was informed an expert would be brought in."

Lockem felt the woman's level of discomfort was
rising so he switched subjects. "Is there anything else
you can tell me about Delilah Cooper?"

"I'm afraid not. She was a member for little
more than a year, only volunteered for one or two
committees and then only for specific events. I
wouldn't have called her an active member of the
congregation."

Lockem turned toward the door and the
secretary followed. "Please understand, I'm not

criticizing her participation. Most members only come to Sunday services and even regulars don't have perfect attendance."

He reached the door, opened it, and stepped into the larger church office where Carolyn Action's desk and the church's files were located. His gaze swept the room as walked toward the hall door. There was a faint sound of young voices raised in excitement at games going on in the big all-purpose room just down the hall. He thanked Ms Action and left the church. He wondered, walking down the walkway toward his car, whether there might be anything else. From experience he knew that people untrained in observational awareness frequently missed visual clues to coming action or peculiar interests. He looked up and visually scanned his immediate arena. With a small sense of amusement he realized he had walked a good distance from the door to the church without surveying his surroundings as had been his habit for years, ever since his military training had placed him in war zones.

In his car he punched in Marjorie's cell phone number. When she answered, Lockem said, "We are going to need some deeper research on Ms Delilah Cooper and on her friend, Lorna Cooper as well. And I am beginning to wonder if the fact these two women carried the same last name might have created a problem for somebody, been a tragic confusion."

"Oh dear," responded Marjorie. "You think Lorna Cooper might have been the real target?"

"Not yet. But we have to consider the possibility. I'm on my way home."

When he arrived in their cult de sac, the garage door was already open and beckoning. Alan wondered about that. Was it a breach of their security system or something else? He had his answer when he arrived in the kitchen where Marjorie was fixing their meal. When she turned to greet him, he saw she was holding

52

a small black control box in one hand, a long wooden spoon in the other.

"I calculated how long it might take you to get here and programmed this new garage-door controller when to open the door."

"I get it," Alan responded. "But I wonder about security if there was a delay, or a change in plans. Suppose I'd decided to stop for gas or get some groceries?"

"When's the last time you just stopped for groceries on a whim?" She dropped the controller on the counter and turned to the stove to stir the pot of steaming sauce. "I decided to make enough spaghetti sauce to freeze some, but it's the menu for tonight."

"Smells good to me," he said. Let me take a gander at the documentation for the controller." He went to the file in his office where the couple kept documents related to all the machines in their lives. Alan knew they could always find information online but he liked a paper-based backup file, and the very time they needed crucial information on a system would be the same time their internet or computer system decamped.

Perusal of the garage door system revealed that an internal clock could be programmed to the minute, or to a voice command. He replaced the document and closed the file. Dinner of home-made spaghetti sauce on pasta with a crisp side dish of salad greens awaited his undivided attention.

During dinner Alan related his conversation with the church secretary about Delilah Cooper and the painting on the wall of the office. "It's a large oil on what appears to be board or boards of some kind. It must be six or eight feet high and maybe three or four feet wide."

"Did you see a signature?"

"Yes. I should have taken a picture with my phone, but it didn't feel right to do so." Marjorie nodded in understanding. "The artist's signature appears to be more of a symbol or a family crest,

53

maybe. I think it's a black C surrounding a stylized T and connected by a sort of wandering tail from the T."

"Odd." Marjorie frowned and scrunched her lips. "Nothing comes to mind, of course, but I'll check some of my art history sources."

Lockem nodded agreement. He cleared the supper dishes while Marjorie went off to her computer. Two hours later Marjorie reappeared with a triumphant expression on her face.

"I believe I found him. A monk or friar, Italian. Actually Umbrian. Thirteenth Century. Name of Communion Georgio Talagiease, or something like that. Nothing but religious scenes. I even found a couple of illustrations that look like what you described." She handed Lockem a sheet of paper from her color printer.

"Naturally, his work is also ascribed to other painters alive at the time, or "from the school of," and like that. Provenance is both important and very hard to come by in many, I'd say most cases. A few paintings have been authenticated, but several in the Vatican haven't been evaluated and there are also some in other collections that are or aren't by this artist."

Lockem looked up at her. "This one looks like the painting in the office. I don't think it's identical, but I'd have to compare them side by side."

"My research tells me it is believed there are a few in private hands." She paused and licked her lips. "If it is an authentic Talalgias', it could be worth more than a million dollars."

Lockem snapped his head up. "A million?"

"Maybe more," said Marjorie. "Even if it's not authentic and it can be proven to be a contemporary copy it would be worth around half a million. Contemporary to an original."

"Holy Toledo, to coin a phrase. Maybe we stumbled on something here."

"Murder motive possibly," agreed Marjorie. "There's controversy over ownership of some of the

54

painter's works. You know, the usual. Passing through family hands for generations, gifts to friends and lovers, donations to a church. Even thefts. Now let me tell you about Edom"

" Oh, yes. Edom. I like ancient ruins as places to visit but that part of the world is a little dangerous right now."

"I did my visit on the Internet, and with a nice old guy in Stillwater."

"Interesting. Tell more."

Marjorie picked up several sheets of paper and settled into her chair. "In approximately the Tenth Century BCE quarreling relatives of a King David got chucked out of Jerusalem. They formed a cult of some kind and went south on the peninsula where they formed a community which grew to become Edom. There are all kinds of references to the place in the King James version of the Bible. Most of the references are negative."

"Where'd you get all this?"

"Patience, my dear." Marjorie gestured at her fist full of papers. "I won't bore you with all the details. As I said, research on the Internet, including a look at a city in Turkey called Ephesus. That comes later.

"Now, according to legend, emphasis on the word legend, Edom grew and prospered in spite of the jealousy of those in surrounding communities. For a time the mentions in the Bible were thought to be just stuff of legend. However, recent archeological discoveries have proven Edom's existence. Anyway, after some time, Edom was overrun and destroyed, possibly as a function of early Christianity. I'm just hitting the highlights here, you understand?"

"Yup. Do continue," said Alan.

"I called an antiquarian book dealer in Stillwater. He was very helpful and explained some things that helped. Apparently, there was a book written around the second or third Century called Ephesus or Epheseum. It was supposed to be included in the ancient biblical texts but got left out at some point. It might have been the original Obadiah."

Alan nodded. "I do remember something about this. When King James created the English Bible, didn't the scholars go back to the original texts wherever they could, but there was disagreement over some of that as well?"

"That's right and apparently a lot of the original materials in Greek and Latin and some other languages were lost over time. So, now we come to the painting called 'Adoration of Odom.'"

"Aha."

"Exactly. The story is some person of high order wanted to recognize the good people of Edom so he commissioned a painting. And that painting of a group of what look like early Bedouins celebrating or honoring an early Christian prophet was created by Talagiease."

"I am amazed at your success. Well, not so much anymore. You always seem to come through."

"As my friendly bookseller in Stillwater reminded me several times, most of this is insufficiently documented."

"Except there hangs the painting."

"Exactly," agreed Marjorie. "And the question of how it came to be in Saint Paul, Minnesota, is still out there. Plunder of some sort, perhaps?"

"That's a possibility," Lockem said. "After every war, soldiers appropriated plunder and carried it home. Obviously, a new line of inquiry, starting with when and how the church acquired the painting. But not tonight.

Chapter 12

The morning sun sent multiple sparkling beams through the unshuttered windows and warmed the meadows that lay next to Lockem's property. Alan Lockem stood with a mug of steaming coffee at the door to their deck. In his hand he held a printed list he'd just retrieved from his printer. Carolyn Action had just sent him names and contact numbers of the nineteen current members of the church board. He was expecting a list of former members to come a little later, as she was able to ferret out the information from the files.

Lockem decided he'd call board members, rather than take the time to locate and physically interview them, at least until he found someone who seemed to have useful memories or records. Several hours of telephoning and repeating over and over the same explanation suggested strongly that the church's records of past and present board members were woefully out of date. After the third discovery that an address was years out of date, he started making notes so he could give his new information to the church.

Finally, after seven calls he actually reached a former member, now resident in south Florida, who had a vague recollection of a twenty-year-old discussion of the painting by the board. "Oh, yes, somebody raised a question," she ruminated. "Was it an important painting, or by an important artist? Might it be worth enough so we could repair the roof, or some such." She chuckled.

"Did the board come to a decision?" At times Lockem could hardly understand the woman. She sounded tired and, frankly, old.

"No. It was like a lot of topics. The subject would come up, we'd discuss it and often decide it wasn't worth the time or, more often, the money. Hmm. Have you talked with Emma Haberly?"

"Who?"

"Emma Haberly. She was on the board. She took it on, to find out the background and other important information about the painting and the artist. I think she discovered some facts, but it was incomplete. I don't remember what she learned. I doubt there's anything in the meeting minutes."

Lockem couldn't find Emma Haberly or any other Haberly on the list so he called the church secretary. "Mr. Lockem, I'm sorry the records are in such rough shape. They just aren't a high priority."

"I'll give you what I've learned," Lockem said. "I was told to talk with an Emma Haberly, but she's not on the list."

"Emma? No, she wouldn't be. Not a board member. She was the wife of our Pastor twenty years ago. More. She came to most of the meetings. The pastor is long deceased, but Emma still comes to services, sometimes. I can get you her phone number at the Senior residence where she lives."

After a brief pause, Carolyn Action came back on the line and read off the name, address, and phone number of Emma Haberly's current residence. He keyed in the Haberly number and gazed out the window. The late afternoon sun sent warm rays into his office window and a slightly breathless voice came to his ear.

"Sorry," she puffed. "Not as spry as I used to be."

"Mrs. Haberly? My name is Alan Lockem. Carolyn Action gave me your number."

"Lockem?" she interrupted. "I've heard of you. You are looking into Reverend Elliot' death, right? I have a friend here, former cop. He told me about you. How can I help?"

"Thank you, Mrs. Haberly. A question has come up regarding a painting owned by the church. The large oil of the people around a sort of crude altar? Near a temple, perhaps. Maybe beside a route marker."

She chuckled. "Pretty accurate. Yes. That oil painting, maybe from the 12ᵗʰ Century, by some friar

58

named Talagiease. I'm not sure how you'd pronounce it."

Lockem smiled. "That's the one. What can you tell me about it?"

"Not much," she said. "I agreed to look into it for the board. That was years ago. I talked to a couple of art teachers, a historian and somebody from one of the galleries in town. They all told me the same thing. The painter was known but not terribly important and they didn't know if that painting is a true original without a serious examination."

"Did they arrive at a conclusion?"

"Oh, a detailed examination of the painting was never done. I talked with a restorer at the MIA who said he thought they had the expertise, but it would cost a lot of money. I took the information to the board and they voted not to proceed."

"I get it," Lockem said. "A gamble. Perhaps a real windfall if authentic, perhaps a significant expense if not."

"Exactly. So the board at the time, opted for alternatives to investment in a painting. Too bad, I think."

"I appreciate your information and insight, Mrs. Haberly."

"Pleasure to talk with you. I'll be pleased to learn the outcomes. Pastor Elliot was a lovely man, Mr. Lockem."

Lockem later related his conversations to Marjorie.

"Sounds definitely promising. Shall we take the painting to an expert?"

"How 'bout this," Alan said. "Let's get an expert in from the "U" and let them look at the painting on the wall, and then if they think it's worth it, have it removed to a lab for real analysis."

"I'll call the University Art Department," Marjorie said, first thing in the morning."

"Works for me," Alan responded.

The next afternoon Lockem and Marjorie watched with Carolyn Action while a tall, distinguished-looking man with a neatly trimmed beard and mustache examined the painting. First, he had merely stood back, hands clasped behind his back and stared at the art. Now he had approached more closely and almost peered at the work. At the moment he was examining the signature in one lower corner of the painting. Or perhaps he studied the frame.

Marjorie glanced at her companion and whispered, "He's humming."

Lockem nodded. The man had introduced himself as Professor McBride, or Doctor McBride, if you prefer. Now he straightened and replaced a magnifying glass in his vest pocket. He turned to the watchers.

"Well," he said softly. "Interesting, most interesting, don't you see. The painting appears old enough and in the proper style to be authentic. Of course, it may be a clever forgery from the time, or as the literature noted, possibly a student work." He glanced back at the watchers. "I looked up the painter and art activity during the period in question. Tests and more examination would be necessary, don't you see. It is my considered opinion that the paint and other elements should be tested. I would be willing to have one of my graduate students do some research, don't you see. Hmmm, for a modest fee."

"What other testing might be needed? Marjorie asked.

"Ah, yes. I would suggest a good restoration facility such as that at the Institute, MIA, don't you know, would be appropriate. That would require the investment of significant funds, don't you know."

Lockem nodded.

"I have a sense this painting illustrates an area in the Sinai near the ancient city of Petra." He frowned and shook his head. "I can't say why, there's just something that suggests Petra.

"I suggest you remove the painting from the wall and examine the back. You may find some useful information, clues, don't you see."

Marjorie and Carolyn both stared at the professor in surprise.

"Yes," McBride continued with a small lift of his thin lips, "notes from the artist, sales, or inventory details, sometimes forgotten by the purchaser. I also suggest that you locate the documentation in reference to the gift, the purchase, any nuggets of information that we might use to authenticate the work, don't you see." McBride took the thanks of his small audience, made sure Lockem had his business card, and then left.

"Well," Carolyn muttered. "That was interesting." She turned to Lockem, "I'll start a search of the records to find whatever we still have. And I'll memo the board."

"I want to examine the brackets and get it off the wall if easily possible," Lockem said, stepping around the desk.

Chapter 13

"I think we should talk to church board members before we go any further," said Marjorie. She and Lockem were relaxing after returning home. They'd discovered the painting on Action's office was well secured to the wall with several brackets so hadn't been able to inspect the back.

"You think this because....?"

"Because more research is going to cost something and there's the problem of publicity."

"I understand about the cost, but publicity?" Lockem frowned.

"More attention means more people learn about the painting. That church is under scrutiny already because of the murders. Is it going to be necessary to pay for round-the-clock security if the art becomes really valuable?"

"Ah, good thinking. What do you propose?"

Marjorie looked down, thinking then she raised her gaze to his. "We could make a contribution in Grace to the church and pay for night-time surveillance."

Alan rotated that turnip in his mind, examining it from several positions. Nothing dangerous or complicated came to mind, and her suggestion paralleled his promise to Myron Johnson. "All right, I'll talk to the church board president and our security company. If the security folks can't do that sort of protection, they'll surely have a recommendation or two."

Alan called the chair of the church board and they agreed to meet early the next morning for breakfast at a small café in the neighborhood of the church. The location was near the home of chairman Myron Johnson. Lockem arrived before the chairman and took a table near the windows with a pleasant view of the neighborhood homes across the busy, tree lined street.

Five minutes later, Myron Johnson, wisps of white hair pointing in all directions from under a dark knit cap, shuffled into the café. He smiled, nodded at Lockem, and waved to the waitress at the counter. "My usual, sweetie," he called. She nodded in response but didn't smile.

Johnson surveyed the room and immediately picked out the stranger in the room as his meet. He nodded and strode to Alan's table, thrust out a hand and smiled, revealing a missing tooth in his wrinkled face.

"Alan Lockem, I presume?" he said. Alan stood and shook the offered hand. Johnson's grip was surprisingly strong. The men sat and the waitress brought coffee for Myron and a refill for Alan.

They made a bit of small talk about the weather and the state of local government and Myron fixed Alan with a direct look and said, "This murder. Terrible, terrible. It has upset the congregation in a very significant way."

"I'm not surprised, and I can understand that having strangers, never mind the police, poking about must also be unnerving."

"Most of us understand the need for the police, of course, and we are satisfied, I believe, that you and your agency are necessary. We are most upset over the death of that young woman. The stranger. I am satisfied that she is a complete stranger to the congregation. And while there have been a few rumors about Pastor Elliot, I am sure they are just talk."

"You are quite satisfied that your pastor is clean?"

"Young man, I've been associated with this church and engaged in its governance for a very long time. More than one or two decades. Pastor Elliot is— was our third scriptural leader. There are almost always some negative comments that surface. Sometimes they are related to scripture, but most often it has to do with some imagined social slight. Real scandal is unknown in this congregation. At least

63

unknown until these recent murders." He bowed his head and swiped at his face. Lockem thought Myron might be tearing up a little.

He leaned in and said softly, "My sympathies, Mr. Johnson. I'm sorry I have to probe so insistently, but we do need to get to the bottom of this very sad situation. Is there anything, anything at all you can tell me about the young woman, Delilah Cooper."

Myron shook his head. "I'm afraid that's a dead end, Mr. Lockem. I never met the woman and I don't believe I ever noticed her at services, although she sure could have been there. Good attendance most Sundays, you know." He waved one hand randomly.

Lockem nodded and pulled at his earlobe. "I also want to get your take on the Talegiese painting in the church office. Again, anything at all however insignificant it may seem to be."

"Hmm. Well, you know, that painting has been in our care since as long as I can remember. The donation papers must be in the files. I'm pretty sure the donation came early in the teens, the nineteen teens. It would have been shortly after the congregation was founded and the building occupied. That must be right around 1920."

"Do you recall who donated the work?"

"Oh, no. It was on the wall when I started going to Sunday school there, you know, and it was just there. It was always there. Like the cross in the sanctuary. Years later, when I was named to the board, somebody asked about the authenticity of the thing and we did hire some expert from, I think it was the University. Of Minnesota. But I don't remember any report."

"Whatever the report, it must have been positive, don't you think?"

"Oh, sure," Johnson agreed. "Otherwise it would have been taken down, I'm sure." He nodded and took a healthy swig of his coffee.

Lockem thought for a minute. He'd learned very little but he was zeroing in on where to look for records of the painting's receipt by the church. There might be clues in those dusty files. But clues to what was still unclear.

"Mr. Johnson, we believe that the painting may have some connection to the murders and I'd like your permission to do further research. I really can't say why we believe that. The thing is, should we learn certain things about its provenance, or a previous owner, that might bring more and unwanted publicity. Plus—"

"Plus, if you discover that the painting is authentic and by a famous artist, it's value may skyrocket which could become a security problem. Yes?"

Lockem smiled. "You have it in a nutshell. I am prepared to donate to the church for the specific purpose of protecting the painting, should that become necessary. Would that be of interest?"

Johnson nodded. "Absolutely. Look, I have pretty good instincts about people. I guess that's why I've been on the board so long. Let us just agree right here, if your inquiries reveal new information and we are required to put in place some sort of protection, the church can come to you for a contribution, yes?"

"That's satisfactory and further, I'm prepared to invest personal time in helping the church secure whatever additional protection may be necessary. All right?

"Excellent. I've had you checked out and I'm comfortable with a verbal agreement until we get our lawyer to draw up a document."

Lockem nodded his agreement. Myron Johnson may be aging; he hadn't lost his faculties.

"Well, Mr. Lockem, there's nothing else I can tell you about that painting. I do know a number of funny stories about our congregation, and I can tell you a good deal about our overseas ministry and other successful projects we've done. I'm particularly proud of some of the youth clubs we've established in South America. I've never been a big proponent of the kind of

65

missionary work some churches did to convert numbers of citizens to Christianity, but they have their attitudes and missions. I get that." He shrugged. "On the other hand, our youth programs overseas do not conceal or shirk their close affiliation with our religious beliefs." Johnson smiled and stuck out his right hand. He shook with Lockem as he rose stiffly to his feet.

"I wish you every good fortune in your search for truth, Mr. Lockem."

"Thank you, Mr. Johnson. And likewise to you." Lockem watched as Myron Johnson slowly crossed the restaurant floor and pushed out the door, thinking the intel dump he'd just received might be interesting, but not particularly useful. From the street came the rumble of a passing motorcycle.

Lockem paid the bill leaving a generous tip for the smiling waitress and went to his car parked a long block away on the street.

Chapter 14

Lockem called Marjorie on his flip phone but when she didn't answer, he left a message that he had had a successful meeting and was on his way to the church. The building was only three blocks distant and Lockem considered walking. In the end, he drove the two blocks and parked on the street directly opposite the side entrance which led to a short stair and the office door.

"Hi, Carolyn, I'm back again. Sorry to bother you, but I need to look into your old files, if they are readily available and you will be here a while."

"Sure," she smiled. "This is my late day. My hours keep me here until the two groups that meet tonight are done at eight."

"Got it. What do you do about supper?"

She shrugged. "Usually I brown bag it with a sandwich. Or, like tonight, I wait until I get home."

"How about I pick us up something a little later?"

"Thanks, that would be nice." She smiled. "Assuming you're looking for more on the painting, I'm pretty sure the files you'll want are in the bottom drawer of that file in the far corner of the closet."

Lockem opened the door to the tiny closet and immediately saw the old metal four-drawer dark green file cabinet under a shelf. He looked at the faded labels. Each had date ranges. The bottom drawer was labeled 1918-1922. He recalled the building had been first occupied in 1920 so this must be the files for the construction of the building after the establishment of the congregation itself.

He dragged the drawer open—it had no roller bearings—and examined the brown folders. He'd guessed right; all the folders appeared to deal with the construction of the building, including furnishing the sanctuary, purchase of the big pipe organ and furniture for a church office.

In the next file drawer above, he found a folder labeled office and inside that several letters and scraps of paper with scribbled and carefully hand-written information about the furnishings. One note referred to a significant donation of a painting or some sort of wall decoration. Lockem smiled to himself and lifted the paper from the folder. He laid it on the table and adjusted the lamp Carolyn had thoughtfully provided.

The document appeared to be some sort of formal or legal writ of transference. What Lockem knew as a bill of sale. The top part was in Italian, a language he recognized but could not translate. However, the bottom half was in English and stated that the painting, authenticated as having been created by the Renaissance artist, one Friar Artolo Talegiease, a teacher and painter of religious works for the church.

Lockem took the document to the office copier and ran two duplicates. When he re-inserted the bill of sale in the file, he examined his copy more closely. The document indicated that the purchaser was an American man named John Jones. Lockem muttered, realizing that the chances of finding Mr. Jones was remote at best. But then, as he paged slowly through the file, he discovered that a John Jones had been a regular attendee at the church in the mid and late twenties right after its consecration. Then Lockem found a folded paper in the file that turned out to be a letter from a John Jones suggesting that he and his wife, Elizabeth, were interested in making a gift to the church. They were, the letter indicated, moving to a warmer climate in Georgia and were selling or giving away parts of their various collections. The letter further stated that while they had been assured the painting they wished to give to the church had been legitimately obtained and its provenance accepted, they could not guarantee there might not be future questions. The writer went on explain he didn't believe it would ever happen but felt compelled to raise the issue, however remote.

Lockem copied the letter and added it to his file. He now knew how and when the church had obtained the painting and that no lawyer was likely to question the legitimacy of ownership. But when he returned home, Marjorie smiled, handed him a glass of his favorite scotch, a twelve-year-old MacCallum, and waved a piece of paper at him.

"You'll be interested in this," she said. "I heard something on NPR and chased it. A gallery in Salt Lake has decided not to resist an ownership challenge from a French family over who owns a painting by some Belgian painter who is pretty well known."

"Who's the painter?" Alan took a sip and eased into his favorite chair.

"I had never heard of him, so I did a little Internet chasing and found him. That's not particularly important, but what may be significant is the increased activity to return stolen art from present owners to original ones. There was a lot of art misappropriated during World War Two and families and galleries are tracking down the works and sometimes suing for return."

Alan nodded and smiled at Marjorie. "I get it. Let me tell you what I found. I have a copy of a bill of sale between the couple who donated the painting on the office wall and the gallery in Tuscany where they purchased the work. We also now have the documents attesting to the donation of the painting to the church. And remember, this all occurred around the beginning of the Twentieth Century, long before the rise of Hitlerism."

"Oh, good. That just makes our life a little easier" she said.

"Anything else before I bring up something that's a little puzzling?"

"Nope. I talked to one of your contacts at the FBI. Naturally, she wouldn't tell me anything on the record, but it was pretty clear there isn't a lot of attention on this situation."

"Seen any motorcycles around?" he asked with a smile.

"Say again?" Marjorie frowned and leaned toward her companion. She knew from experience he was leading her on. A little.

"I just wondered. When I concluded my talk with the board chairman, and we were leaving, I noticed a motorcycle going down the street."

"And?"

"It's probably just my paranoia, but ever since we met Mrs. Elliot and those bikers, I've had an uneasy sense of more frequent sounds of a motorcycle engine nearby. As I say, it's likely nothing to worry about. Just a little puzzling."

Marjorie stared at Alan and he stared back. Neither of them believed it was nothing to worry about.

Chapter 15

Early the next morning, Alan had just finished his second cup of coffee and was contemplating the bagel, cream cheese and two sizzling rashers of bacon on a plate before him. Marjorie was still in bed and the early sun was sending dazzling rays across treetops in the nearby park.

The doorbell chimed and a heavy fist sounded an authoritative banging on the front door. Alan rose, deposited his napkin on his chair and shuffled to the door. He had neglected to dress before deciding to feed himself. Wrapping his robe more closely around his waist, he checked the video screen and then unlocked and swung open the door.

A tall slender young man wearing a nicely tailored suit stood smiling on the front step. He stepped back slightly when Lockem opened the door. "Good morning," Lockem said. "What can I do for you?"

"Mr. Lockem, I presume." The man did not wait for a response. "I am here representing an international organization dedicated to the location and restoration of stolen art works. I have come here to talk with you because we have received valid information that you may be in possession of information regarding an ancient painting that may have been stolen centuries ago."

When the man paused for breath, Alan smiled and stuck out a hand to greet his visitor, a man for whom English was not his native tongue. The man recoiled slightly and Lockem said, "Why don't you come in and we can talk about this. I'm sorry you caught me not quite fully dressed, but I'm sure we can ignore that small discomfort." He smiled some more at the young man and held the door wider in a clear invitation.

The young man hesitated and then nodded once, stepped forward and walked into the house. Alan directed him to a comfortable seat in the living room. He sat and said, "I must apologize." He reached to an inside pocket in his neatly tailored brown suit jacket and extracted a small leather folder.

He opened the wallet and said, "My name is Karl Markel. Here is my identification."

Lockem looked at a clean new-looking credential, recognizing the official symbols of Interpol. Opposite the Interpol identification he saw a credential for another organization. "Yes, I am here representing International Properties. IP is dedicated to the area of fraud and restoration to legitimate owners of stolen art works. Have you heard of the scandal in England over forged art works at the Tate Museum?"

"I have law enforcement friends in Britain. As a result, I have heard a bit about that rather extensive fraud."

"Our organization played a small part in helping bring some of the perpetrators to justice. But that is history. I am here today to discuss with you a painting by a Renaissance Italian painter, one friar Giorgio Talagiese, who taught painting and produced a number of paintings of important scenes of religious events in the Christian history. Our information indicates that one missing work may have come into your possession." Markel paused and licked his lips.

Lockem had the impression he was dealing with a somewhat inexperienced agent. He smiled and said, "Would you like a glass of water; or perhaps a cup of coffee?"

Markel nodded, looking grateful. He said, "Thank you. Coffee would be much appreciated."

Lockem turned and went toward the kitchen. He poured a second cup of coffee and glanced at the plate of rapidly cooling rashers of fried bacon. He handed his guest a mug of coffee and set down a small tray with milk and sugar and then returned with his own mug of coffee. Lockem briefly considered excusing

72

himself to get fully dressed, then decided against it. He sat across from his guest.

"I assume you have a specific reason or target for your appearance here today, correct?"

Markel nodded. "Oh yes, of course. We believe a church organization for which you are working owns a large religious painting that may have been created by an Italian friar in the Twelfth Century."

"That is correct. It is an oil on cloth and or canvas and purports to depict an adoration."

"Yes, the blessing of Odom."

"Odom? I'm not familiar with that term. Is that a place?"

Markel fished a folded piece of paper from an inside pocket. "Odom is referred to in Ephesus, one of the books of your Old Testament. Odom, sometimes spelled Edom, was a kingdom created after a falling out among the leaders of the Israelite Kingdom. The painting was named Odom or perhaps Sins of Odom."

Lockem raised his eyebrows.

"Yes," Markel said. "It has also been referred to as Adoration of Odom, but that title has been called into question. There is some evidence that the painting was misappropriated from an abandoned church or priory in central Tuscany by passing English knights returning from their Crusade." He paused and looked at Lockem as if he expected a response, possibly a protest."

"You must also be aware, then, that the church is in possession of a valid, notarized bill of sale for the painting. That bill of sale describes the painting but does not give it a name." He delivered this information in a neutral, non-belligerent tone.

"Ah, yes," Markel said. "We presume the sale or donation of the painting was legitimate and that none of the parties questioned its legitimacy or ownership, at the time. I am here because the International Properties would prefer to handle the return of the painting in the most logical way. We recognize and assume that the congregation would prefer to handle

73

this as discreetly as possible, as would International Properties. The corporation has no wish to engage in a public controversy over the artwork."

"Assuming it can be shown to be an object improperly obtained by the donor. Do you know a woman named Cooper? Lorna Cooper?" Lockem watched Markel closely when he asked the question. The was a response, not a guilty start, but he—Lockem—had the impression the name was not unfamiliar to the other man.

Markel shook his head. "No, I do not know such person."

"She's a redhead, very bright hair. I just wondered."

Markel checked his wristwatch and stood. His actions were smooth, giving Lockem the impression of a well-kept, athletic body. "I must go. I wanted to do you the courtesy of alerting you to our coming efforts to retrieve the painting."

Lockem stood and turned toward the door, ushering Markel out. "Thank you. I appreciate the warning." Markel strode down the walk to a dark sedan with tinted windows. Lockem couldn't see if there was anyone waiting in the vehicle, but someone started the engine just as Markel opened the front passenger door and slid inside. The vehicle accelerated smoothly away from the curb. Lockem focused his gaze on the rear license plate. It was a Minnesota plate.

He closed the door and turned to pick up the coffee cups in the living room. Reaching for the cups he paused when Marjorie said," I think we may want to preserve that coffee cup for fingerprints and maybe even DNA. Don't you agree?"

Lockem smiled, nodded, and left the visitor's cup until he could preserve it in a paper bag.

CHAPTER 16

"The timing of Mr. Markel's appearance is interesting. Don't you think so?" Marjorie stood in the doorway to the kitchen holding her favorite coffee mug. She was dressed casually in hip-hugging dark grey slacks, a pale blue blouse, and her usual minimal makeup.

"I do. Did you hear most of his questions?" Lockem took his own coffee and went toward her.

"No. As soon as I heard the door open and somebody come in with you, I decided to dress. I wasn't ready for a visitor."

Lockem nodded and briefly related his conversation with the man from IP. He concluded after a pause with a request. "I think we need to know some more about this company, International Properties."

"Happy to do the research," Marjorie responded. She took her coffee and retreated to her office and her computer.

A minute later Alan followed her, saying, "That woman, Lorna Cooper? Didn't she say she worked in the IDS for one of those global firms?"

"Yes, she did, something called Worldwide, or Worldwide Enterprises."

"Right. Markel, Cooper, and Cooper. Sounds like a law firm. One interesting aspect is that all three of these people are employed by companies that are multi-national and their corporate names are unspecific."

"One is no longer employed. International Properties, Global and Worldwide. And each has a name that could mean anything," Marjorie looked thoughtful. "It reminds me of the guys who'd come into the clubs looking for a date. They made up names, theirs and who they worked for. At least that was our automatic assumption."

"We need to know more about all three of these companies," Alan said. Merkle gave me a business card, but there's nothing on it except a phone number and the name of his company. I'll get it for you."

When he returned to her office, Marjorie was already busily plumbing the depths of an international company list to locate corporate information about the employers of the deceased Delilah Cooper and Lorna, the other woman named Cooper.

"I decided to start at ground zero. I'm searching on-line databases of corporations world-wide to try to discover how well-known and connected they might be. Later, I'll examine their Internet information. And, if we decide we need to, I'll drill down even more into what these operations are all about, or not all about."

"Good," Alan said. "I'm going to try to trace our Mr. Merkel and see if his agency is legitimate. That may require some cyber dancing if it's a small or one of those front groups."

"Front groups?"

"Yeah," Alan smirked. "Remember, dozens if not scores of organizations with innocent-looking names and offices appear around political campaigns and associated with military operations, especially when there's controversy of seriously different views on the action. Sometimes they are just ordinary folks getting together to promote something, like Clean Water, Incorporated, or People for Freedom. Now that was a subversive group, trying to torpedo support for the Korean War back in the fifties. There was some evidence it was funded by the Chinese government and that they mounted other espionage ops here in the states."

"Huh, and I bet with the advent of the Internet and the communications revolution, even more of that occurs," Marjorie nodded. "We will root them out and terminate their ops." She raised one fist and turned to her computer keyboard.

Alan smiled at the back of Marjorie's head and walked along the hall to his own office. His computer was already turned on and the monitor screen displayed another pastoral scene of an island beach

76

that curved into the foreground, edged by beige sand and the deep blue water of the Pacific Ocean. Over the sunny scene, a few white clouds punctuated the expanse of blue sky.

He opened his email and discovered a long list of unread messages. Frowning, Alan punched up first his Twitter account, then Facebook. He disposed of the few messages and returned to his email account. His frown deepened when he discovered he'd been bombarded with warning missives from several sources that purported to be religious and political organization which he'd never heard of and of which he quickly became convinced were probably phony.

He decided to scan them all and save them in a file instead of just deleting them all at once. That was his inclination after reading the first two, filled with warnings and gratuitous, thinly veiled threats. It was fortunate he did so.

A third of the way through the messages, he saw a name in the heading he recognized as vaguely familiar. The message, an aggressive warning, had come from somebody named Profit Obadiah H. when he attempted to respond with a simple one-word question, the address came back as nonexistent. He then searched online for Obadiah with a last name beginning with H. He found a few but none with even a hint of a possible connection to the Obadiah who had sent him a quote from the English Bible. "Thus saith the Lord concerning Edom: Arise ye and let us rise up against her in battle." He didn't recognize the quotation, but he took it as a warning, or possibly a threat. He moved the message to a separate folder in his computer and continued to read the file titles. Advertising, political and fund request e-mails filled the screen, but there were no more personal entries or anything that might be directed toward the services he and Marjorie often provided. He closed the program and signed off.

Staring thoughtfully into the depth of the blank screen, Alan thought about his life and whether he was doing, in his retirement, what he wanted. He wondered what Marjorie felt, what she thought about the work they did, the responsibilities they assumed. He rubbed his sore knee. Had they allowed themselves to be drawn too deeply into the swampy morass of violence and criminal elements? That was a question for a later time. First, he and his companion had to resolve the questions around two murders in a sacred space. The next step toward a solution required a meeting he faced with reluctance. He had to sit down again with the widow of the slain pastor, Melissa Elliot. Even with Marjorie's constant support, this action would be emotionally fraught. From time to time, during his active years in the service Alan had been called on to personally notify relatives of their loss. Frequently the deaths occurred during secret operations not known to the press or even regular military authorities. Decisions about what and how much to reveal of the circumstances of a loved one demise could only properly be revealed in any detail or meaning by someone with knowledge and understanding of the mission.

Chapter 17

Alan rose and walked across the house to Marjorie's office, a converted bedroom. The house, when first acquired by Lockem while he was still serving in Southeast Asia, had been a three-bedroom layout. Alan had converted one bedroom to a workout room and when Marjorie moved in she chose the smallest bedroom as her own private office where she installed a computer and files that carried information and even some exhibits from the couple's growing services to people in need of creative and sometimes unusual salvage services.

Alan's service in the army had left him with intimate knowledge of law enforcement and useful contacts across the continents in many military and law enforcement agencies. His chance encounter with retired, wealthy, civic-minded showgirl, Marjorie Kane, only enhanced the capabilities of an odd agency they called Lockem and Kane. Marjorie, who spent time backstage between shows pursuing her own interests and often fending off the advances of lecherous males, became adept at the intricacies of the Internet. She also enhanced her abilities to judge people and their intentions on the fly. Working with Alan improved her powers of observation and the couple came to depend on each other's separate strengths with frequent consultation as they worked their cases.

He found her sitting at her computer, staring at the screen, shoulders relaxed, fingers on the keyboard. The screen was blank. Dark. No icon floated in the environment. "Marjorie?" He said softly. You okay? Everything all right?"

She pulled her hands back and swiveled in her chair. He could see that her eyes were moist, brimming with tears. She nodded. "Yes, honey. I'm okay. I just got to thinking about Melissa, the pastor's wife. And her kids. And the Cooper woman's family. Delilah. I assume she had family somewhere. Or a close friend. Someone who will miss her."

Alan nodded. I hope so. I've just been thinking, it's time to have a lengthier conversation with Melissa Elliot."

"Do you think she's involved? I mean more than simply as wife of the victim? Also a victim."

He nodded. "I get you. No, I don't have any sense that she's involved otherwise, but she is likely to have some useful background. Maybe something that goes to motive."

Marjorie grimaced in sympathy. She agreed but knew her companion disliked probing backgrounds of damaged victims. And Melissa Elliot was surely a victim. "Do you want me to join you? Or should I see her alone?"

Lockem thought for a minute and then said, "Yes, I think that's a good idea. She may respond more easily to you at this time. I sensed some resistance when we were there the other day, even before the bikers showed up. Would you call her and go see her or meet for lunch or something? Today, if possible?"

"I'll get right on it," she responded, and reached for the telephone.

Two hours later, as the late November sun began its fall to the horizon west of Minneapolis, Marjorie Kane sat balancing a delicate cup of Lapsang tea on her knee. Melissa Elliot, dressed as if she'd been out or was going out, sat opposite Marjorie in the Elliot sunroom. The sun sparkled off Como Lake, speckled the ceiling with restless spots of light.

"Yes," Melissa said, "that group of boys still comes around frequently. Sometimes they bring a box of groceries." She smiled and shook her head. "It's not that we need the help, and I suspect Obi knows that. But he and the other two formed a tight friendship or comradeship with Obi and JJ especially." She smiled sadly.

"I take it the boys biker group were sort of rescued—by the reverend? By Pastor Elliot?"

80

"That's right. Several years ago, right after we moved here, Marty did some pastoral work on the East side. There was some gang activity surging and he wanted to get involved."

"And that's where he engaged this biker group, we met the other day?" Marjorie sipped her tea, watching Melissa process her question. It was a simple straight-forward question. Was there something else there? An unseen layer of anxiety?

"Yes, I guess that's right. That was several years ago. I can't remember all the details of every project my husband got into." She shook her head slightly. "When we took this calling, Michael was excited to see all the possibilities. He made so many contacts and organized several projects very early. I have trouble remembering all of it. But yes, I remember he brought Obi and one of his buddies' home and it just grew from there."

"So this connection goes back ten years or so." Marjorie consulted her notebook. "Were they always bikers?"

"No. In the beginning I think JJ always drove them in an old camper van when they came here. But one day, oh, probably three years ago, Obi and JJ and three others all showed up on motorcycles." Melissa looked at Marjorie. "I'm sorry. That would be Obadiah Hassen and Jacob Judah Hamilton. JJ always rides with his brother, Henry."

"Do you recall the names of any of the others in the ga—group?" She didn't want to risk offending Melissa by referring to the bikers as a gang, even though all her instincts had led to that characterization.

Melissa frowned in concentration and took another drink of her cool tea. She twisted her lips. "Oh dear, our tea is cold. Here. Give me your cup and I'll rinse it out and pour us fresh from the pot." She reached for Marjorie's cup. Marjorie realized the other woman was trembling slightly. She was upset. Over what? So far, the conversation had been relaxed and seemed non-threatening.

"How are the children coping?" She watched Melissa pour steaming tea into their cups.

"The girls? Oh, they are recovering nicely. Young, they're used tOo their daddy being absent. I sent them to my parent's. Outside of Chicago. It's hard, you know? I thought it would be better if they were with their grandparents while I wrap things up here." Melissa paused and then nodded as if she were having a silent conversation with herself. "Of course, you wouldn't know. I've decided to move back to Chicago as soon as I can pack up and sell the house."

Marjorie raised her eyebrows. "I'm a little surprised. I guess I just assumed you'd keep the children in school and not make any major decisions until next spring."

"Oh, well, I guess it seems a little abrupt. We have no ties here, except to the church and now that's gone. My parents are finding us a place and I've already been in touch with a local school. I believe a change as soon as we can arrange it will benefit the children." Melissa's tone seemed almost self-congratulatory.

Marjorie wondered if the police had been informed. It almost seemed as if Melissa and her family were running away. She leaned forward and set her empty teacup on the table in front of her. "If you are comfortable with my request, can you give me names and phone numbers or contacts for people your husband was counseling or working with? I don't mean church members. We have that information."

"Yes, of course. If it will help."

There was a soft rap at the back door and it opened to admit Trevor Howland. Melissa brightened immediately.

"OH. Sorry. I didn't know you had company."

"Hello, Mr. Howland. You aren't interrupting. I was just about to leave."

"I have Elliot's address book here. Marjorie, why don't you just take it and maybe copy it? You can return it whenever you finish with it." Melissa stood up, walked to another room, and retrieved a small black address book which she handed to Marjorie. Trevor watched, looking a little concerned.

"Thanks, Melissa. I'll return it as soon as we can make a copy." She didn't mention she might have it tested for fingerprints and DNA. She dropped the book into the outside pocket of her purse, said goodbye to Trevor and made her own way out the front door and down to her car.

Chapter 18

By the time Marjorie returned to Roseville, the autumn twilight was fading fast into darkness. Alan's SUV was in its customary slot in the garage. She closed the overhead door and walked up the half flight to the center hall. The fragrances of rosemary, roasting lamb and a tomato-sauce-based salad dressing greeted her. Alan was busying himself in the kitchen. Kitchen magic often presented a sign of his mild frustration over lack of progress in a situation they were engaged in. Marjorie smiled to herself as she shucked her coat and draped it on an antique rack in a corner of her office. Alan's frustration often resulted in a culinary masterpiece from their kitchen.

"So, my favorite chef is preparing a celebratory dinner? Hast thou made a breakthrough?"

"'Fraid not. My afternoon consisted mostly of cleaning out a bunch of crap in my e-mail folder."

"Really?" She grabbed the utensils and set the small table in a corner of the big kitchen. The round polished oak table had been her mothers. It didn't quite fit the décor of the more modern house, but it's design and attraction more than compensated. Neither Marjorie nor Alan were particularly concerned about having a coordinated décor.

"So, tell me about your afternoon with Mrs. Elliot. Were you productive or wasting time?" Alan grinned over his shoulder from his place at the stove.

Marjorie glanced back from the glass-faced cabinet where she was selecting goblets for the wine. "A nice merlot, don't you agree?"

"Yes but I want to hear about your day."

"Bring the dishes and sit. I will tell all when we have a little less distraction."

Alan pouted at her in the way he had and finished dishing up. He had selected the large dinner plates and sliced each a generous piece of rare lamb from the roast. They also had a nice green salad and a baked potato smothered in sour cream and butter.

He graciously pulled and held the chair for his companion. They sat and Marjorie took a generous mouthful of the glowing merlot.

"There is definitely something going on around the Elliots. The widow has sent her girls to their grandparents in Chicago and she told me she expects to move back home next spring at the latest. Apparently, her parents are seeking an apartment for her."

"Doesn't that seem a little abrupt?"

"Yes and no," Marjorie responded. "She has no real ties here, except through the church and that was mostly the church people. I did get a faint suggestion she didn't really have much of an emotional attachment to the people there. And there's something else. Her husband extended the church resources all over the city. Very active guy, apparently. Lot of expressed interest in social issues. That's how the connection came about with the bikers. I got the impression she hadn't been too happy about that."

They ate in silence for a few appreciative moments, savoring the mixed aromas, the tender lamb, the crisp salad, and the wine.

"It sounds like there are some more trails to check," Alan said. "I've been wondering about those bikers, how they showed up at the home the day of the funeral."

"There's more. Just as were concluding our tea, excellent, by the way, a former friend of her husband showed up. Remember Trevor Howland?"

Lockem frowned then nodded and swallowed. "Yeah, a college friend of Elliot's, right?"

"Right. He seemed a little ill at ease or at least surprised and uncomfortable when he walked in and discovered I was there. And he did just walk in. Well, he rapped on the door as he opened it. I think there's a connection between Melissa and Trevor that isn't exactly kosher. I'm not saying they're having an affair.

85

It may be that they just feel a growing attraction that is stronger than they expected. Whatever it is, is certainly bothering Trevor Howland."

"Do you have feeling she's running away from something?"

Marjorie smiled. "Yes, but I'm not sure what. It may be the current circumstances, her husband's death. It may be worry about the bikers or this relationship with Howland."

"More trails to follow. Maybe all of the above. I've been able to do some searching. Oddly, I can't find anything on International Properties. They have no corporate web site. There are some references to IP in a business development site. I called our acquaintance at the Minneapolis Institute. She didn't know anything and didn't recognize Lorna Cooper's name. So I called a couple of galleries here and one in Chicago. People at two thought the name and person was vaguely familiar. The owner of the Sandling Gallery in Minnetonka was the only person I've found who tipped to the name."

"What kind of gallery? I don't know the Sandling Gallery."

"Sculpture mostly. It's a small gallery, three years old." Alan poured more wine. "The owner said she was expanding into art glass next year. Lorna Cooper is on her mailing list as an interested patron."

Marjorie rose to clear the table. "Did you ask how long Ms Cooper an interested patron has been?"

"I did. Ms Cooper has been an interested patron and buyer for almost five years."

"So, that means she's been around for that long, at least. Pick up any threads? Any lint?" She bent to place the used dishes in the dishwasher.

Not yet. She frequently attends shows at the gallery and has purchased a few small items. Her employment record here is interesting. I haven't been able to learn much. She appears to be a mid-level officer in a corporation with a useless name.

Worldwide Products is recognized as a wholesaler of stuff."

"Stuff?"

Alan chuckled. "Yeah. They have connections to manufacturers of casual items all over the world. They sell Christmas decorations, some small toys, greeting cards, casual clothing, cheap art reproductions and other stuff. I ordered a catalogue. They also handle stock order of supplies for various retail distributors. We've probably bought things from our local hardware store that were wholesaled from a Worldwide affiliate. Lorna Cooper works in the area of fine art acquisitions."

"How does Worldwide function?"

"Let's say you are a retail store that wants to sell reproductions of paintings by a friend or relative. You think his art is pretty good and you want to support the artist. So you buy the rights, commission reproductions, and sell them through your existing outlets. I'm pretty sure they also initiate such operations."

"I get it. Maybe that's what Ms. Cooper does, buys and validates art for the company. We don't have any links to this big painting in the church, do we?"

"Not yet, but I'm betting we will find some, and I have news regarding our Mr. Merkle."

"Ah." Marjorie waited.

"He's a phony. Or he may be undercover. I'm betting it's the former. Interpol agents do not have part time jobs or second, simultaneous, careers. I think he ginned up a credential from Interpol's Internet information. I just called a couple of small favors."

Alan grinned and waved one hand. "As far as the painting is involved, I guess it's just gut-level instinct. Experience. I think all of this is somehow connected. I just don't understand what the bikers have to do with anything."

"I think it's probably just because of Pastor Elliot's outreach. They may have a feeling of closeness they didn't want to let go of."

"Agreed," Alan said. "Unless one of the bikers was involved in the murder. Suppose one of the bikers came to the church planning to murder Pastor Elliot and killed Cooper as well?"

"Far-fetched, I think. What could possibly motivate a biker to do that?" Marjorie shook her head.

"Suppose Pastor Elliot discovered something bad about the bike gang? Something seriously illegal. So the bikers decided they had to shut him up. Do you think it's a possibility?

"Barely. I just don't see anything that even suggests something like that." Marjorie shook her head. "There is something going on here that we can't see yet. Cooper is still an anomaly. Although, more and more I think she's quite possibly another tragedy."

"An innocent who got caught in a cross-fire you mean."

"Yes."

"Okay. I'll sleep on it. But her cleaned out desk is still an unanswered puzzle."

Marjorie smiled and picked up the TV remote. "Maybe that's just a fat mistake." She pressed a button and the TV went dark.

Chapter 19

The next day Lockem decided to visit the Sandling Gallery. He had no specific reason that linked to the murders, but if there was a connection, he might find it at the gallery. Marjorie declined to join him, having a full schedule of her workout at the gym and meetings in the late afternoon. They decided to find their own separate evening meals. She did promise to do some research on Edom, Odom, or whatever it really was.

Lockem discovered that the Sandling Gallery would be open from four in the afternoon until ten in the evening. By four he had spent several hours in the Hill Reference Library, at the Saint Paul police department headquarters and scarfed down a tasty fried lunch at iconic Mickie's Diner on ninth and Saint Peter.

His time at the library had resulted in nothing directly tied to the church or the two murdered citizens but he did have a higher appreciation for the art of the Twelfth Century. The officer in charge of the double murder had no update, but Lockem was able to meet several officers in administrative services and a few new recruits. He knew maintaining contacts within local law enforcement agencies could, at times, be valuable.

Later he had located the small single floor Sandling Gallery on a winding highway on the east side of Lake Minnetonka, with a broad visual expanse of a bay on the lake. It was prime commercial real estate.

He found a parking spot in a far corner of the small, paved lot and walked toward the front of the building, past an ornate and solid side entrance. As he walked along the driveway, he realized that the building had once been a mortuary. Inside he tried to avoid looking too curious but scanned the hallways and rooms he passed. His impression of the origin of the building was confirmed as he passed an office space that clearly had started life as a small chapel. The outline of a Christian cross that had hung on the wall, surrounded by a plaster relief of an arch still remained to anyone with a sharp eye, even though the original decorations had been removed and the walls painted.

Lockem strolled down the wide carpeted corridor and followed the signs around a corner into the large gallery. This space had apparently been the main lobby or perhaps a meeting hall. When he looked at the walls, there were signs from the placement of windows that interior walls might have been removed to enlarge the gallery. Here there were dozens of glass-topped cabinets in almost random fashion, or wandering rows, interspersed with sculpture and round display platforms. The display units were mostly round flat disks waist high on three crossed slender legs. They held small sculptures. A few also held artfully displayed jeweled necklaces draped on small, polished pottery lumps or craggy rocks combined with a dead twig or two. Some were accented by carefully aimed spotlights from an overhead grid.

Lockem swept the room with his appreciative gaze, recognizing the considerable effort and no little expense that had gone into the room. He wondered how much money was on display in the carefully crafted jewelry and other art. Four large original oil paintings hung on the walls. A discreet printed label near the main entrance told Lockem the paintings were all by the same artist, John Hockley, a name he didn't recognize. It didn't matter. He noted the several surveillance cameras positioned above the lighting grid. When he had stepped closer to the front entrance portico to read the piece about the painter, he registered the metal security gate suspended over the entrance and the bars on all the windows. He had no accurate idea of the value of the art, but it was obvious the gallery operators took security seriously.

"Hello," he called. The murmur of voices halted and for a moment there was only the gentle sounds of the building systems.

"Just a moment, sir," came a melodious voice. "I'll join you in a moment."

Lockem waited and after a few minutes, he heard the snap of hard heels on the tile floor and a tall slender Asian woman dressed in a sleek, long form-fitting dark blue dress appeared. Her gown was slit up the side to mid-thigh, giving an appreciative observer a glimpse of the woman's slender legs when she moved. Lockem wondered briefly if she was dressed for a coming evening event. Then he thought that perhaps she always dressed in such an elegant fashion. Perhaps it was just her style.

"Welcome to Sandling Gallery. May I be of assistance?" She smiled and her long dark hair swayed when she turned and minimally gestured at the room.

"Thank you." He paused, expecting she would give him a name, but the woman only glanced over his shoulder, retaining her smile. "My name is Alan Lockem. You have an unusual and spectacular display of art objects. You also are housed in what I would term as an unusual building, unusual, that is, for an art gallery."

The woman smiled and nodded. "Yes, adapting a former mortuary to the needs of a fine art gallery turned out to be more trouble than we anticipated. I think it has turned out quite well, don't you? My partner got the idea from that restaurant, the one in Brainerd, I believe? It was popular and had quite a wide reputation, I understand."

Lockem vaguely remembered reading about the restaurant conversion in a newspaper article some years ago. That wasn't the purpose of his visit. "I will take the time to look over your collection, if I may, but I also have a few questions. My partner talked to you a day or so earlier inquiring about a woman named Cooper, Ms....?" His obvious attempt to elicit her name resulted only in a demure smile and a nod.

"Oh, yes, Lorna Cooper. I don't know her really, at all, although she is an occasional customer and frequently attends gallery openings when we feature new artists or new collections."

Intrigued, Lockem asked, "Do you carry artists other than glass and sculpture talents?"

"We do. This is our main gallery and the only one open at the moment, but as I will show you, this room is designed to be flexible and we are converting three other viewing rooms. One will become a small theater for lectures and the other two for separate shows."

Lockem thought she was shifting into her sales role.

"One of our designers suggested we put the display cabinets on wheels so they can be more easily moved about for different emphasis, different kinds of displays, or removed from the room entirely." She smiled and walked to the nearest cabinet. She placed one foot on a lever at the floor and pressed down. There was a loud click and she was able to easily move the cabinet off a small piece of tape affixed to the floor. Alan glanced at the tape and smiled at the woman. She then moved the cabinet back to its original position and pressed down on the lever. There was another loud click.

"Is there anything you can or are willing to discuss regarding Ms. Cooper?"

The woman looked at him for a silent moment, then appeared to relax a bit. "Ms. Cooper concentrated her interest on smaller sculptures and some jewelry. In several instances she requested and received information about some of the artists who have placed work with us."

"Is some of the work here on consignment?"

She smiled and nodded. "Oh, yes, unless an artist is nationally known with a strong reputation, we would accept jewelry and other art only on consignment. We do buy some jewelry that we like and have some indications there is interest in the artist

92

and his or her work. Art jewelry and sculpture are pretty limited fields and this gallery doesn't have the funds to invest in highly speculative art. Tastes in jewelry change constantly, artists rise and fall. I'm proud of the support we are able to offer some artists, but we are limited by our funds."

"Can you tell me what sort of jewelry Ms Cooper was interested in?"

"Not really, Mr. Lockem, although I do recall that she sometimes requested the contact information for artists who also offered lower cost, more popular pieces. We are always pleased to support artists who have other work not of the kind we would display."

Lockem and the woman had by now moved slowly to the other side of the gallery where she indicated some of the pieces displayed on a craggy shard of pumice rock. "Here for example, are four pins we purchased from the artist two years ago. Originally, we had eight, having sold four. When I inquired of the artist if she was interested in selling more pieces she declined. I later learned she had signed a contract with Worldwide Products."

"And do you happen to know anything about that company?" Lockem was discovering more and more links to other players in this case, but the links weren't as productive as he hoped.

"Not a great deal except it is a conglomerate that deals in part with costume jewelry. One of the ways they acquire new products is to hire artists to design pieces for them. I believe the company often contracts with new artists they find in shows like ours. Ms Cooper saw some jewelry here she liked and negotiated a contract with the artist. It's a way for a good artist to make some money. Most jewelry artists are interested in that, of course. Very few resist the idea of mass duplication of their designs although there are some who prefer to provide individual pieces for individual customers."

"Anything else you care to tell me about Ms. Cooper?"

"There is nothing more to tell you. Ms. Cooper comes to the gallery occasionally and sometimes buys some jewelry."

"Thanks for your help. I know my companion will want to visit your jewelry display and I'll be sure to encourage her to visit." The woman nodded goodbye and Lockem exited through the main door to find his car

Chapter 20

Driving home from Sandling Gallery, the harsh afternoon sun sent mysterious messages through the back window of Lockem's vehicle. A few blocks into the city, he heard and then saw a motorcyclist behind him. Under normal circumstances in a more benign season, he might have paid the rider no mind but with temperatures trending downward and the days growing shorter, plus remembering the biker gang the dead pastor had engaged, he wondered. He decided to avoid the freeway route home and drove sedately through the city, keeping track of his two-wheeled shadow. He noted the rider was well protected against the icy wind with goggles, a heavy hat pulled low on his forehead, thick appearing gloves and pants, and a bulky coat.

Lockem eventually decided to ignore the rider, turned into the next north-bound freeway entrance, and increased his speed toward home. The rider disappeared from view after a few miles. Lockem smiled and continued home.

Later over dinner, he reported to Marjorie. "I think the gallery is interesting. You should go and see some of their jewelry and glass offerings. I don't believe the people there have anything to do with the murders. I did get some insight into Lorna Cooper's job, but I can't see it has ought to do with the church or even with the old painting on the wall of the office."

"So it's a dead end?" Marjorie asked.

"At the moment, I label the Sandling Gallery as a likely dead end. I will not take it off the table entirely, but I think we have other more profitable possibilities. It was a little odd she didn't introduce herself. And she was dressed for an up-scale evening event." Lockem chewed silently and then swallowed. "I want more information about the Pastor's local activities outside the church. Yes, those motorcycle guys, and also the other organizations and neighborhoods he may have engaged with. The church secretary can help there. I also think Ms Cooper's friend bears closer examination.

Marjorie nodded agreement. "Why don't I reach out to Lieutenant Gage tomorrow? He can probably give me some contacts. Both cop and civilian contacts. Then I'll see who might have some dirt on the mysterious Ms Cooper. Lorna Cooper."

"And I'll look into Reverend Elliot's neighborhood social work activity. I'll call Ms Action tomorrow," Lockem responded.

**

"Good morning, Mrs. Action. Alan Lockem here. I need some information on Reverend Elliot's non-church related activities, and I hope you can help me with that."

There was a short pause. The woman sighed and responded, "Here's the situation. The church constantly receives requests for help of various kinds, from shelter to food drives, like canned goods for Christmas gifts. Then there are individual and group asks. Can the Reverend help us organize a group counseling effort for new neighborhood mothers, or troubled teens or...? You get the idea. Then, active boards and pastors often have their own interests. Reverend Elliot had several interests that took up part of his time. When he was in Chicago. he worked with youth gangs and he carried that interest over when he moved here to our church."

"Did the board review his activities? Do they have any say over what their pastor does in this regard?" Alan bent his head and held the phone with his shoulder so he could make notes.

"Yes to both questions, Mr. Lockem. He discussed his activities regularly with board members. I know his calendar shows a lot of regular evening meetings." Lockem could hear her rattling paper.

"I'd greatly appreciate it if you could put together a list of the groups he interacted with."

"Take me a couple of hours. Should I mail it to you?' She seemed to be in a more cooperative frame of mind toward him, Alan thought.

"Oh, no. I'll drop by before you leave today if that's okay. I can pick up your list then."

"I'll be leaving about four-thirty today. Does that work for you?"

"Perfect," he said. "Excellent and thank you so much. I'll see you then." He closed his flip phone and turned to his computer. He knew he could have asked her to fax or email the information, but he favored a personal touch and he was getting internal vibes about security of the information. While he waited for the time to pass and the church secretary to compile the requested information, Lockem decided to explore what he could find online about Obadiah Hassen and the other members of the motorcycle group.

He already knew they might not be a gang that fit the popular perception. Motorcycles might simply be the preferred mode of transportation for some of those young men. But he needed to know more, in order to build a full picture of life around the victims and the church.

Two hours of intense searching, scrolling through many different web sites, blogs, social media, and other Internet channels only raised his level of frustration. Other than biblical references generated by the given names of some of the members, he could find no entries by the bikers or others. If they communicated electronically, it might be possibly using private channels.

The day waned and he closed the computer. In the car, heading toward the Saint Paul neighborhood where the church stood proudly on a large evergreen tree shaded corner lot, the fall sun weakly penetrated the treeless branches of large elms marching along the boulevards. Lockem parked directly in front of the building between the sidewalks that split the boulevard and allowed more ease of curb-side drop-offs. Two large entryways stood above stairs in the dark brick façade. They were arched in medieval European style with heavy carved oaken doors. Lockem knew they provided direct access to the rear of the sanctuary where at least one of the murders had taken place. Instead of mounting the stairs, he walked to a smaller wood paneled door that faced the cross street. This door led to an elevator and short staircase that would take him to the office where the church secretary, Carolyn Action waited. He hoped the list she had created would prove to be reasonable in length. He did not care to contemplate a list of several pages that could take days or even weeks to check out.

Up the short flight of stairs, he turned right into the office and opened the door. The long narrow office had windows overlooking the stairs and was crowded with two desks, two computers and a row of four-drawer file cabinets. Carolyn Action's desk sat at one end and on the plain stucco wall behind her, hung the religious scene of the prophet with several names and his adoring acolytes kneeling at his feet.

"Good afternoon, Ms Action. I hope you had a decent day."

"I did, thank you. My day has been uneventful. The printer is just spewing out the list you requested." As she spoke, the printer dinged and stopped issuing out pages.

Carolyn collected the four pages into a neat stack and slipped a paper clip on them, then handed the pages to Alan. He flipped through them, skimming the entries for anything familiar or unusual. On the third page his progress was stopped by the name, Odom.

"Huh," he murmured, glancing at Carolyn. "An odd name here, Odom. Biblical, isn't it?"

Carolyn smiled, "I had to look it up. Odom is the name of an ancient kingdom that was south and a little east of Judea. According to the legends, it was founded by a disgruntled family related to the ruler of Judea. There's a reference to the kingdom of Edom in the chapter of the King James Bible titled Obadiah."

Lockem raised his eyebrows and stared at the woman. "Isn't that also the name of one of those bikers? The one they call Obie?"

She shrugged. "I suppose that might be. I really don't know. That's a group Pastor Elliot listed, but they weren't connected to the church. He and Melissa worked with them independently of the church."

"Okay. I'll get out of your way. Thank you for putting this list together." Lockem smiled at her and folded the list into a jacket pocket. He turned and started out of the office. At the door he stopped, turned back to her, and said, "Let's not make too much of this, just let me caution you to remember this is a murder investigation. It's probably better to not mention this list to anybody."

"Mr. Lockem, without specific direction, nothing of church business is discussed with anybody, other than those directly involved." She smiled in a self-satisfied way and Lockem, nodded again and left the office.

Chapter 21

Marjorie sat across the desk from Roseville Police Lieutenant Vernon Gage and gazed calmly into his face. He looked back, waiting.

"I see. I have to form my questions in such a fashion that you will determine whether to answer me. Is that correct?"

"Not exactly, ma'am. I'll tell you as much as I can about this case. But you have to remember that you are a civilian and you are inquiring about an open case. I must be very careful to not reveal something that might later compromise our investigation."

"Or result in a court challenge," she said evenly. An observer would not be able to detect that the two were really friends who enjoyed their occasional social interactions. "I wasn't aware you had an active case involving Ms. Cooper."

"In fact, Roseville does not have an active case involving Ms Lorna Cooper. And, as you are well aware, the other Cooper, Delilah, is deceased."

"Hmm, yes. I am aware that the live Cooper was involved in an altercation at a local bar some months ago. I wondered if you have any additional information you can share."

Gage glanced at a file in front of him. "As you already apparently know, she was transported here to the department by our officers after there was an altercation."

"But she was not charged with anything."

"That's correct. She had a small cut or abrasion on her forehead as a result of contact with an empty beer bottle."

"If she was brought here to the station and not charged, she must have been released immediately."

"That's correct. According to the report, there were no EMT's or ambulance available at the time. We are a small city, as you are aware. Our officers did the neighborly thing. After they determined she was not drunk and the persons who initiated the brawl had already departed, the officers brought her here and allowed her to clean up a bit."

"Was her head injury treated by a physician?"

"No, Ms Kane. The female officer used a first aid kit in the office to put antiseptic on the wound and cover it with a small bandage. Her friend arrived and they were allowed to leave."

"And there was no formal report?" Marjorie raised her eyebrows in simulated concern.

"No. Once the officers determined neither woman was inebriated and the wound was minor, they decided no formal charge or report was necessary. A younger, less experienced officer might have charged Ms Cooper, which would have been lawful, but in this case it didn't seem necessary."

"I see, just citizens helping out. Small town and all that." Marjorie smiled.

"Correct. Ms Cooper declined to press charges against her unknown assailant. She declined to file a complaint against the bar and said she couldn't identify the man who struck her."

"Do you have any other useful information?"

"Only this," Gage leaned forward and lowered his voice slightly. "the officer noted that she seemed a little anxious about being approached by the officers. That was at the bar. Reluctance to be helped, was the way he put it in his notes."

"Where is the bar that was the site of this altercation?"

"Oh, that small place out on north Rice. It's, hmmmm, not unknown to us."

Marjorie made another note in her notebook and smiled at the Lieutenant. "Any other bits you'd care to add?"

Gage smiled again and looked away from Marjorie. "No, nothing else. Her friend took her out and we've had no contact since. Further, according to the file, no other law enforcement agency has inquired about Ms Cooper." His lips twitched, "neither Cooper, until the murder."

Marjorie rose. They shook hands and without further conversation he escorted her to the department door. Outside, she sat in her car in the parking lot and typed notes into her I Pad. It didn't take long. She drove home then and turned her thoughts to supper. Inevitably, after deciding she'd make a green salad of fresh spinach, celery and some other crisp veggies topped with a few bacon sprinkles and their favorite salad dressing, her thoughts returned to the murders.

From what she and Alan had learned so far, the connection between the pastor and the woman were so tenuous as to be almost non-existent, except for where their lives ended. Still, there were intriguing threads to be pulled from the fabric of their lives. Pastor Elliot had a relationship with that biker gang, the group Alan was exploring and there were those unexplained holes in Ms. Cooper's life, the gaps in her bookshelves and the months when she was off the radar and out of sight. Marjorie thought that the possibility that she was actually some sort of agent was farfetched. Pretty remote. Which, she mused, left wide open the question who she was and what was she doing at that church on that fateful afternoon. Marjorie twisted her lips in frustration, an unconscious habit. Still more questions than answers.

Alan Lockem stood on a street corner high on a hill north of the capitol dome. He'd parked down the hill in the big lot managed by the hospital where his mother had been born. The future of the hospital, he'd read, was in some question. His connection to the hospital was faint at best but he yielded to impulse, parked in their lot, and hiked four long blocks uphill to where he could see the older residential neighborhood that covered the hill and was limited by a freeway on the south and east sides and a major city boulevard on the north. He turned around and looked back the way he'd come, over the houses and businesses that stretched out west into the rest of the city.

He stood at the crest of the hill, above a series of government buildings that occupied the land between this hill and the freeway. The site of the former Mechanic Arts High School now occupied by a modern state office building, reminded him of bygone athletic events in the medium sized gymnasium of the school. His gaze swept the neighborhood where he knew at least some of the members of the motorcycle club lived. Trees along the boulevards pointed their slender leafless fingers at the gray sky. The sun appeared as a pale orb behind the screen of clouds.

Abruptly, Lockem heard the racking cough of an engine issuing from the nearby alley. It sounded like an automobile engine sans muffler. The rising and falling cacophony of sound indicated that someone was playing with the accelerator, goosing the rpms up and down. Lockem started toward the alley, hoping no one was trying to sleep in nearby homes. Many of the residents of this neighborhood worked late and overnight shifts at some of the medium sized manufacturing operations along the major streets in the valley.

He turned into the alley to discover the source of the ratcheting noise came from a trembling automobile engine mounted on a wooden test frame in the mouth of an open garage. Beside the engine frame rested a gleaming, dark red, Harley Davidson tricycle. Lockem recognized the man leaning over the rumbling engine. David Kline, the biker who had been leaning on their car outside Melissa Elliot's home looked up. He looked mildly startled.

"Well, Mr. Lockem, isn't it? The private Dick?"

Lockem smiled slightly and walked slowly toward the other man. "Investigator, if you please. Dick seems so dismissive. I wonder if we could have a short conversation?"

"I guess. Your time, but I gotta get this engine tuned up and the rest of it cleaned up. We're goin' to a rally up near Itasca. Starts tomorrow early."

"I understand. I just have a few questions about your group. Your motorcycle group."

"Club. We're not a gang." Kline waved at the street. Some people here and Saint Paul cops sometimes call us a gang, but we're nothin' like them Hell's Angels." He shook his head and bent back under the hood of the car.

"How long have you been a club?"

"Dunno, three, four years, maybe. Would you hand me the wrench on the fender, there?"

"This one?" Lockem picked up the only wrench on the fender and placed it in Klein's upstretched fingers. He stepped back a pace, recognizing the device as a possible weapon. But Klein ignored him and worked on something Lockem couldn't see. "What do you guys do? Get together and ride around the neighborhood?"

"Yeah, we do that. We do highway rides. Go to some town or other. A park for a picnic. We meet, mostly at Obi's. He has a room in the basement of his ma's—his house. Sometimes we toss a football around."

"So nothing illegal."

Klein pulled his head out of the engine compartment and stared at Lockem. "Why would you say that? We aren't a gang. We don't harass people. Not since I joined."

"Before you joined?"

"There were rumors. Nothin' to find, that I saw. We do funders."

"Funders? What's a funder?"

"Raise money. Sometimes for a neighbor, sometimes for a cause. Like we raised money on the web to help pay for some kind of new machine at the local hospital." He nodded toward the big beige hospital down the hill a few blocks and across from the state capitol building. "We rode in a funeral

104

procession last summer for a GI from overseas somewhere. Afghanistan, I think."

"What about earlier? Before you joined up?" Lockem watched Klein closely, looking for any sign of nervousness. He didn't see any.

Again, Klein shook his head in negation when he raised up out of the engine compartment. "Naw. I heard Obi and the brothers, they all grew up together, had some juvie trouble when they were little."

"That would be Henry and Jacob?" Lockem hoped he had the names right.

"Yeah, H and JJ."

"Interesting names those men have," Lockem remarked.

Klein grinned. "Yeah, their mom's and Obi's all belong to some small church where a lot of the kids have old biblical names. Dunno why."

Lockem smiled another nod in Klein's direction and said, "Well, thanks. Appreciate the info. I'll leave you to it." His glance slid across the open garage, over the door to the backyard. The shadow of a young woman at the edge of the open door, had appeared there. Lockem was sure she had heard Lockem's voice or seen him from the house and had been listening to their conversation for the past minute.

He raised a hand and turned back into the alley in the direction he had come, glad he hadn't asked Klein anything to raise suspicions. The late sun splashed off the uneven dusty alley sending Lockem's shadow ahead of him toward the street.

Chapter 22

"I think the motorcycle club may not be involved," said Alan. Marjorie had just reported on her conversation with Lieutenant Gage. He went on to relate his conversation with David Klein while they stood over the automobile engine Klein had been adjusting in his garage.

"Isn't he the young man we encountered outside Melissa Elliot's home?"

"That's right. I didn't press him on his background, and we had a short conversation in which he mostly told me about the club. It turns out the boys grew up in the same neighborhood and their parents all attend a small evangelical church. That's why several of the members have biblical names."

"Like Obadiah, you mean," said Marjorie.

"Like Obadiah," agreed Alan. "He's sort of like the leader of the club. I'm going to talk to the city police about them, probably tomorrow."

"Good. I don't disagree with your assessment, Alan, but I have this persistent feeling there's something about those riders we're missing.'

"Well, they're going out of town today. They have an appearance in Bemidji where they've been asked to ride in a funeral procession for a biker up there."

"Interesting. Any indications about Mr. Klein?"

Alan shook his head. "Nope. Another subject to raise with the authorities."

Alan Lockem crossed his legs and adjusted the crease in his slacks. He looked toward the door to the interview room on the fourth floor of the Art Deco tower that was the Saint Paul and Ramsey County Administrative Center. He'd expected to meet his contact at police headquarters across town, but just as he prepared to leave home for the drive to Saint Paul, he received a call to go to an office on the fourth floor of the center. He knew he was now located in a chair right over the head of the massive statue of an Indian Chief that stood at the head of the ground floor gallery, a vast gloomy space that dominated the principal entrance to the building.

He found the office to which he'd been directed, entered, and identified himself to the woman at the desk. She directed him to the single door behind her. He went into the empty room, found a chair, and sat down to wait.

After a brief time, he heard footsteps, the door opened and a man Lockem judged to be about fifty, entered holding a beige file folder. He nodded and said, "Mr. Lockem? You can call me John." John took the only other chair in the small office and sat, after dragging it a few feet closer to where Lockem sat.

"You've been vetted, pretty completely, but I'm going to tell you right up front that I'm not going to give you much. Some pretty weird things are happening in regard to this situation."

Lockem nodded, noting the stranger hesitated before uttering the word "situation."

Without waiting for Lockem to respond, he opened the file folder and glanced down at a sheet of paper. "The man you refer to as Klein is indeed a source. More detail than that about his circumstances or our relationship I'm not willing to provide." He looked up at Lockem, stared unblinking into his face.

Lockem had the sense the man was unhappy having to reveal anything at all. "I can assure you our interest is peripheral, but I'll appreciate any help. I'm not convinced those motorcycle men are involved with the murders. At least, there's no direct link."

"Except," nodded the officer labeled 'John' "we have an eye on some of their associates, three of whom are currently in prison for auto theft. None of the present membership have indictable offenses that we've observed. They are working with some local non-profits as well as a connection with that church on the west side of the city."

"We're planning to talk with Pastor Elliot's widow in more extensive interviews because we're assuming his actions outside the church are most likely connected to his death," said Lockem.

The other man flipped a sheet in the file folder on the table and said, "We expected that. I believe you have been cautioned about interference with our probes."

Lockem nodded. He knew he wasn't going to get any more useful information, but he asked anyway. "Is there anything else you can tell me that might help?"

John shook his head. "No, sorry, we also appear to have reached a dead end for the moment." Almost simultaneously, the two men rose, shook hands and Alan Lockem exited the room, closing the door softly after himself.

Striding down the hall toward the elevator Lockem wondered what kind of impression he had made on the police representative. Almost traditionally, he knew, law enforcement people looked askance at private investigators as interfering civilians. He didn't usually worry about such impressions, but he hadn't had any recent interactions with the Saint Paul police and early impressions sometimes hung around. Well, it was done now, time to move on. His stomach messaged it wanted something so Lockem decided to walk the five blocks past his car and see if he could get a sandwich at historic Micky's Diner.

The wind whistled down the canyons of the city. Even though it was a pleasant fall day, the early afternoon breeze carried a bite. He strode purposefully along the street, thinking about the circumstances and the questions he and Marjorie had to answer if they were to successfully address the two primary issues, who had murdered Pastor Elliot and Delilah Cooper, and why?

He found a single seat at the counter in Micky's, received an unordered mug of steaming black coffee and then ordered a hot ham and cheese sandwich. The sandwich arrived with surprising alacrity and he quickly satisfied his hunger. Returning to his car, which he'd parked at a meter on the street, he discovered the time had expired and a ticket for unmetered parking had been placed on the car under his windshield wiper.

He walked around his car, a habit he'd acquired years ago while on active duty in a war zone. He found nothing suspicious except it appeared someone had wiped the dust and rain drops from the right rear taillights. The sun had disappeared and Lockem smelled rain in the air. He slid the overtime ticket into his briefcase and dove north toward the entrance to the freeway.

Chapter 23

At home in Roseville, Alan settled down with Marjorie and a glass of wine. "The officer seemed forthcoming on the one subject I asked about, but he refused to say anything about Mr. Kline. He wouldn't even acknowledge he knew the man."

"Where is he in department level?" Marjorie always wanted to be able to construct a vertical hierarchy of people's positions. She said it helped her analyze possibilities, as in who knew what when, and how that influenced sequences of decisions and action.

"I don't have an answer for that. In fact, now that I reflect on it, he said I could call him John and not Sergeant or Captain or any rank."

"So, we don't know if he's civilian, city, county, state, or....," her voice faded, and she looked across at Alan.

"Federal," he finished. "Huh, I guess I'm slipping a little. Should have thought of that possibility while I was with him. "Oh, I hope not. I've had enough federal stuff for a while."

"Maybe the painting has something to do with this."

"I take your point, Marjorie. The issue of that painting in the church office has to be solved, but I still don't believe it's connected to the murders."

"Agreed. I am planning—" whatever she was planning to say didn't materialize when the land line phone sounded an incoming call that seemed to demand immediate attention. Alan shrugged at his companion and rose to reach for the instrument hanging on the wall of the kitchen. He'd decided that while they had a multitude of modern methods and means of communication, retaining an "old-fashioned" telephone service would at times be advantageous. One of his business cards carried three means of reaching him and included Marjorie's name and number as his equal partner in their investigative enterprise. The other card, the one he only handed out judiciously, displayed a single international telephone number and no address.

He recognized the voice on the telephone, it was Sergeant Caplan, his contact with the Minneapolis police. He identified himself and heard the sergeant sigh into the phone, "We are interviewing a woman tomorrow who is or is likely to be important to the Delilah Cooper murder. She and her lawyer are scheduled to be here at nine. I thought you might want to observe."

"Yes, indeed. I appreciate being asked. I wonder if I might impose to bring my partner to observe, as well?"

The sergeant sighed into the phone again, apparently suffering from some level of sleep deprivation. "I think that will be all right. Naturally, I'm relying heavily on your discretion, here."

Alan nodded in satisfaction. "Thank you. Much appreciated. Try to get some rest." He replaced the phone in its cradle and turned to his companion.

"Minneapolis PD is stretching things. We're invited to observe an interview—not an interrogation— of an individual important to the murder investigation."

"Do you know who?" Marjorie raised her head in the way she had when something excited her interest.

"Caplan didn't say, but it's an interesting development."

"I'll say." Marjorie shook her head slightly. "Interesting is an understatement. Letting civilians into an interview process must be really rare."

"Except that investigators commonly interview people at the scene of a crime, especially those with no direct connection to the crime. Like somebody who heard the short and possibly saw a stranger in the neighborhood at the time of the assault."

"They always interview young people and children in the presence of a parent or responsible adult." She smiled. "Are we responsible adults?"

111

Alan smiled. Sometimes we might imbibe a little too much wine and cheese, but in general, I'd say we're pretty responsible."

"I'm in a mind to review this case, you with me?" Marjorie swung around and picked up her notebook, the one she carried to most interviews, the one where she almost always started her case notes. Other investigators or interviewers might have moved to smaller electronic devices like I-pads or laptop computers but as she sometimes liked to say, "I'm an old-fashioned burlesque dancer, not a stripper. I prefer to use pen and paper to take notes." Marjorie didn't find it necessary to add that her notes were promptly transferred to computer disks and stashed in various locations for later retrieval as needed.

With notebook sheets in hand and Alan with his own record, the couple sat down at their dining room table to examine what they had on the Marjorie had dubbed Murder in Church. She never used names of victims or of specific locations in her notes to avoid revealing too much private information, should the notes be confiscated or exposed.

"Okay," Alan started, "the pastor of the church, site of two murders, is shot to death in the robing room behind the altar. The room is at the northwest corner of the sanctuary. The other victim, a somewhat mysterious woman named Delilah Cooper, was discovered on the floor of the sanctuary near the door to the robing room. Both had been shot once." He stopped and looked at Marjorie who nodded at her notebook.

"Right. We know from the police report that the bodies were discovered by Carolyn Action, the long-time church secretary, that each died of a single bullet wound and that you found what appears to be a bullet scar high up on one of the recently cleaned display pipes."

"No resolution of that little mystery, either" muttered Alan.

"I get asked by a group of the church women to solve the mysteries and you discovered that Delilah Cooper lived in Minneapolis and worked at that PR agency in Minneapolis as a respected account agency exec."

"Yeah. And that reminds me I've made two calls for an appointment and haven't had a call back yet. Could they be avoiding me?"

"You can ask, once you finally get to talk to someone." She scribbled a note. "Then we talked to the widow and met members of the biker gang."

"Club," Alan corrected. "Klein insisted they're a club not a biker gang."

"Okay, I have no problem with that. I do have a problem the way those guys turned up at Melissa Elliot's and her relationship with—*apparent* relationship—with that Trevor Howland."

"What do we know about him, about Trevor Howland?"

Marjorie frowned and turned pages in her notebook. "I found his face page. He's local, a businessman went to school with the dead reverend Elliot. Howland also went to divinity school and college. The same one Elliot graduated from. But Howland's not listed by the college with a divinity degree. I can't see how that has anything to do with anything."

"Probably not," Alan agreed. "Let me address Ms. Cooper, the dead one. She was a successful businesswoman at that agency downtown. I haven't found anything to connect her with the church or anybody else connected with the church. However, there are a couple of doors I will still go through. Her apartment, once I got access, was the peak of ordinary, except for the gaps in her bookcase, gaps we subsequently learned had contained several bibles of various ages and linked to a variety of religious sects. There was a Koran, and some of Christian denominations and ages and who know what else. There was even a bible in Chinese. Only a little odd.

What was odder was that we learned that indeed, her desk had been professionally cleaned out."

"Odd indeed. Then we met with the other Cooper, Lorna." Marjorie picked up the narrative. "We learned she'd been involved with Delilah after she'd been detained by the Roseville cops from an altercation at a local bar. But Lorna's link to Delilah is tenuous, or at least obscure."

"We know we have questions about Lorna Cooper's life, the gap on the East Coast."

"But that's so old, that reference must be wrong or on somebody else.

Alan nodded again and said, "then we have this gang of bikers that may just be a social project of the good reverend."

"Which leaves the question about the Artolo Talegiese painting in the church office."

"Oh, I think we'll leave that to the church directors and staff to sort out, although perhaps a donation to cover restoration might be in order."

Marjorie smiled and nodded, closed her notebook and said, "That would be nice. So, next up, the interrogation of somebody."

"No, no," Alan said. "Caplan said it's an interview, not an interrogation. If it were the latter, we wouldn't be allowed to observe.

CHAPTER 24

The chairs in the observation room were plain, hard un-cushioned side chairs. Apparently, whoever in the Minneapolis Police Department charged with furniture had assumed nobody would spend much time in the room or there would not be lengthy interrogations to observe.

Marjorie squirmed in a vain attempt to entice a little more comfort out of the seat. She hooked her heels in the brace that spanned the legs. Since she was wearing a pants suit, her unladylike but more comfortable pose didn't expose anything private.

Lockem entered the room a minute later. He'd been detained for a private word by their host, Sergeant Ed Caplan. Marjorie looked a silent question at him. Lockem shrugged and slid into the chair next to her. He looked around the small room again. There were four more unoccupied chairs and two uniformed officers standing at the back. Both the man and woman displayed emblem on their uniforms that designated them as having command rank. The woman nodded at Lockem and reached to adjust the volume on the wall-mounted speaker.

"If it's not loud enough, let me know," she said, directing her gaze at Marjorie.

The door in the side of the room in front of them opened and a uniformed policewoman escorted another woman into the room. She placed the subject into a chair at the center of the room beside a small table with a scarred and stained top. Three other chairs in the room faced the first and were partially obscured by a video camera mounted on the wall just below the window to the observation window. After a few minutes during which the lone occupant shifted her skirt after she sat down and then waited placidly for the next action. She did not appear to be even slightly nervous.

The door opened and a woman in civilian clothes with the bearing of an officer entered, followed by a uniformed man Lockem and Kane both recognized as Sergeant Caplan. The officers of the Minneapolis Police Department sat across from the unidentified woman. Caplan had a file folder with him which he laid on the table and did not open.

Marjorie leaned to Lockem and murmured, "Her hair is the wrong color, but she looks like Ms. Cooper.

Lockem had been staring at the woman. The high angle distorted her features somewhat and she didn't look up, appearing to direct her gaze at the table, or her interviewer. She didn't seem to have any curiosity about the interview room in which she now sat. The woman wore heavy rimmed glasses. Lockem raced through his memory trying to remember if Ms. Cooper had been wearing glasses when they saw her after the memorial service. This woman, in the room before them had dark hair that was worked into a tight bun at the back of her head. Lorna Cooper had worn her hair in a loose, curly halo that fell to her shoulders.

Lockem knew the difference in hairdos didn't necessarily mean anything, one way or another. He concentrated on the woman's movements, especially her hands where they rested on the table. He couldn't at that moment say what he was looking for—a twitch, a way of holding her fingers, anything that might link her to Lorna Cooper. At the same time, he had no basis or information that she *was* Lorna Cooper or somehow linked to the death of Delilah Cooper. Marjorie nudged him. "No lawyer," she whispered.

The voice of the police interviewer crackled from the speaker, "Good morning, Mrs. Johnson. My name is Caplan, Ed Caplan. You have been advised that this is an informal interview and you are assisting the police in our inquiries into the unfortunate death of Ms Delilah Cooper. Am I correct?" The woman nodded and reclasped her fingers on the table in front of her.

116

"Okay. First, tell me about your relationship with Ms. Cooper."

"Well, as you now know, I am the librarian at the Walker Regional Library near the building where Ms. Cooper lives—lived. I got to know her a little when she became a frequent visitor to the library."

"How frequent?"

"Last year, she was only an occasional visitor, but in the last six or nine months she came in every week and even two or three times a week. You should realize that Ms. Cooper may very well have visited our library at other times, times when I was not present."

Caplan nodded. "I imagine traffic is pretty strong at that library. How is it you came to know her? Did you two form a connection of some kind?"

"I believe we did, after a few weeks. I noticed she seemed to have a very specific and limited area of interest. She never showed any interest in fiction or any of the special sections, like the art or children's or the audio books."

"Did she seem to show an interest in any specific authors or subjects?"

"Yes. Not authors. Her major interest was in the Middle East and its history. Ancient history, mostly."

Caplan shifted in his chair. "We found a fair number of books in her apartment, but they covered a wide range of subjects," he said.

"Yes, and I believe you may have found there to be some gaps."

"Really? Care to explain that?"

"Yes, sir. This gets to the reason I am here this morning. Apparently, you found evidence that several books may have been removed from Ms Cooper's shelves. Many of those were likely library books about ancient history of the middle East. I believe you also noted there was no bible in her apartment."

Caplan nodded. "That's correct. However, that isn't at all unusual. As to the missing library books, I understand you have submitted a list of ten books that belong to the library that are now overdue. The library presumably would like them back."

"Indeed so. At least four of the missing library books are from the reference section and were not available for lending. They should not have been removed from the building."

"I'm afraid I have no information about those books at the moment, but your request is on file and if we locate them, they'll be returned." The silent audience in the viewing booth watched as Caplan opened and scanned the file of papers. "There's no mention of specific titles in the file here, but a detailed inventory of her belongings will of course, be developed."

"What about her bibles?"

"Excuse me?"

Mrs. Larson leaned across the table toward the policeman. "She had a collection of bibles. I don't know how many, but she told me she owned several. Some were not in English. Her copy of the Koran was in Arabic. She had a religious volume in Mandarin, she said. But she focused on the Middle East and the religious movements there, especially the ancient movements, that were happening before the Muslim converted the entire region." The woman sat back and stared at Caplan. "Maybe that's why she was killed, because of her interest in the ancient world."

Caplan raised his head and appeared to stare back at the woman. "If there's nothing else, Mrs. Larson, let me just say how much we appreciate your help. I assure you, when we retrieve those missing books, you'll get them back as quickly as its possible to do." They rose almost as one and he escorted the woman to the door. A policewoman was waiting to escort Mrs. Larson out.

Caplan turned around and looked directly up at the observation window. Then he shrugged. Neither of the two police officers in the booth with Lockem and Marjorie said anything. One switched off the speaker.

They nodded to Lockem and Marjorie and exited the booth.

Chapter 25

"We learned some more," said Marjorie. "Should we go find Ms. Larson and maybe buy her some tea? Or?"

"I want to wait. Grabbing her here at the police department might rattle her cage."

"I agree," said Marjorie. "We know she works at that library on East Hennepin, just a few blocks from Cooper's apartment. Let's give her a day to sort of wind down from this experience."

Lockem nodded. "You know her comments about Cooper's biblical interests is intriguing because of the connection to the guys in the motorcycle group. Obadiah, Esau, Abel and Judah."

"That's right! And the connection to the church as well." Marjorie raised her voice over the echoes in the cavernous lobby as they made their way down the main staircase toward the large statue in the entrance to the building. "It's kind of an odd coincidence, isn't it?"

"If it is," said Lockem. He took her arm, as he habitually did, to cross the street to their vehicle. She almost always allowed him to do so. He'd parked on the street at a convenient meter. Crossing with the light, they had to stop briefly when a motorcyclist turned the corner and rumbled by. Lockem looked at the rider, but his helmet totally obscured the driver's face. Lockem and Marjorie glanced at each other as unspoken questions flashed back and forth. They had both become much more aware of motorcycles in their immediate presence, although without any overt threats.

As they drove through the city on their way home, Lockem and Marjorie were silent, each with their thoughts about the questions that remained foremost in their case. Who would want to kill the pastor and the Cooper woman? Were the victims linked in some other way? It would be unusual if they were not, but so far, the evidence wasn't there. How was the church involved if it was? Why was Delilah Cooper's apartment cleaned so carefully of all the bibles and other religious texts? The librarian had insisted Ms Cooper had a strong interest in biblical subjects. What sparked her apparent intense interest in religious history and religious writings? How were those texts linked to her death? If they were. Were the individuals in Pastor Elliot and his wife Melissa's orbit, in his social community services, somehow also linked to his untimely death?

So many questions. So few answers.

Lockem swung the vehicle into their cul de sac, slowing to let the garage door completely open, then drove precisely into the designated slot, leaving sufficient room on the right for Marjorie to exit.

"I need a drink." Lockem's voice was laden with the frustration he was feeling. "I'm coming to the reluctant belief we aren't competent to solve this case."

"It's hardly noon, my dear." Familiar with his moods, Marjorie looked away and smiled.

Ignoring the flashing red numeral on their landline phone cradle, Lockem stalked into the living room and threw himself into a chair. He grumbled softly, meanwhile staring out the front window at the empty house across the cul de sac.

In the kitchen, Marjorie drew a glass of water, added two ice cubes, and carried it to her companion. Her lips twitched as, without a word, she returned to the kitchen to prepare a light lunch. After a few minutes, during which she went almost automatically through the motions of preparing sandwiches, she called Lockem to the table.

"Lunch is ready, Alan."

When they were both seated and he had taken a first bite with the scowl still fixed on his face Marjorie said, "I think there are two areas we still need to explore. One is that painting in the church office."

"Oh, yeah, I thought about it, but I can't see how it connects to the murders."

"Maybe it doesn't" Marjorie said. "But it came up and you know it should be resolved. What was the name of the gentleman who visited early the other morning?"

Lockem stared at Marjorie for a silent moment. "Good grief, my mind must be going. Age, perhaps? Karl Merkle. He is in the file. He purported to represent Interpol with an interest in the painting. Huh. Another twist to unravel. What's the other?"

"School and history. I think I should do a deeper dive into Reverend Elliot's background."

"Huh." Lockem looked over Marjorie's head and then back into her eyes. "You are, as usual, absolutely right. That's a segment we haven't covered. Nor did the police. I'll follow up on the painting if you are willing to go down the lumpy historical road of the dead Reverend."

"Deal," she said, "even if it's a long shot. We know he graduated from White Bear Lake High School so I'll start there. A long time back, but maybe I'll turn up somebody with long-festering resentments who finally slid down the ethical slide until he saw an opportunity."

"Or she did," amended Lockem. "Regardless of the probable lack of connection to the murders, that painting is an interesting object. Now, about that interview this morning."

"We'll need to talk to her, that's for sure. Maybe a list of the missing library books will tell us something."

Marjorie took another bite of sandwich and when she had swallowed, said, "She didn't admit to it but I wonder if she knows the other Cooper. Lorna."

"I'm not convinced the viable Ms Cooper has anything to do with this at all." Lockem frowned and shook his head. "I'm also not convinced that guy Merkle, who showed up early the other morning, remember him, has any direct connection with the murders. He may be connected somehow with the painting or the artist, or even with the company Ms Cooper works for."

"Marjorie looked at her notebook. "Hmm. I do not believe in coincidence, but sometimes stuff happens. Just maybe the investigation into Ms Cooper's firm, International Products is linked to the painting which is tied to the church which links to the bikers which..."

"Wait, wait," Lockem grinned and waved his hands. I'm more inclined to believe the painting and the church and the investigation is all coincidental timing. No links."

"Well, onward. I guess we'll find out." Marjorie rose and cleared their plates to the kitchen sink. Lockem turned away and walked to his office. Then he turned and went back to take Marjorie by the shoulders, turning her to face him.

He leaned and kissed her forehead. "Do you know how much I prize our relationship? I get in a funk sometimes and you always seem to know just what I need—how to bring me 'round."

On tiptoe, Marjorie planted a soft kiss on his lips "My friend, you still don't know, and maybe never will, how you helped me out of a bad situation when we first met. And how you treat me all the time. I've never felt so equal, so appreciated, so happy. I'm just pleased I can get you out of an occasional funk." She softly punched his chest. "Just don't make a *frequent* habit of it." Grinned up at him.

Lockem grinned back and turned again, to his office, aiming at consolidating his notes on the issue of the painting by Talegiease or a contemporary forger, He knew Marjorie already had worked out a strategy aimed at dissecting Elliot's education and the people connected.

He opened his calendar on his laptop and made some changes from his notebook and then updated his case file to reflect what they had learned at the police interview. He had a feeling that a talk with the librarian in a few days would reveal even more. The telephone chimed and he picked up without checking the readout.

"Ed Caplan here."

"Ah, sergeant. Thanks for allowing us to be witnesses to the interview."

"You're welcome. I hope it helps, but in any case, it's not something we need to mention further, since you must realize it isn't kosher."

"I understand," Lockem responded. "I did have a thought about the case. Because of the gaps in the Cooper woman's bookshelves, I wondered if she might have been borrowing from the library."

"Borrowing. I see." Caplan's remark was carefully noncommittal. "Interesting."

"I'll be following that lead in a day or so and if anything turns up, I'll be sure to inform you."

"I'll appreciate that. Just wanted to touch base. Give my regards to Marjorie." Caplan severed the connection and Lockem smiled. The threads that had been established in earlier cases were still in place. He turned to his own library to find a large and heavy, well-illustrated volume of Middle Eastern art from ancient times.

After several minutes of consulting the index, several pages, and some chapter headings, Lockem found what he sought. The Friar's name was not referenced in the index. Apparently, he had not been considered an artist of sufficient importance to receive his own index entry. He was mentioned in the chapter on religious art of the tenth and eleventh centuries. There had been some small controversy, since the leaders of the school had encouraged students to paint religious art depicting figures from religious movements other than their own. If Lockem interpreted the entry correctly, that could mean students like Friar Talagiese had been creating paintings of Semitic or even Pagan figures, Hebrews, perhaps. Lockem was not well-read in early religious history and he had no reason to believe religion, ancient or modern, was a motivating force behind

124

these murders. He did wonder if the painting was a depiction of a historical event or a myth or just an illustration from the mind of the painter.

Chapter 26

A police officer stopped Marjorie as she entered the sprawling school building. A phone call had sent her to this campus building. She explained to the officer her mission and he directed her to the administrative offices. Even though it was still fairly early in the day, several students and teachers flowed in and out of the office and two adults were seated at desks using their phones.

A smiling young woman who must have recognized that Marjorie was neither faculty nor parent approached. "Good morning. How can I help you?"

Marjorie explained what she was looking for and why. "Oh, yes," the woman responded. We were so saddened to learn of Pastor Elliot's death. In a way it was a blessing that his parents had already passed."

"Did you know Mr. Elliot as a student here?"

She shook her head. "Oh, no. He graduated years before I moved to Mahtomedi and came to work here. I'm finishing graduate school at the U. In education," she said unnecessarily. "Here. If you fill out this form, I'll get you a hall pass and take you to the library. The storage room where we keep all old school records and a shelf of yearbooks is there. There won't be any faculty or staff here anymore, I'm afraid, who knew Martin Elliot as a student, but the archives are extensive so you should find quite a bit of information on him. I got the impression he was pretty active in school. So I bet you'll find some leads." Marjorie had only said she was doing background research on the murdered man. The school secretary had apparently automatically assumed she was with a police agency.

The school library was large and airy and quiet. A young man and woman whom Marjorie learned were both licensed librarians, acknowledged her and took her to a table in a corner of the storage room where she could stack or arrange the materials she might need to read. The woman brought Marjorie two yearbooks and showed her how the files were organized, indicating the cabinets that might hold the most useful documents. She sat down to read the yearbooks, make some notes, and learn what she could about the high school years of the murdered pastor and some of the people who might be important sources.

After two intense hours in the library, Marjorie had scribbled a profile of the deceased pastor in a notebook, including relevant and potentially helpful names. She made four phone calls from the privacy of her car, reaching out to former classmates and one teacher. Only the former teacher remarked that she had been contacted by a police investigator. Then Marjorie phoned Alan and when he picked up, she smiled and said. "I have enough, I think, to conclude this phase. Now it looks like calls to a couple of out-of-town numbers. How are you faring?"

"Pretty well, but nothing that can't wait until you get home."

"Okay, toots, I'll see you in a few."

Marjorie closed her flip phone and opened her small laptop. She rapidly entered her notes into the file she'd already created. Mark Elliot, oldest child of a quiet family that had lived in White Bear, apparently for many years. One of the yearbooks Marjorie had perused indicated that the Elliot family lived on the ancestral farm with Mark's grandparents. Mark had been moderately active in school as a member of the debate team and as a short distance runner on the junior varsity track team.

Other school sources indicated that Mark had been active in church-related organized activities outside of school, some of which appeared to conflict with school connected events. He missed a regional track and field meet due to a student retreat connected to his church. His senior yearbook gave some indication he had an interest in college and possibly a Divinity School program.

127

Marjorie placed a call to the northern Illinois college the boy had attended for several years. She'd hoped to quickly confirm Mark's attendance but the dean of students she talked with had been reluctant to provide any information over the phone. She wanted something for the file that proved Marjorie had a right to the information, even though Marjorie knew if she could acquire a yearbook for the school, it would likely give her everything she needed.

"Will you accept an email from the authorities, attesting to the legitimacy of my request?"

"Oh, sure," the dean said. "Anything that I can put on paper and stick in the file."

"Okay. Thanks for your cooperation." Even though the woman in Illinois hadn't been very forthcoming. Marjorie emailed the Saint Paul police Lieutenant in charge of the church murder case with the name and address of the college dean and requested that he verify that she had a legitimate reason to get the public information on graduate Mark Elliot, late of Saint Paul.

She was pleased that only a few minutes later her email program pinged and she saw a copy of the request land in her inbox. The garage door groaned and rattled open and she knew Alan had arrived. Just as she rose to greet him, her mail program pinged again, and she saw that an email with attached document had arrived from the dean of the college.

"We have made some progress, I think," Alan greeted Marjorie with a hug and then turned toward the kitchen and the bar. "Scotch?" He queried.

"Thanks. I've a roast in the oven along with some baking potatoes. "'Bout another half-hour, I think. I had to get the police to email Elliot's college for them to send me his records."

"That's odd. Aren't the records public?"

"I thought so, but apparently this dean wanted something for the file. So she didn't come off as having made the decision on her own. I asked cop on the beat

128

to email her. He did and the requested documents now reside in my email."

"That was fast," Alan said.

"I think she wanted to send the information, she just wanted something to CHA."

"CHA? Cover her—oh," Alan laughed.

"As far as his high school record goes, it's pretty uninteresting," she said. She bent slightly to peer into the oven window at the roast. When she turned her head she saw Alan gazing at her hips and backside. "Ahem," she said. "Are you listening to me?"

Alan flicked his glance back to Marjorie's smiling face and he winked. "Yes, my dear, I am listening and I'm certainly paying attention." The oven timer dinged and dinner was soon served.

After dinner, Marjorie laid out for Alan what she had learned about Mark Elliot's teen years growing up in White Bear Lake. "He was reasonably popular, ran track, and my overall impression is that he was a good student. Not spectacular. B-plus I'd say. His track partner, the boy he usually worked out with was a kid named Trevor Howard."

I think a few calls to some classmates, if we can find them, would be a good idea. His college will be the next step as well."

"I'll work the locals in the morning," Marjorie said. "You call the college."

***

"Oh, sure. I remember Mark. He was a good boy. I'd see him in church, and he helped some of the neighbors with snow shoveling their driveways in the winter."

"So, you can't recall him ever getting into trouble of any kind?" Marjorie wasn't probing for dirt, but she was a little tired of hearing the pastor had been a total saint, growing up.

"Oh, well, he and his best buddy, Trevor, I think his name was. They were picked up one Halloween, I guess it was. Just pranks, though. Nothing serious."

129

Marjorie made another note, thanked the woman, and replaced the phone in its cradle. She looked and saw her mug was empty of coffee and the wall clock displayed 11:30. Enough, she thought. She collected her notes and sauntered down the short hall to Alan's office.

"Trevor Howard's name came up again. Some Halloween prank apparently. Have you gotten anything useful from the college?"

Alan swiveled in his chair to smile up at her. "There you go, with that modifier. *Useful* can have so many different meanings. Anyway, I'm waiting on a call back from a dean, or the provost, or a vice president, somebody who is empowered to answer my questions. I called the U and some other locals looking for yearbooks for the years Elliot was in school at that college. No luck. Two librarians didn't even know the college existed."

"What about the Divinity school?"

Alan nodded. "Good question. Elliot took college-level credit courses in high school. Then, when he went to a small liberal arts college in Illinois, Knox, Knax, something like that, all those credits transferred, so he was able to get his B. A. in three years plus some summer school. I'd love to see his transcript, but I don't know if that will happen. Main thing right now is to get his theological school information."

Marjorie glanced at her wristwatch. In spite of the many technological changes that have brought time keeping to a multitude of electronic sources, she preferred the small, diamond-encrusted watch with a narrow leather strap she wore on her right wrist.

"I've called the secretary at the church, Carolyn Action? I was thinking on it today and I've never seen the actual site of the murders, or at least that robing room where Elliot's body was discovered. I'm going to go take a look at it."

Alan nodded. He'd been wondering when Marjorie would decide to visit the church again. He

130

knew it wasn't ghoulishness or reticence. Usually, when their projects involved death, she insisted on visiting the scene. It gave her useful perspective, she insisted.

Chapter 27

Church secretary Carolyn Action welcomed Marjorie with a smile. This time. She'd been surprised and concerned to learn about Marjorie's former profession when the couple first appeared following the double murder. After her initial feelings of discomfort about welcoming a former dancer into the church, she had displayed toward Marjorie, her rejection had gradually been replaced with acceptance and, as she now recognized, more than a little curiosity about Marjorie's background.

"Good to see you again, Carolyn. As I said on the phone, it may seem a little ghoulish to some people, but visiting the locations where the murders happened may help me answer some of our questions." Marjorie said quietly.

Carolyn smiled back. She had resolved her reservations and responded to Marjorie's unfailing sense of fairness and calm demeanor. "We've just been given the okay to start using the robing room where the Pastor was found and that section between the robing room door and the end of the choir section where Ms. Cooper's body was. I have our regular cleaning crew scheduled for day after tomorrow. Finally. I really thank you for the reference to that specialized company that handles crime scenes. Our regular cleaners were reluctant to even go into the sanctuary."

"I'm glad we were able to help," Marjorie said. "And we are much appreciative of your help in getting to the bottom of these crimes."

Together the two women walked across the wide room that presented several doors to one side of the sanctuary, heels echoing off the hardwood floor. Carolyn reached the panel of switches beside the wall of doors and flicked on the general lights in the sanctuary. She pulled open the nearest tall door that reached fifteen feet to the richly paneled ceiling.

Marjorie hesitated in the door frame, breathing in the dusty odor of an unused space. Her gaze took in the row of pews, the altar, and the pale pads in all the pews she could see. Carolyn stood at the door and watched as Marjorie walked slowly along behind a long-curved pew to the center aisle that bisected the entire room. This would be the path down which a bride would proceed to the waiting arm of her groom at the steps to the altar. Marjorie could see evidence that the forensic specialists from the police department had swept the aisle and probably vacuumed it as well. Faint traces of temporary tape lines were still visible along either side of a line that ran up two steps and across the platform to the robing room door. Marjorie stopped and looked over the altar platform and then up at the rack of organ tubing.

"You see something?" Carolyn's voice, quiet and tremulous, drifted around the space/

"No, just wondering why the police seem to have limited their deep search for evidence to the direct path the killer must have taken."

Carolyn walked closer and the women went to the door of the robing room. "The police report suggests that Delilah Cooper was killed first. She was standing at the door here, much like I am now," said Marjorie. She heard Carolyn close behind her draw in a deep calming breath.

"The Reverend Elliot must have turned toward the door and the killer shot him over Cooper's falling body. Two shots for him, one for Cooper." Marjorie turned her head to observe Carolyn Action clutching a crumpled handkerchief and holding it to her face.

"Oh, God. I wonder if I'll ever get over this?"

Marjorie reached out a hand to the other woman and pulled her into a quick embrace. "The turbulence will fade, eventually," she murmured. "But you will probably always experience some emotional recollection here at this spot. Even reconsecration won't completely erase the tragedy."

Big sigh from Carolyn. "Thanks," she said, straightening and stepping back. "The Bishop has been pressing for a date for the reconsecration ceremony." Marjorie nodded and walked over the space on the floor where Delilah Cooper had fallen and entered the small robing room. Two sides of the space were taken with racks holding robes, shawls, boxes of clothing, surplices, and banners. A long length of one rack held identical dark blue robes on hangars. Two metal folding chairs occupied about half the space. Street or civilian clothes hung on one of the racks.

"Choir robes?" asked Marjorie, pointing at the rack.

"Yes," said Carolyn.

"Why are there still street clothes on the rack there?"

"A few people who volunteered sometimes left a change here."

"Is the room just as you found it when you came across the bodies? As far as you can remember?" She knew from the police report the room was essentially undisturbed. She still wanted Carolyn's assessment.

"Ah, yes, I think so. The pastor wasn't changing so he was dressed in street clothes. I found him right—right there." She pointed to a spot on the floor.

"Carolyn, you can leave if you wish. I'll be a few minutes."

"Thanks, I'll just sit over here, if that's all right."

Marjorie nodded and stood in the middle of the room, scanning the entire space. She couldn't say what she was searching for, but she'd learned from Alan to use her senses and let information and ideas come to her. After a moment, she stepped to the tiny table in the corner under the rack where the minister's robes were hung.

"May I ask you something?" Carolyn's voice was quiet and firm. She'd apparently tamped down her emotions.

"Of course," Marjorie pulled open the drawer in the table. It was empty. She wondered if the police had taken the contents.

"I hope this isn't embarrassing." Marjorie heard the hesitation in the words and raised her head. She knew what was coming.

"I know you used to be a dancer."

"Yes, a stripper." Marjorie smiled to herself. She was comfortable with the coming conversation.

"Oh, well, what was that like? I mean, oh, I don't know just how to ask this—"

"Marjorie smiled at the wall and said, "Carolyn, I often am asked that, about my previous profession. What was it like, being a dancer on stage, scantily dressed? Stripping."

"Yes, well—"

"They really want to know how a young woman becomes an ecdysiast. A stripper. And of course they often make assumptions. There are a lot of ways it happens, of course. Some are sordid and awful. You hear stories about gorgeous, abused girls who get forced into it or try dancing to get away from prostitution. There are some girls who start out dancing, get into drugs and prostitution. There are also women who become dancers and don't do any of those scurrilous things. I studied dance in high school. Turns out I had an aptitude for it. So I took a chorus line job in Nevada. From background dancer, I became a headliner. I worked hard, developed a persona, and became comfortable around strangers, even wearing very few clothes. In some really classy places in Europe, wearing scanty costumes and mingling with customers off stage was the norm."

"But what did it feel like? Stripping I mean. On stage in front of strangers?" Carolyn's gaze and tone were intense, focused.

"Carolyn, do you go to the beach in the summer?"

"Of course."

"Wear a bikini? I can tell you have a nice figure."

"Oh, well. A bikini. Sure, sometimes. Often."

"And when you get to the beach, you are usually wearing shorts and a top or some kind of coverup, right? You must be, what, twenty-six?"

Carolyn nodded.

Marjorie smiled and said, "And when you are disrobing, stripping down to your bikini, are you aware of the people around you? Maybe the young men your age? Aren't you aware of whether they are checking you out?"

Relaxed, now, Carolyn smiled, nodded. "Sure. I guess it's almost automatic."

"Even if you are with a man or aren't looking for a hookup, you are still aware of who is watching. So, now add some dance steps, some music, lights, maybe some applause."

"Oh, I get it. But what about nudity?"

"What about it?" Marjorie had been running her fingers over the choir robes. In the lining of the robe she was holding was a thin bit of what might be padding. Or was it something else? She turned her attention to the seam of the robe and quickly found a defect. The seam had been opened about an inch and a tiny pocket of filmy material had been sewn inside over the opening. Her questing fingers found the pocket empty. She peered closely at the neck of the robe. A number was sewn into the top edge so it could be easily seen. "I see a number on this robe. Do you have a record of which member got which robe?"

Carolyn said, "Yes. We issue robes that fit to individual members so large or tall folks get larger robes. Pastor Elliot recommended that after an incident in which a tall tenor stepped out to sing a solo and he was wearing a robe way too short." She smiled at the memory. "When he raised his arms at the end, it might have been unfortunate if he hadn't been wearing pants. Hairy knees."

"Does that ever happen?" Marjorie looked mildly alarmed.

Carolyn smiled more widely, nodding. "The building isn't air conditioned and sometimes in Spring and fall it can get really warm, so choir members wear shorts under their robes. Pastor Elliot wanted us to maintain a little decorum, especially in services when the choir parades through the sanctuary."

Marjorie had been running her fingers over the side seams of other robes and not finding similar little secret pockets. She turned her attention to the paneled doors on the wall opposite the door to the short stair of six steps that led to the room outside the sanctuary. Then she turned around. The door at the bottom of the stair was open letting daylight into the space. The steps looked worn and well dusted. She stared at the short entrance to the robing room. "Is that door ever locked?" she asked.

Carolyn shook her head. "Never. There's no reason to lock it. I'm not even sure there's a key."

Marjorie turned her attention back to the cabinets in the opposite wall. She pulled open an unlocked door to see shelves crowded with candlesticks, glassware, small cups, pitchers, and folded clothes. She recognized the church's collection of stemware and other items commonly used for various services. It would take hours to examine all of it and Marjorie knew the police report stated the doors to these cabinets had been closed when the bodies were discovered. She blew out a frustrated breath and looked at Carolyn.

"Can you tell if these shelves have been rearranged or disturbed?"

"Sure. It's one of my jobs to keep the inventory and because we often change the design of the altar area, depending on the season, I need to know about our inventory of stuff. We use several different bibles." She pulled out a drawer and showed Marjorie the three big volumes nestled there.

137

Returning to her examination of the clothing hanging on the rack, Marjorie also returned to the subject of their earlier conversation. "A lot of people just automatically assume that strippers are drunks, dopers or prostitutes, but in my experience, it isn't so. Sure, some are, just like the rest of the population, but dancers have to stay in pretty good shape, or they don't work. Miss a show, you get fired. When I traveled with a chorus to military bases, I met a lot of well-educated women and others who seemed to spend every off-stage minute either exercising or studying some college course. Carolyn, the job of dancer looks glamorous and it is, but it's also a lot of work. Most dancers recognize pretty early that the career can be short-lived." Stopped, realizing she'd started preaching. "Sorry."

"Don't be. I—" the look on Marjorie's face stopped her.

"I found this piece of paper in a pair of pants on this hanger." Marjorie unfolded a sheet torn from a notebook. She discovered someone had written down a telephone number. "The number on this hanger is 10."

"Oh. That's the pastor's other hanger. He has a narrow locker there, but it's always stuffed with robes and his extra clothes so he has that other hanger."

Marjorie smiled. "Let's go to the office and see what this number tells us."

Chapter 28

The women stepped into the church office and Carolyn went to her file cabinet to search for the file of choir members. Marjorie sat nearby and watched.

"I remember a friend when I was in college. She earned money as a figure model for students in art classes and for commercial artists as well. Sometimes I'd see her walking about the campus in a ratty but really long raincoat and those short rubber boots. You know the kind I mean?"

"Sure," Carolyn responded. "I have a pair, somewhere."

"Well, I knew she was between sittings and she was naked under the coat."

Carolyn popped her head up from a file she was examining to stare at Marjorie. "Really?"

Marjorie grinned and said, "Yep. It was a little risky, especially on a college campus connected to a religion, but she never got caught." Carolyn giggled.

"Sometimes it would be funny. We'd be walking across campus together and see an art student who realized she didn't have anything on under the raincoat. Talk about double takes."

Carolyn continued to look thoughtfully toward Marjorie and then she said, "Our society has a lot of contradictions, doesn't it? I mean, it's okay for people to look at naked bodies in an art class or in a painting, but we frown at and regulate strippers in night clubs."

Marjorie smiled, "Back in the Twenties, you may remember learning, there was something called prohibition and then there wasn't. We all make lots of judgment calls based on our social class, you know, upbringing, and schooling. The dancers I have known performed over a range of venues from back street strip clubs to high-end so-called Gentlemen's Clubs. Two of the girls I toured with had advanced degrees. They were both smart, as well as beautiful and sexy looking. Good dancers. Good actors. Their dancing paid for advanced degrees and eventually both left dancing for more traditional and acceptable professions. A lot of society doesn't approve just like they don't approve of nude models." She shrugged and smiled. Morality, like art is a constantly moving target."

"Art is in the eye of the beholder. Here, I found the list," Carolyn said. She took several sheets from a file folder and brought them to Marjorie. "It's up to date as of August."

"Most of the time when I was touring, I studied." She grinned at the memory. I didn't call it that, I just got interested in psychology. Then it was computers." Marjorie scanned the list of choir members. The number she had found earlier in the robing room was assigned to an unfamiliar name. Two names jumped out at her. "Can I assume this choir member, Melissa Elliot, is the wife of the pastor, Martin Elliot?"

"That's correct. She could have had her own permanent robe because she did a fair amount of solo work, but she insisted on being part of the group with no special treatment."

Farther down the list, Marjorie saw the name Trevor Howland. "Do the numbers have any meaning? I mean, have members with lower numbered members been here longer?"

Carolyn shook her head. "Not anymore. Now when a member leaves the robe number is reassigned to whoever shows up next to sing. There are a few people in the congregation who only want to sing in special programs or when certain songs are scheduled. They just get whatever robes are available."

Marjorie didn't respond, she was recalling her own youthful experiences as a member of a college chorus and how close some members had become as a result of the rehearsals, the performances, and the occasional trips to other towns. She wondered if any liaisons developed in the church choir. Church choristers were not automatically less subject to romance and jealousy than other members of society. She wondered if her suspicions were enough to invest the time and energy in pursuing possible liaisons.

"Scandal," Marjorie said abruptly. "Any gossip about members of the choir?"

Carolyn stared at her in silence as if assessing what and how much to say. "No," she shook her head finally. "Oh, every so often somebody will giggle about a couple with their arms around their shoulders. I can't recall any scandal at least not in the time I've been here. This is a pretty conservative congregation."

Or pretty careful, Marjorie considered silently. "I appreciate your help—Carolyn? What is it?" The woman was staring at the empty wall behind Marjorie, small tear drops making shiny tracks down both cheeks.

Marjorie walked around the desk and dropped one hand on Carolyn's shoulder in silent understanding. "Look, long as I'm here You think I could have a closer look at the painting in the other office? Carolyn nodded. "Door's unlocked," she said in a hollow voice.

Marjorie opened the door to the Pastor's office and looked up at the painting looming, it seemed, over the room. But first, sat at the desk and pulled open a drawer. "Do you have a magnifying glass in your desk?"

Carolyn nodded and produced a large round magnifier with a short black handle from her lap drawer. She handed it to Marjorie. Then she snatched it back, found a tissue and wiped off the glass surfaces.

"By the way, his wife wondered about a bracelet. Do you know it?"

Carolyn nodded. "Yes, a copper-colored band he wore all the time. I haven't seen it."

Marjorie took the magnifier and moved behind the pastor's chair and approached the painting. With the help of the glass, she examined the group of figures that appeared to be concentrating their

141

attention on a single robed figure standing on a mound or earth or perhaps a rock outcropping. She quickly looked over the lower part of the canvas until she found what appeared to be a signature painted in a lower corner of the desert sand. The signature seemed to her unpracticed eye to be contemporaneous to rest of the painting. She traced the lines with her forefinger without actually touching the surface. She could smell dust and something else that might have been old paint fumes.

She pulled out a pen and her note pad and tried to reproduce the scribbles. What resulted looked like a child's scrawl of Adorati-something-something and then either Odam or Edom. Staring at the fragmentary letters she realized she had expected Latin or some other ancient language. Still, it was interesting. How it might be connected to the murders, she had no clue at the moment. Below that line and partially entangled, there appeared to be long name. It was so faint and faded she gave up trying to reproduce the letters.

Marjorie handed the magnifier back to Carolyn. She pulled her phone from her purse and snapped a couple of pictures of the signature area. "Thanks for your help, Carolyn. I'm sure this has been such a difficult time for you and all our questions and presence hasn't made things any more comfortable."

After glancing through the desk for the bracelet, she left Carolyn and the church and drove home where she typed up her notes and saved them to the appropriate case file. Reviewing again everything she knew Marjorie experienced a sense of frustration or impatience. So far, they had managed to turn up several possible alternative theories, none of which seemed grounded enough or solid enough to propose to the authorities, or their clients, for that matter. In fact they seemed to be getting deeper and deeper into more and more alternative theories. Theories were fine, she thought, the problem was she felt farther from identifying a killer and a motive than when they'd started.

142

CHAPTER-29

Alan's snuffles in a broken rhythm woke her. They'd stayed up late tossing theories and fragmented ideas back and forth in a vain attempt to breach the fences they'd both perceived around answers to the case.

"Dammit," she heard softly from her companion in their big bed. "What time is it? I can't see the clock."

"How'd you know I'm awake?" Marjorie rolled onto her side and squinted at the bedside clock. It showed an orange 4:12. "Four-ten."

"Heard your breathing rhythm change. I'm gonna go for a drive. Clear my brain."

Marjorie knew he sometimes went for late-night drives, even as a kid while still in school. During and after his time in the Army Alan had continued the occasional habit. He said it helped clear his mind and organize his thoughts around whatever problem was uppermost at the time.

He drifted about the bedroom dressing and she fell back asleep, partially rousing again when he kissed her goodbye and slipped silently downstairs.

The garage door slid up almost noiselessly and Lockem piloted the C-RV neatly out of the driveway and turned toward the nearest freeway entrance. He took the exit north onto the freeway.

The pavement already carried a fair number of vehicles. A lot were headed south into the city, but he had plenty of company driving north, at least until he passed the main east-west Interstate bypass. He continued north toward the melding of the two north-south Interstate branches that bisected the cities. They joined in the northernmost suburbs. As he approached the exit to the highway that went to Chisago City, Taylor's Falls and the river border with Wisconsin, a touring Harley Davidson motorcycle roared by on the left, cut across two lanes and

144

disappeared over the hill toward the small eastern communities.

Lockem noted the lights of the machine as it disappeared into the distance, briefly outlined against a lightening sky. Soon he was almost alone on the highway, boring toward the north, headlights sending high intensity beams many yards up the concrete. He didn't set the cruise control, preferring to remain in full control of the vehicle. His hands were light on the steering wheel and he relaxed more and more as time and the countryside smoothly passed. The sounds of tires, engine and wind whistling past the side windows had the hoped-for effect. Alan's mind began to slow down and part of his attention turned to the still unsolved elements of the double murder. He stayed in the right lane, obeying the speed limit. He was in no hurry to get to where he was headed. Indeed, he wasn't headed anywhere in particular.

Some distance north of the suburbs, the developments faded away and the forest and wetlands drew closer to the edges of the highway. At North Branch he left the freeway and turned east on the state highway, sailed through Palmdale, and headed down the long grade to the valley of the St. Croix River, just north of Taylor's Falls. As he hummed along the nearly deserted highway and began the descent, he became aware of what appeared to be a truck or van pulling closer behind him. Its headlights were not quite aligned, and one appeared brighter than the other.

Moments later the following lights disappeared even though the two vehicles were on a straight section of the highway, heading down the bluff to a sharp bend near the bank of the river. Alan felt a bump. Had he been rear-ended? There came a harder bump and he heard the screech of tortured metal. He seemed to be losing control of his vehicle. He tapped the brake but didn't slow. Then came a sudden lurch and he turned the steering wheel right to correct his direction. The CR-V refused to respond and Lockem realized in that second he had lost control. Trees and underbrush appeared in the windshield, streamed by the side window. He threw up an arm to cover his face.

Long shadows and dappled rays of sun sprayed warm golden dawn over part of the large bedroom when the insistent sound of the telephone penetrated Marjorie's sleep and roused her. Unlike other phones in the house, this one had been programmed to command insistent attention. She sat up, threw one hand at the place where Alan should have been lying. Then she remembered he was out driving about.

Grumbling at the early time she rolled over to the other side of the big bed to grab the telephone, still yowling, and vibrating insistently. "Yes," she said tartly.

"Mrs. Lockem?"

"Speaking," she responded. They'd learned that explaining their relationship on first contact was frequently lengthy and sometimes got things off to a rocky start.

"This is the Chisago County Sheriff's office. You are the Marjorie Kane, listed as second contact for an Alan Lockem, of Roseville?"

"Yes, I am." Alarm rose, and she glanced at the clock which read 7:40 am. Alan should have been home long before now. When he went for an early morning drive, it never lasted more than an hour.

"Uh, Ma'am? I'm afraid I have some disturbing news. Just please bear with me here." She thought he sounded young and uncertain.

"Officer, please just get on with it"

"Yes ma'am. Does your husband own a dark blue late model Honda CR-V with a Minnesota license plate—" she heard the number as her heartbeat increased and her hands began to tremble.

"A patrol unit discovered the vehicle about twenty minutes ago well off the highway and smashed into trees and underbrush."

"Oh, God. Alan was out driving last night. Is he all right?"

"Well, that's the thing. The vehicle is empty, and we haven't located the driver."

"What? Wait. Alan is missing?" Her breathing surged.

"If he was driving. There is some blood on the windshield and driver-side seat."

The appalling thought of Alan lying injured and unconscious out there spurred Marjorie to action. She tossed off the coverlet and her nightgown. Still holding the phone to her ear she said,

"Do you have pictures?"

"No ma'am. I'm up on the highway looking for where the vehicle went off the road."

"I'm coming out there. Check nearest facilities while I'm on the way, will you please? Alan would call as soon as possible if he's able. I'll be there as quick as I can." Without waiting for the officer's measured response, she dropped the phone in her purse, scrambled into jeans a shirt and shoes and ran for the garage.

Their neighbor, Lucy was standing on her front stoop when Marjorie's gray mustang screeched out of the garage and tore west toward the nearest freeway entrance. Once on the freeway, Marjorie punched up the mobile phone and called Lieutenant Gage at Roseville PD. He answered promptly.

"Marjorie? I just saw an alert about your CR-V found off 95 up near Taylor's Falls. What's going on?"

She tersely explained what little she knew and asked, "Do you know the sheriff up there? Would you call him?" Listening to her voice she realized she was close to tears. She took two deep calming breaths and waited another moment for Gage to come back on the line.

"Done," he said. "The sheriff is being alerted and he'll handle things. Go up to North Branch then turn east on the highway. Drive safely and please keep me advised."

147

She took the exit at North Branch and noticed a local patrol car blocking crossing traffic at the main street. The officer standing by the front bumper waved her through the intersection. The highway heading east was empty. She barely slowed, whizzing through two small villages next to the highway. When she approached the scene of the wreck, she found four patrol cars parked, lights flashing, on the shoulder of the road. Marjorie hit the brakes and skidded to a stop. She slammed the control into park and jumped from the car.

CHAPTER 30

A tall impeccably uniformed deputy intercepted Marjorie as she trotted across the highway toward the patrol cars. "Ms. Kane?"

"Yes. What can you tell me? I left my phone off on the way here."

"Good thinking. Come this way, the CR-V is down here. But we still don't have anything further on the driver."

"What do you mean, nothing further on the driver? I told you Alan was driving this morning."

"Yes, ma'am but the vehicle is empty. We don't have the driver yet."

Her heart raced and her gut lurched so strongly she expected to be sick. Gulping, Marjorie fought to repress her feelings of nausea.

Down the slope, they came to a torn gap in the underbrush on the north side of the highway. Other deputies were just beginning to string yellow crime scene tape around the track of the vehicle. Her stomach lurched again when she saw the glossy blue rear end and her mind registered the license plate. No question, the vehicle was definitely theirs.

"Normally, we wouldn't close off the site, but the Sheriff said in this case we'd better." He stood uncomfortably close, as if he feared she might collapse.

Forcing her voice toward its normal tone and cadence she asked, "What do you know so far?"

"Call came in about six about a vehicle off the road. We sent the nearest patrol car. The deputy radioed in the crash and that there was no sign of the driver. Half an hour or so later, she radioed in again that she found blood in the front seat and on the windshield but no bod—no driver in sight."

"It's definitely our CR-V. I want to inspect it more closely." She waved one hand, forcing the tremor out of her voice. "Yes, I'll be careful. Check with the

Sheriff. He knows our background. You can stay right with me." She began to pick her way down through the tangled brush. The deputy, frowning, stayed close. Stopping just outside the tape at the rear she stared at a long dark scar on the left rear panel. Then she slid down the hill a little further until she could see into the front seat of the vehicle. The front driver's side door hung wide open and she could see dark spots on the seat and window, and on the floor under the steering wheel. It looked like dried blood. Her breath caught and more tears tracked down her cheeks. She struggled to repress her feelings. The van had been stopped on its careen down the hill by a stout tree bent over by the front end of the Honda.

Marjorie dried her eyes and turned her attention to the ground beside the driver's door. Bending, she peered at the damp ground searching for footprints or anything to indicate Alan had managed to extract himself from the wreck. Where could he be? Did somebody pick him up? Was he lying concealed in the underbrush, unable to call out? She was sure he'd been run off the road so maybe person persons unknown had taken him away. Too many questions.

The deputy slid down beside her. "BCA is sending a crime scene truck. Should be here within the hour. A Lieutenant Gage? From Roseville, he said with a message. You need anything, just call on him."

She stood and stared down the hill through the dark underbrush, hoping to catch a glimpse of Lockem.

After a minute, "Let's go back up to the road," Marjorie said. "Can we see where he went off the highway?"

The deputy nodded. "Sure. Here, let me help." He offered his hand. Struggling back to the shoulder of the highway the deputy turned and made a visual sighting to the rear of the vehicle. Then he walked a few yards back. "It looks to me like he must have veered off right about here. The car was airborne for just a second or so," pointing.

150

The image of their vehicle being airborne made Marjorie's gut clench again.

"It's possible he fell asleep a few yards back because the road is smooth and straight for at least a quarter mile." The deputy glanced at Marjorie's face and grimaced.

"Mmm," she said. Marjorie bent her head and stared at the road surface. Then she paced a good hundred yards west. She saw no evidence that a vehicle might have been forced off the road by collision. No skid marks, no broken glass or car parts. If Alan had been run off the highway, it had been an expert and careful move.

"I'm going to wait and talk to the BCA people." She sighed. She wanted to run back down the hill and start a search for Alan. He might be seriously hurt and unable to respond. He might be lying alone down there in the woods, unable to call out, alone and dying. Her need to find him and help him in any way she could remained her primary focus.

The rumble of a large truck momentarily distracted her. The tow truck driver parked a few yards away at the side of the highway and spoke with the deputy. Moments later crime scene technologists from the Bureau of Criminal Apprehension arrived and began their examination of the wreck. Barely able to contain herself physically, Marjorie sat in the front seat of her vehicle and watched. Her mind played scenario after scenario, over and over. Some of them were tragic, some merely painful. Maybe Alan had walked into town, perhaps he'd found a local resident who treated his minor wounds and was about to carry him to report to the county sheriff. She couldn't decide. There wasn't enough evidence of anything. Except Alan was missing, there was blood and time was passing. She sighed. A tear tracked down her cheek and she swiped at it.

A tech in a standard state coverall trudged up the hill and came toward her. Marjorie stepped out of the car. "You might want to come look at this" he said.

151

"We found tracks sort of stumbling down the hill in the brush."

She followed him to the front of the wreck and stared at the faint indentations the tech pointed out on the ground. "Those look like the tread of the kind of shoes Alan would have worn when he's casually dressed," she mumbled, staring at the indentations in the soft soil. "Might be his."

"Okay. We haven't tracked them very far down the bluff yet, but the Sheriff's office is on it."

Outside the crime scene tape, Marjorie squatted in the dirt and placed her fingers in the faint shoe print as if she could somehow get a message from it.

Farther down the hill she heard shouts from deputies and a few civilians recruited by the county sheriff's office to search for the apparently severely injured driver of the wrecked van.

She rose and looked to the young deputy who had been hovering near and said, "I'm going down the hill and join the search." Her tone of voice brooked no objection and the deputy simply nodded and pointed down the hill toward a clearing at the bottom.

As she stumbled through the underbrush to the clearing at the bottom of the hill, she heard the bass rumble of the tow truck maneuvering into position above her, preparing to drag the wrecked CR-V out of the brush.

At the bottom of the hill she met four young men. Another, the man who appeared to be in charge, was an older appearing deputy. He stepped forward and grasped her hand in a clasp that was somehow comforting and reassuring.

"We've tracked Mr. Lockem several hundred yards to the north. Found some clear prints in the mud I'd like you to look at, ma'am."

She went and knelt at the muddy patch. She stared briefly at the clear tracks in the puddle he pointed out. The prints were clear and familiar. "Yes. These tracks are from Alan's shoes." She peered at the impressions. How was it she was so sure? The tracks

152

looked odd, as if he might have stumbled. One print seemed deeper than the other. Was he limping?. Out-turned toe of one shoe was unlike him. His stride, from the shoe prints, was off, somehow. Injured? She couldn't tell. The tracks raised her feeling of need to find him soon.

Questions flooded her mind. How injured was he? Were people after him? Maybe he was disoriented from the crash. And most important, where had he got to?

The deputies and the volunteer began to beat a path through the thick underbrush until they reached a more heavily forested area that was less clogged with weeds and low growth. But that also meant the ground was firmer and the footprints disappeared.

"What's in that direction?" she asked, pointing upriver.

"Local road, a few cabins scattered along and eventually, the river." The deputy glanced at the sky, pulled his phone, and called in for a vehicle to meet them in an hour. He relayed the name of the corner where an even narrower road branched off toward the river and a pair of old private cabins.

The lead volunteer searcher, who had moved ahead more swiftly, trotted back toward the small group. "Look, he said. "There are broken branches and drag marks along the edge of the road."

He paused to get his breath and one of the deputies said, "Makes no sense. If I were injured and down here, I'd want to use the easiest path. Wouldn't you? Why doesn't he head back to the highway to flag down a ride?"

The volunteer shook his head, addressed Marjorie. "He's former military, right?"

"Yes."

"So was I. He might be layin' a trail but tryin' to stay concealed. If he'd been run off the road, he might be afraid to try to climb the hill." He turned and trotted back down the dirt road. Marjorie and the rest spread out across the road and moved a little faster,

153

looking at the ground, the bushes, even the tree trunks.

An old cabin built partly of pine logs and finished lumber came into view through the trees. It was set back almost twenty yards from the road. The volunteer who told Marjorie to call him Sid ran to the door and pushed. It didn't move. A deputy stepped beside him and pounded on the door, shouted "Police! Anybody home?" The only response was silence, except for a whisper or a sigh from breeze high up in the trees.

The lead deputy commanded, "Break it in."

Sid, the volunteer, had already picked up a stout log. He reared back and slammed one end into the lock slot above the old-fashioned door handle.

Marjorie hardly noticed the action. She was staring at the wall beside the door frame, at an almost dry smear of what she knew was blood.

Chapter 31

A second slam from the log broke the latch, but something kept the door from swinging wide open. The deputy stepped up, put his shoulder against the door and shoved hard. The door gave way and the men surged into the single-room cabin. When Marjorie stepped inside she saw that a chair had been placed to hold the door closed except from a determined assault. She looked up to see an old cookstove against the opposite wall, a small table and several straight chairs scattered about the room and a stacked pair of bunks against another wall. The two windows opposite each other in the side walls admitted some light but she could only see a large untidy lump of bedding and blankets on the lower bunk.

The deputy made a futile effort to restrain her. Marjorie lunged across the room crying, "Alan!" When she reached the bunk, her foot slipped in a small pool of blood and she grabbed at the bed frame to steady herself. Tearing the bedding aside, she saw the pale slack face of her lover. "Alan! Alan," she cried.

Lockem's face was bloodied and when she put her face to his, she barely detected shallow breathing. One of the men pulled down the rest of the bedding. Lockem's pants were shredded and the anxious searchers saw his belt formed a tourniquet around his right thigh. It had been positioned near his crotch above a long gash in the flesh.

The deputy grabbed his phone and bellowed, "Get me an ambulance, stat!" He took a deep breath and continued in a somewhat more normal but still urgent tone. "Looks like a fracture of the right leg. Serious blood loss. Other injuries unknown." Marjorie had put her hand gently over Alan's heart and was somewhat relieved to feel a faint but steady beat. It looked like he'd lost a good deal of blood. His pants and the bedding under his thigh were wet with dark moisture and he appeared pale.

The volunteer named Sid gave the deputy the name of the cabin owner and the fastest way to get the ambulance and EMTs to the scene. Another deputy gently moved Marjorie aside and examined Lockem. He adjusted the tourniquet, releasing a small pulse of blood.

"Can we get some water in him?" someone asked.

"He's unconscious," someone else said. Marjorie wet a cloth from an offered water bottle and gently cleaned Alan's face. It became clear that much of the blood had come from his bloody nose.

A long half-hour passed while they tended to the fallen man and waited for the ambulance. EMTs arrived with a rush of siren and flashing lights. The EMTs set about placing tubes and needles to supply vital fluids and they professionally bound up Lockem's wounds. Marjorie was reassured to be told that Alan's vital signs were recovering although he was in need of immediate medical help. The ambulance team called in a medical helicopter to a landing location, a nearby clearing in the forest. The ambulance took Lockem to the clearing and he was lifted into the helicopter and flown off to a hospital in Saint Paul. Marjorie made arrangements with the Sheriff to have her car returned to Roseville while she was driven directly to the hospital by a deputy sheriff.

After Lockem was moved to the ambulance, the local volunteer took the deputy aside and pointed at a branch that had been kicked partly under the bunk. "Look at that. Could be used as sort of a crutch."

The deputy peered at the branch and nodded. He pulled his baton and dragged the branch from under the bunk. The men looked at it without picking it up and satisfied themselves that Lockem must have used the branch as a cane or crutch to help him navigate from vehicle to the cabin.

Lights and siren helped reduce the time to get Marjorie to the hospital in the city. By the time they arrived in Saint Paul, Lockem had been processed in and moved from the ER to an operating suite.

Marjorie marched across the floor, intending to enter the surgical suite and see her companion when the door swung open and a large black woman appeared, holding up one hand in an almost imperious motion to stop Marjorie. The woman was clad in light blue scrubs.

"I know you want to see him right now, but you can't. We're about to operate to repair his leg and other injuries."

Marjorie took a gulp of air and then another. The woman opposite her watched calmly. Marjorie steadied herself and looked at the other woman. "And you are?"

"Doctor Sandborne, Ms. Kane. I'm Mr. Lockem's surgeon. Would you like to sit down?" Indicated a pair of padded chairs.

"Tell me," Marjorie commanded, and sank into the nearby chair. She sighed and said, "sorry, I don't mean to be rude."

"No problem. Your husband is stable and from my initial examination, we should be able to restore his leg to full function. He has a fracture of the femur and soft tissue damage. His recovery and rehabilitation may take a considerable amount of time."

"But he'll live? He'll be all right?"

"Yes ma'am. I'm quite confident of that. He must have put the tourniquet on almost immediately. He's in good physical condition, otherwise. I'd suggest you wait in the surgical lobby out there and I'll come see you when we're through. It'll be a while so you might want to get something to eat. All right?" The surgeon's voice had softened she laid a large gentle hand on Marjorie's shoulder. "Is there somebody we can call? You should have somebody wait with you." Marjorie felt like crying, but she wouldn't do that right now. Could she call Lucy? No. Fact was, there was no one. The few close friends and relatives were scattered

157

across the nation, none close. There was no one except the man on the operating table.

"I'll be all right. Thank you.

The other woman nodded and turned back into the operating suite.

***

Several tedious hours past, more slowly than she could ever remember it happening like that. The sun had begun to fall slowly onto the horizon when Dr. Sandborne reappeared to sit beside Marjorie and smiled.

"Your guy is going to be fine. He's obviously in good shape, physically. It will take a while for that leg wound to heal, but if he exercises and watches his diet, he'll walk again. Maybe even jog."

"May I see him?" Marjorie's voice betrayed emotion and a measure of weariness. Dr. Sandborne nodded and walked her to the ICU where a nurse took Marjorie in hand.

She softly entered the room where Lockem lay. His breathing was deep and steady. Tubes and wires ran from racks suspended over his bed to his body. For a long minute she stood motionless, staring at her friend, her lover. After decades of resisting attentions from all manner of men, here lay the one man she had chosen, the one with whom she expected to spend many years. She knew his love for her was strong, just as her love had become a live presence in her existence.

He sighed in his sleep, as he often did, and she knew then, somehow that their lives would go on together.

Chapter 32

TWO days after Lockem's surgery to repair his damaged leg he rested comfortably in his hospital bed grumbling to anyone within occasional earshot about the inaction. He had no one to talk to at the moment. Marjorie had just left the hospital to pursue information on the accident. Or, as she continued to insist, the attempt on his life.

Lieutenant Gage had suggested he accompany her to the Highway Department garage where their CR-V was under examination. She had been glad for his interest. There was no way, she'd told the police, that Alan Lockem could have fallen asleep at the wheel and run off the road. He would have stopped to nap if he'd become sleepy, she'd snapped. And what about the scar on the rear left panel? She hadn't been sure, after the conversation that the authorities would take her concerns seriously, that the wreck hadn't been an accident.

Gage knew the analysts would have been reluctant to examine the vehicle just on her request, so he decided to apply a little subtle pressure. When the two of them walked into the garage in New Brighton, the badly damaged blue vehicle was on a hoist and two mechanics were peering at the undercarriage. One of them pointed a small high-intensity flashlight at the rear axle.

They both glanced at the couple and nodded. "Yours?" One asked.

Marjorie reckoned he meant the case not ownership of the vehicle, and that could mean there was a case. Lieutenant Gage smiled and said, "What can you tell us?"

"Whoever noted the mark on the left rear panel was correct. We took samples. Lab says its old tire rubber. Looks as if somebody driving a vehicle with an old truck tire hung on the front end, hit your vehicle, and knocked him off the road. Tricky and dangerous if deliberate."

"Any way to tell if it was accidental or deliberate?" Gage asked.

"'Fraid not," the mechanic said. "There is a technique some patrol learn. It gives them a way to short circuit a high-speed chase, but it takes a lot of skill and it requires a good place on the highway or street. We may be able to trace the tire to where it was sold, but that's problematical and won't be much use, anyway."

Suspicions confirmed, after looking over the written reports on damage to the vehicle, Gage and Marjorie left the garage.

"It appears you're right, somebody targeted Alan." Lieutenant Gage headed into Saint Paul, intending to accompany Marjorie to the hospital. "Assume somebody followed him from home. How long was he gone?"

"According to the speedometer and the garage-door timer, Alan drove about sixty miles over two plus hours."

Gage looked a question at her.

"We've been upgrading our security systems. Computer logs times doors are opened and closed and dates."

"Wow, expensive, yes?"

"Yes, but worth it."

"Do you think it has to do with these church murders?" Gage asked then.

"I don't know," Marjorie said. "We don't have anything else on, right now, but that seems to be a stretch. I wonder if we can find out if any of the bikers have the kind of skill necessary to force a vehicle off the road without causing a big wreck. And how did they find him? Four o'clock this morning, Alan went out for a drive to think about stuff. He usually just wanders when he does that. He doesn't remember exactly where he drove—not unusual—so he must have been followed a long time because we know the attempt on his life happened about three hours later, around seven."

Gage nodded. "Makes sense to me. It's also possible somebody else connected to the murders was responsible for this." He checked his phone. "I have to get back so I'm going to leave you here at the hospital. Can you find your own way home?"

"Oh, absolutely. Don't worry about me. I owe you for all this help." She patted Gage's arm and slid out of the car. When she entered the lobby of the hospital she scanned the scattered groups of people coming and going. It had become her habit, since the attack on Lockem, to pay more attention to the people around her, even in ordinary circumstances like crossing the hospital lobby. The woman at the desk waved and smiled. Marjorie waved back and continued to the elevator.

Exiting the elevator, Marjorie walked along the hall to just outside Lockem's room. There she encountered Lockem's slender young Physical Therapist in a white coat that was too large for him.

"I am impressed with his progress. I truly didn't expect he's be able to stand this soon." He glanced at the clipboard he held. "Still, when I was at the VA in Philadelphia, we saw any number of marines and soldiers with massive physical damage who were anxious to get out. If Mr. Lockem continues to improve, he should be able to go home in a few more days. I'd recommend you rent a hospital-style bed and hire a nurse part-time, one with physical therapy experience."

"Thank you, Doctor, I'll take your advice." She turned to the large lounge on the same floor to have coffee and wait for hospital staff to finish their morning examination. Seated alone at one of the small round tables with a large cardboard container of sweetened coffee, she consciously took a break from worrying about Alan's leg and his mental condition to observe the few people in the lounge. She'd already rented a

161

hospital bed and rearranged the small office on the main floor of their home into a place for Lockem.

The sounds of a measured pace, hard heels on the tile floor came to her and she swiveled her head to see a tall gray-haired man displaying military bearing crossing the space directly toward her table. Marjorie tensed up until the man smiled down at her and without asking, sat in the chair across the table.

"Marjorie Kane," he said, staring at her face. "I knew it must be you."

"Excuse me? Do I know you?" She glanced over his shoulder toward the woman at the coffee counter.

The man across from her leaned forward and his smile faded. "Oh, God. I'm sorry. I should explain. My name is Harry. Harry Hines. I'm head of Neurology here. When I saw your name in the patient's file I just had to find out." He stopped, took out a large white handkerchief and wiped his lips. Then he exhaled and shook his head.

Marjorie, beginning to realize what was going on, began to relax and offered a smile. "I think it's perfectly all right," she said. "I bet you recognized the name."

Hines nodded. "I did. I thought, could that be true? Could you be the Kandy Kane I met in Seattle? Of course, you won't remember."

Marjorie's smile broadened. "Seattle? Sometime in the 1960s We were appearing in a club downtown. Some Army officer came backstage and asked if some of us girls could visit the fort the next day because his company was shipping out at the end of the week. Right? Fort Lewis?"

Hines relaxed and smiled. "That's right. You and several of the chorus girls came to the base the next day for lunch and then we had a social time at the canteen afterward. I was one of the G.I.s in the company. I was so in awe. I'd seen you dance in San Francisco and in Seattle. When I saw your name in the file I couldn't believe it."

"Well, it's nice to meet a fan after all this time," Marjorie said. "Tell me, why did you have Alan's file?

"Hospital policy. Older patients with serious trauma get checked for mental stability. Your guy is in good shape." Hines smiled, checked his watch, and shook her hand again. "Well, forgive the intrusion, but I am so pleased to meet you again, Kandy Kane." Hines jumped out of his chair and strode off grinning. Marjorie watched him go, knowing he would never realize how much she appreciated his brief visit at this time.

A nurse came to the door and signaled to her she could rejoin Lockem in his room.

#

Ten days later, a private ambulance and crew transferred Lockem to his new bed in what had been his office on the first floor of their home in Roseville. With the help of the private nurse, Marjorie was able to keep him focused on rehabilitation and recovery of full mobility. Several law enforcement personnel and others came by to see him and commiserate over his accident. He and Marjorie avoided revealing beyond Lieutenant Gage and state police investigators that he had been deliberately forced off the highway. Whether it had been an attempt to kill him or just warn him off was still unknown.

Lockem and Marjorie spent a couple hours each day reviewing their case notes. xcept the mark is higher than a tire contact would be. Tire must have been installed on the front of the vehicle that hit you. Not a hard smack, the driver hit you just hard enough to cause a swerve and an over correction."

Alan nodded. "Sure. I took a driving course in the service. We learned how to force vehicles into spins, sliding changes and real wrecks."

"The State Patrol believes you were forced to crash. But we don't know why." She took a breath. "Now tell me why you left the car? We had a hell of a time tracing you down to that shack."

163

"I thought the driver was trying to either seriously injure me or kill me. When I got out of the car I thought I saw stop lights flash just down the hill. I figured the driver might come looking for me so I hightailed it out of there, as best I could."

"Something for me to add to the list of who and why?"

He smiled at her, leaned back against his pillows. "Yes, and we will discover why and who." He reached for the glass of orange juice and took a long drink that drained the glass. "Refresh me as to where we are with Trevor Howland."

Marjorie turned another page in her file on the case and said, "I've traced him to his BA degree from the U. After a year's hiatus when whatever he did, I haven't yet discovered, he entered the same Divinity school his best bud, Elliot was in. I don't think Trevor finished his degree, so I don't yet know if he's a licensed pastor or not. I also haven't traced him back here yet."

"Mister Trevor Howland may be more involved than we know, right now."

"Yeah, I get that. I found his name on a label in the robing room at the church. He apparently sang in the choir on a regular basis. As did the Pastor's wife."

"Ah, the plot twists."

"No thickening?"

Marjorie giggled. "To hear this old couple here in this bedroom, you'd think we were in our dotage."

Alan nodded, reaching overhead to stretch his shoulder muscles. "The incident is peculiar. I have the impression the driver tried just about everything to make it look accidental. Even though I'm confident he—or she—wanted to kill me."

"Absolutely!" Marjorie sat down on the bedside chair. "Eat your breakfast, will you?" Given this thing started with two killings, it shouldn't surprise us you became a target."

"Sure, but you know as well as I do we aren't frequently targets of physical attack. I think it must be the painting." Alan grunted and stretched arms overhead again.

"Usually, we are on the same trail," Marjorie said, "but I disagree this time. I think it has something to do with the relationship between the Elliot's and this Trevor Howland."

"Hmm, Alan mused. He stuck a backscratcher under the edge of the cast on his leg and tried to alleviate the itching of his skin. "It's worth following up, but it sure widens the investigation, 'cause you'll have to include that motorcycle gang."

"Club," Marjorie interjected.

"Yeah, club," Alan amended. "So, what's your plan for today?"

"I think I will call the women who hired us in the first place and enlist their aid in getting the painting evaluated by experts at MIA. Then I'm off to the gym. After that, I'll come home and make us a meal."

"Seems like a plan. I'll use the resistance bands to exercise and watch a little TV, think about this thing and maybe take a nap." Alan sank a little lower in the bed, Marjorie removed the tray and took the dishes to the kitchen.

She returned with Alan's cell phone, the bedroom tv remote and one of his pistols. He set the gear on the bedside table in easy reach and slid the pistol under the bedclothes beside his left thigh. "I called Lucy. She's home all day, she said, no big surprise. She'll happily come over and do for you if you just call her." Marjorie hesitated by the bed and then leaned in and kissed him murmuring, "be careful with the gat, meds, you know." Then she went to her office to do some online research.

Alan slid down, switched on the TV, and immediately dozed off.

Chapter 33

Marjorie reached out to one of the women who had originally entangled Lockem & Kane in the church murders. After two phone calls which yielded no new information but were staunchly supportive of the investigators, she called Lieutenant Gage, their Roseville Police contact and friend.

"Glad you called, Marjorie. How's Alan doing?"

"Better than I expected. But that was an ugly fracture and as you know, injuries at our age don't heal as quickly as you young fellows."

He chuckled. "You sound more like your old self. I'd like to stop by later today if that's acceptable?"

"Absolutely. I'm going to find a home health aide to be here to look after Alan so I can get some more work done on this investigation."

"I might have some help for you there," Gage muttered. "See you this afternoon."

Marjorie called Carolyn Action to advise her of Alan's injury and explained she wanted to have the painting more closely re-examined to determine if it might be the reason for the killings.

"I thought we'd done that," said Carolyn.

"Well, yes," Marjorie agreed, but even if we aren't sure there's a connection, I don't like leaving loose threads, so I'm getting an expert in." She doubted it would matter but crossing every T and dotting each and every I was important. Alan had impressed that fact upon her early in their partnership. She also called the president of the church board to be sure he was still okay with a close examination of the painting.

A call to the Minneapolis Institute of Arts elicited contacts to find an expert in painting of the period. Marjorie soon had an appointment in a few days to meet a woman who believed that she could determine the authenticity of the painting without removing it from the wall. Along the way she had to

166

explain and reassure several contacts that her partner had survived and was recovering from the automobile crash near the border with Wisconsin. She also related that their independent investigation of the murders in the church would continue. She adroitly avoided specific questions about the progress of the Lockem & Kane investigation, leads they may have developed, and information acquired.

The researcher from MIA called and she and Marjorie arranged to meet at the church in two days' time. She told Marjorie she expected she might be able to make a preliminary determination that same day. Marjorie spent some time with Alan, restless and grumpy in forced inaction. She had brought him one of his laptop computers so he could review some of their files and make recommendations. She also moved his phone charger to a more convenient place in the room. Privately, she hoped he wouldn't make too many suggestions or call many people. She thought she had enough on her plate and Alan needed rest as much as anything else.

The day arrived when the restorer from MIA was scheduled, and Marjorie was at the church half an hour early. She and Carolyn muscled the desk away from its position in front of the painting and cleared space they thought might be needed by the examiner. They head the door open, and the elevator grind up with its load. The middle-aged woman who appeared at the door, carrying a big satchel grinned when she came in.

"Hi. I'm Amanda from MIA. You Marjorie Kane?" She was looking at the wrong woman and Marjorie stepped forward to take Amanda's offered hand for a brief squeeze and shake. Amanda swung the satchel off her shoulder and said, "I have another bag by the door." When she returned with an even larger suitcase, Carolyn stepped forward with a smile and held the door open so Amanda could bring her equipment into the crowded office.

167

While she set up Marjorie watched her and talked with Carolyn.

"I've never even read about this. What kind of analysis do you do to authenticate a painting?" Carolyn wondered.

The woman donned a plastic apron and set up a small collapsible table and a portable microscope. "There are a number of ways, some of which are broad strokes like does the piece look the way it should? I once examined a painting that was supposed to be from the nineteenth century of a cowboy, only he was wearing jeans with a zipper." She smiled, continuing that zippers hadn't been invented yet. "You understand that we could do a more thorough analysis if we took the painting to the lab?"

Marjorie nodded.

"Unless I find some seriously questionable elements, I should be able to make a preliminary judgment. Subject, history, does the painting look right. Technique, style."

"Not just dress," Marjorie interjected, "but materials, like is the canvas the right age."

Amanda nodded and went almost nose to the canvas, peering through a loupe. "I look at paint, strokes, at the frame, if it has one."

Marjorie nodded again, briefly wishing Lockem could be present. He had the most curiosity about the provenance of the painting.

Amanda stood back to don rubber or plastic gloves and gazed fixedly at the painting. Finally she nodded and spoke into a small recorder she had set up. She gave the date and location and the title and basic dimensions of the artwork. "The painting is oil on canvas, backed and framed in wood that appears to be early twentieth century. Ladies, I saw a ladder in the hall. I very much want to examine the back of this painting so I'll need your help to remove it from the wall."

As if on cue, the church janitor stuck his head in the door.

"Good, timing," Carolyn said. "Bring the ladder in and help us take the painting down." In short order they had the painting off its brackets and leaning against the wall, backside exposed.

Amanda nodded. "Just as I expected. These stretchers help keep the canvas taut under this broad plank the frame is fixed onto. Look here." She pointed to two small pieces of paper glued to the back of the frame. One appeared to be in a foreign language and was so faded it was unreadable. "And here, this is an export document that allowed the painting to be legally removed from the country of residence by a recognized dealer. I recognize the name. MIA has some art from that gallery. The dealer is now out of business, but he was known for traffic in middle eastern art. I'm sure that's a real dealer label."

Marjorie peered at the old labels. "What language is that, Arabic?"

Amanda smiled. "Probably." She went to work, snipping some tiny threads from the edges of the canvas and carefully scraping tiny bits of paint from edges of the frame and the fabric. She quickly made slides and placed them under her microscope. Humming softly she went about her analysis, had the painting reversed so she could make a series of high-definition photographs of various parts of the work.

Two hours passed almost unnoticed while Marjorie and Carolyn watched Amanda work, occasionally helping by holding a piece of equipment for her. The odor of chemicals permeated the office atmosphere, a not unpleasant smell.

Amanda peered for several minutes at her slides then straightened, smiling. "No question. This is what it's supposed to be. It's been restored and cleaned, but that happened years ago. Decades. It definitely could use an expert cleaning. She glanced at her tablet and scribbled the time on her I-pad. "I love it when these things pan out. It's a very nice scene, authentic, painted during the appropriate period by the artist who's signed it. Congratulations. I'll write up my

169

analysis and send it along with the bill." She went to work packing up her equipment with practiced efficiency.

"How soon will you get back to us?" Marjorie asked.

Amanda raised her eyebrow, smiled again and said, "'bout a week."

The custodian returned and helped re-install the painting. After Amanda finished packing and left the church, Marjorie and Carolyn shook hands ceremonially with big, satisfied smiles on their faces. "She didn't mention value," Carolyn said.

"I expect an estimate will come with the bill. I imagine that will require some additional research outside the church." Marjorie drove home, eager to share the results with Lockem.

CHAPTER 34

When she entered the bedroom, Lockem was sitting on the edge of the bed, a bemused look on his face. Marjorie frowned. "Trying to get outa bed, fella?"

Lockem nodded and flashed her a brief smile. "I thought I'd test the leg."

He didn't have to say which leg. The cast bulked against the pale blue flower pattern of his favorite pajama pants. He'd insisted on wearing those after the operation to repair his fractured leg, even though the pants leg had to be cut from ankle to hip to accommodate the cast.

"And?"

"Well, I got the blanket and sheet back and swung my good leg to the floor. Nice height, the bed, by the way."

Marjorie smiled. The hospital-style bed brought in allowed them to raise and lower the bed as needed to accommodate dressing his wound had been a useful addition. She hoped it would be only temporary.

"But when I tried to stand, it was a bit of a problem." Lockem stopped and licked his lips. Marjorie peered closer and realized he looked a little sweaty.

"I got dizzy. Frankly, it was more painful than I expected. So I sat back down on the bed. After a while, the dizziness went away, sort of, but every time I tried to stand, it came back."

"Any specific pain in your leg?" she asked sympathetically.

"Stiffness when I flex my knee and I guess pain at the incision as well, but nothing I can't handle."

She nodded and took a tissue to wipe his face, but he batted her hand away. "You up for supper?"

"Matter of fact, I am getting hungry. How'd it go with the painting?"

"Complete and unhesitating validation. Old, authentic, painted by Friar Talegiese. Two old but good

171

dealer's labels on the back. I could see a reaction from Amanda when she found them. She'll send a written report. We didn't talk much about value," Marjorie went on, anticipating his next question. "She suggested that would require some time for research with art historians and curators familiar with the period. Maybe the donor would be a source. But eventually we'll get a valuation."

"Donor is dead," Lockem said. "If the historians can validate the location of what the painting depicts, it's a very valuable piece of art. The painter, a friar and teacher, lived and worked in what once was the Kingdom of Edom. My quick research while you were in Church suggests the painting might be worth north of a million bucks."

Marjorie stared at Lockem. "Jesus! You should excuse the expression. The value will go up and the church members will be happy. Maybe I'm wrong and the painting is central to the murders.

"I'm going to put a big potato in the oven and create a salad and probably carefully pan fry a couple of lamb chops. Okay?"

"Mmmm, I'm drooling already. And what do you mean, 'probably carefully?' When have you ever not been? I hate to impose, but could I have a small scotch?"

"Comin' right up." She leaned forward and kissed his clammy cheek. "Get yourself back into that bed and we'll proceed. Your memory must be dipping if you don't remember the ruined dinners. A million dollars, huh? Do you want me to help you back to bed?"

"I think I can manage." Lockem's grin was almost a grimace. After dinner we can go over what we know so far and make some plans."

Succulent dinner finished, Marjorie cleared the dishes from the tray on his bed and her own tray and brought in her file of notes on the double murder. The couple often maintained their own separate files on projects or cases. In this case, Marjorie had a thicker,

172

more comprehensive file. She shuffled notes and looked at Lockem. He appeared to be a little unfocused.

"Leg hurts?" she said.

"Not really. More like it's a drag on my mobility, and it uses some of my awareness. What's up?"

"We now know the painting is authentic and valuable. We know there's a bunch of bikers—maybe not a gang, exactly, that are linked to the deceased pastor. So far, we haven't turned up anything that suggests the bikers were involved in the murders, but my instincts persist in telling me to look deeper."

"Ah, yes, your instinct. I think that librarian needs talking to. She came forward to the police because she thought Lorna Cooper might have taken some of the research bibles from the library's collection."

Scribbling in her file, Marjorie nodded and said, "and you think the gaps in Cooper's bookshelves were the spaces where she stored the purloined bibles. But why would anyone else want them? For that matter, why did Cooper? What in heaven's name would she do with them?"

Lockem shook his head slowly. "Suppose she was trying to find information to support authentication of the painting? But why did she steal them if she did? Unless she wanted to do her research in a more private setting? Since the bibles couldn't be checked out, perhaps she wanted more access to them and she intended to return them later. And where are they now?"

"The other piece we haven't discussed is the choir and the robing room," Marjorie said. "I didn't really unearth anything about the choir. Carolyn did say she occasionally sings with them, but rarely has time to practice with them They do assign robes, but it's not a strict system and the robes are pocketless so I don't think there's anything there. Carolyn said there weren't any current liaison's among members that she was aware of. No gossip, just the usual low-level jealousies around solo assignments. The Pastor's wife, Melissa, often sang with the choir."

Lockem scratched his ear, the one with the abraded lobe, damaged when he'd been ejected from the car on the hill overlooking the St. Croix River. "Have you discovered anything that links Pastor Elliot to Ms. Cooper? Something that could have led a double murder?"

Marjorie shook her head. "Not so far. And I'm beginning to feel as though that's a loser. I'm keeping an open mind—sort of—but I bet we'll discover she was just in the wrong place at the wrong time."

"Your research turned up nothing?"

"So far, that's true," she said. "I could still do a deeper dive into her background, but except for her apparent intense interest in religious history, she seems to be a normal ordinary sort with an ordinary background and only casual connections to this local church."

"I think we need more on her. I'll sit here, stewing in my cast and travel the Internet, finding her roots." He yawned and stretched overhead, winced, and asked for a fresh glass of water. The time for his evening pills had arrived.

The doorbell chimed. Marjorie trotted to the door. She knew the security folks parked outside would have observed, evaluated, and possibly stopped any unknown or dangerous-appearing individual. She swung the door open.

"Hi. Good evening. Oh, Doris. I'm surprised to see you this late."

Doris Toltec smiled and came through the door. "I'm later than usual but the surgeon messaged me and wanted me to do an occasional evening eval. So here I am. Hope it's not too inconvenient."

"Sure. No problem. He's in there." Marjorie pointed toward the bedroom where Lockem sprawled on the bed, muttering at his cast.

Toltec, Lockem's visiting nurse, stepped around Marjorie, and walked into the other room to be with her patient. Marjorie closed the door and went to her own office.

There are no patterns, she murmured to herself. Alan taught me to look for patterns. It made sense, because patterns were an integral part of her dance routines, even the most direct and unsubtle strip tease routines had patterns. The number of steps, the number of times the band played certain sections of her music selections, the way the drummer sometimes was required to emphasize a certain move or pose.

But here, she could see no patterns. And that was why she felt the tragic incidents in the church were happenstance, probably unplanned and opportunistic. Which might mean, Marjorie reflected then, that murder had never been on the table at all. Maybe the whole thing was accidental? No, that couldn't be. Who would shoot and kill two people by accident inside a church? And why was that person, male, or female, going into a church carrying a weapon? This was not the Middle Ages when kings sent knights to dispatch offending rivals at their private devotions.

"Gahhaa," she said out loud, an occasional habit when her frustration reached high levels. She heard a faint curse from the temporary bedroom where Lockem was working with his nurse to maintain his physical health while his fractured leg healed.

Chapter 35

Standing on her front steps, Marjorie Kane gazed around her serene, sun-bathed cul de sac. Flowers bloomed in carefully edged beds, the lawns were green and well-trimmed. Looking at the placid scene, she momentarily found it hard to imagine that behind her, her boon companion was struggling, albeit successfully, to regain his health and heal his fractured leg. She sighed, hitched up her holstered pistol, now riding in plain sight on her hip. The small Sig Sauer P320 was light enough she could almost forget she was jogging through the park behind the house, armed and alert. Almost.

Lieutenant Gage had recommended the smaller, lighter weapon to her after the traffic incident that had injured Lockem. He'd showed up with the weapon as a hastily wrapped gift package. Although she'd resisted at first, he'd persuaded her that she should carry the weapon whenever she left the house. It had been her own decision to wear the weapon in a holster clearly visible to passersby, at least for the immediate future. Marjorie hoped, that rather than allow her confrontation with a surprised aggressor, enemies would avoid her, knowing she was armed. Retying her tennis shoes she jogged around the house and crossed the expanse of lawn at the back of their lot to step onto the path that wandered around the lake and through the small park that surrounded the lake.

After her run, Marjorie showered and dressed. She gave Lockem a vague indication that she was merely running a few errands. In fact, she had decided to have a face to face with David Klein. She had considered every aspect of the case as they knew it and in spite of a lack of compelling evidence, had almost persuaded herself that he and his motorcycling buddies were responsible for Lockem's crash. Proving it could be a problem unless she found some compelling evidence.

***

She parked in front of the Klein address. When she exited the car and crossed the verge to the sidewalk leading to the two-story, white-painted house with a small porch enclosing the front door, she saw the window shade on a second-floor window shift slightly as if someone had just stepped back from the window. Or, she thought, if someone had slammed a door to the upstairs hallway. If it was a small room. Too many ifs.

As she started up the two cracked concrete steps onto the private walkway leading to the front porch steps, she heard a roaring pulsing sound issuing from the back of the house. To her experienced ear it sounded exactly like what she expected to hear from the vicinity of the motorcycle group she and Alan had encountered at Pastor Elliot's home, someone pulsing the accelerator on an unmuffled internal combustion engine with a tuned exhaust pipe so the sound resonated at a low frequency.

Instead of mounting the porch steps, Marjorie turned and walked across the grass around the house toward the garage. As she walked, she mentally returned to her previous profession, straightening her back, walking like a model, swaying her shoulders just a little and thrusting her chest forward a little more. Even at her advanced age Marjorie could project attention-getting sexuality. Drawing closer, she saw a figure seated astride a parked Harley-Davidson motorcycle. He was resting one hand on the throttle and was twisted around to appear to be peering at something beside the engine. Smoke puffed forth from the tailpipe. Beside the cycle stood an old gray GMC pickup truck. The truck appeared to be resting its dual rear wheels on makeshift ramps that elevated it a foot or so off the cracked pavement in front of the detached garage. What interested Marjorie the most was the ancient truck tire attached to the front of the vehicle. She went closer. The hood of the pickup was up and a man in jeans was bent over the fender, head deep

177

inside the engine compartment. She stared briefly at the frayed rope that tied the tire to the grille. It was an old, heavily worn truck tire with almost no discernable tread. In fact the cords that underlaid the original tread were visible in several places.

Marjorie saw the man on the motorcycle saddle twist back and she lifted a hand in a casual wave, watching recognition dawn and roll across his features. His mouth fell open and he revved the cycle engine in quick bursts. Marjorie could tell by the expression on his face that she was making the impression she wanted. The other visible figure lifted his head out from under the hood of the truck and bellowed. "JJ! Knock it off, dude."

JJ immediately killed the engine. "Dave," he said in the silence.

"Hello," said Marjorie in a voice near the bottom of her range. "I guess you're David Klein. I think I recognize you." She smiled and turned her gaze to the other, a boy, really. "You're JJ, I think we met at Pastor Elliot's." JJ didn't respond, he just stared at her chest with a mixture of awe and alarm. Marjorie straightened again, still almost grinning at the two. She knew the reaction she often got from that move.

"So, Mr. Klein. I'm sorry to interrupt your afternoon, but I have a few questions." She stepped closer to the front bumper of the pickup and put one hand on the worn tire. Even a quick look told her there would be no hope of linking this tire to the attempt on Lockem's life, unless one of these two became a suspect and revealed something.

"Uh, Ms Kane, that tire is old, tired and dirty. You want to be careful touching it." There was nothing in his tone that remotely suggested menace or a warning.

"Problem with this old thing?" she asked. She hoped she sounded as casual as she tried to be.

178

"Yeah. It's gettin' too old. Tired. We own it collectively and so she has several drivers. More wear and tear than ordinary."

"Ah, I understand. Perhaps she should retire."

Klein grinned and said, "yeah, I think so. There's a problem with the differential so long as I had her up on blocks last couple weeks waiting for parts, I decided to do some work on the ignition."

JJ had stepped around the garage door and now returned, shoving his cell into a hip pocket. "Obi picked up some scrap an' he wants me to help him at the yard. He'll be here in a few."

Marjorie had planned to quiz David Klein about their vehicles but now she felt she had better depart before the odds changed. She plucked at the frayed ends of the loops of rope around the bent and damaged hood ornament that stuck up on the body panel that covered the radiator.

"You better replace this tie, lose that tire while you're driving and you could have a serious accident. Anyway, I was wondering. I know my partner talked with you, but I just wondered if either of you have any idea who had it in for Pastor Elliot."

The reaction of both young men was neutral. Klein shrugged. "I've thought about it. We liked Mr. Elliot. We all got along really well." Out of the corner of her eye, Marjorie saw JJ open his mouth as if to object. Klein cut him off with a sharp gesture that could have meant anything.

"Well, you guys are obviously busy so I won't take up any more of your time." She had no indication how soon Obadiah would drive up with more of their members and she didn't want to be there when the group got bigger. Larger numbers sometimes gave a group courage. "Look, nobody seems to be making much progress finding his killer so I'd appreciate it if you guys would think

179

about it some more and let us know if you come up with anything we should know."

She waved a hand and walked swiftly back across the lawn and into her car. She drove around the block and parked at the corner on the next side street. In her rearview mirror she had an image of the Klein driveway and part of the pickup. Sure enough, a few minutes later, an older, dark brownish–green Chevy pickup truck came past on the street behind her and turned into Klein's driveway. She could see untidy piles of something in the bed of the truck, but not what it was. The truck stopped nose to nose with the GMC sitting on blocks. Obadiah Hassen stepped out of the vehicle on the opposite side and she lost track of him. A small figure swung slowly out of the passenger-side of the truck and dropped to the ground. Marjorie didn't recognize him, but he appeared to be older than any of the members of the motorcycle group she had encountered thus far.

She didn't have her digital telephoto camera with her, just her cell phone. Moreover, even at the distance of half a block, if one of them noticed her making photographs, that could lead to a confrontation. She didn't want that, but she raised her phone and grabbed a couple of snaps without carefully framing the image.

She watched the man or boy amble along the side of the vehicle toward the garage and disappear from view. She considered driving back to the Klein's to look more closely at the pickup that had just arrived. Chances of learning anything important were too remote to make that move and it would likely rile up Klein and the others in the group. She suspected there would be other opportunities. With no real evidence in hand, she still thought it likely that somebody standing in that yard had driven the vehicle that almost killed Alan. Thinking hard she started the engine

180

and drove away. As she negotiated the ramp to the freeway she felt disappointment. This probe had neither confirmed nor uprooted her feeling that the cyclists were involved in the murders.

Chapter 36

When Marjorie walked in after garaging her car, she was met by the excited voice of Alan Lockem calling her from his temporary bed.

Marjorie discovered Lockem sitting up, bedclothes crumpled around his waist, injured leg almost straight out from his hip, a lively look on his face. "Been dancing, have you," she inquired with a smile.

"No, no. But listen. On a hunch I called Interpol in Paris and got a really clear and reliable connection with someone who has apparently a lot of interest and knowledge about world-wide art theft. I got several questions answered by the woman I talked to."

"So I can assume this woman is not only interested but has some level of responsibility for art theft traffic as well." She smiled again at his enthusiastic response.

"Yep. Remember the young fellow who came early? The one who said he was an Interpol art investigator? Well, Ms Delgado told me there is no Interpol agent named Karl Markel working on any art theft projects. There is, however, a Karl Markel, probationary employee assigned to the New York office. Second, there is some interest in the painter of a work called "Edom." She wouldn't give me a lot, naturally, but I gather there is traffic in the friar's work on the dark side. What is of interest to us is that the painting in the Church office is probably worth something north of six figures."

"That's exciting. How does it help us?"

"Ah, I'm saving the best for last. It seems that this painting has been referred to in various historical and biblical texts written over the past few hundred years. The references may be to a similar work by the same painter and his helpers called "Sins of Odom." Further, Ms Delgado said they have records of researchers looking for information about the painter and the painting."

"Okay, I get it," said Marjorie. "There could be several people interested in protecting the reputation of this painting because of its relationship to Friar Talagiese and other, possibly similar paintings. Authentication will mean a value can be assigned."

"Correct. And, it turns out, there are numerous references to that historical period in some ancient editions of Christian and other biblical literature. So now I'm wondering if our deceased Ms Cooper wasn't on the trail of this thing, hence her examination of Bibles at the library and even the theft of some of them."

"And that's why they were removed from Cooper's apartment? Possibly. Changing the subject, I've ordered a nice dinner from that new place in Rosedale. They told me to give them a heads-up half an hour before we want to sit down to dinner and they'll deliver it all hot and ready to eat."

"Sounds good. I know it's more work, but can we set a small table in here so I can sit at a table like a regular person? Meals in bed are getting to be a drag."

"Consider it done."

Marjorie checked her watch, dragged a small side table into the bedroom, covered it with a nice white tablecloth, and set out good china settings and fine crystal. Then she called the restaurant to arrange delivery. Almost as an afterthought, she ran to the bedroom and changed from her pantsuit to a very nice cocktail dress. As advertised the doorbell rang, the dinner was delivered in perfect form as requested and Lockem and Kane were able to enjoy a companionable and excellent dinner evening together. They mutually agreed to set aside discussion of the rest of their case until the morning when rest and a little distance might yield fresh insight.

***

"I waited a block away until Obadiah drove up in a second pickup. It had a truck or car tire on the front bumper. I'm betting that was the truck that forced you off the road." It was morning and Marjorie was completing her observations on the cyclers to Lockem.

"I think we need to find a reason and a way to put some pressure on that gang to learn more about their roles in all this. If any."

The telephone rang on Lockem's desk. He rolled over on the bed and grabbed the receiver. "Yup." He nodded. "Yes, hi. This is Alan Lockem. Yes, I'll hold."

He glanced at Marjorie and silently mouthed "F.B.I."

A moment later he nodded at the phone and said, "Sure, hello, Agent Torgerson. What can I do for you?" He listened a moment and smiled, "Thank you. Yes I'm recovering and looking forward to getting on with my rehab." He stopped and listened for a minute, then he said. "Thanks for the heads up. Once less piece on the board."

When he severed the connection, he smiled at Marjorie and said, "It's good to have friends in high places. Especially ones who are helpful. That was an agent from the FBI. They've been advised that a person of interest, a man named Karl Markel has been detained by Immigration. It appears there are problems with his visa. He'll probably be deported, eventually. With patience and a little luck we may even get some relevant facts from their interrogations."

"Well, good," Marjorie smiled back. "One less character in this cast to worry about. I'm going to the gym for my workout. See you in a couple of hours."

Leaving the house, she checked carefully using her mirrors and direct vision to stay alert for any potential threats on the road. Somebody had run Lockem off the road and they had no way of knowing if that somebody would try for her.

Nothing untoward happened and she concentrated on her routines, all the time puzzling over the actions of the motorcycle boys. She still believed it was likely one of them had been driving the vehicle that had forced Alan off the road at the river. She also knew it was going to be tough to identify the culprit. She huffed over the weights on her ankles and realized she'd extended the number of reps well past the requirements of the routine. She reset the machine and walked to the other room at the gym to cool down and complete her workout. A warm shower would feel good about now.

On the short drive home Marjorie considered the other major player in the drama, the dead pastor's buddy, Trevor Howland. She'd learned that his presence appeared like a shadow or a wraith in nearly all the corners and corridors of the case. She braked at the intersection four blocks from home. Trevor Howland. There he sat in her mind. Had they overlooked something? Perhaps they needed to take a closer look at Mr. Howland, a much closer look.

CHAPTER 37

"I think you are right," said Lockem. "Although there may be nothing there, we really don't have much in the case file on Howland except his high school record and that he went to college in Indiana."

"Illinois," Marjorie corrected him. "And there's a little more there. He and Elliot went to the same college. I just pulled up my file on him." She stared at the screen. "Actually, I don't have much on Howland. After high school he went to work, then a year later followed Elliot to Illinois and to that nearby divinity school. Apparently he didn't finish at the divinity school because there's no record of a degree."

"Did he ever graduate from any college?" Lockem asked.

"Yeah, his resume indicates a business admin degree from Minnesota."

"Pastor Elliot came to Saint Paul to a church, but we don't know which one."

"We have holes in the fabric," Lockem groused. "Need to crank up the research."

"Ah, my love. I gotchur back—or front—or whatever. I'm about to take a deep dive in computer land and see what can be unearthed on this Howland guy."

Lockem grinned with appreciation. "Excellent, because I'm frustrated with the Internet."

Marjorie smiled, mostly to herself and went to her office and her computer. After organizing the high school records she already had, she proceeded with Wikipedia and Trevor Howland. Then she checked Facebook and LinkedIn and went on to a host of other sites. She collected a list of nearly a dozen Internet sites that offered information about her target, Trevor Howland. Even though the name was a little unusual, she was confident most of the sites would prove to be unproductive. One or two, however might lead to other sites or information that could be useful. A trail was opening.

She settled into her chair and continued her search. She found information protected from anyone without a necessary password. Calling on some techniques taught her by Lockem's hacker friend, she penetrated a few sites and together with information from open sites gradually developed a profile. After high school Trevor Howard has been something of a wanderer. His post-high school education had involved a half-dozen institutions of higher education. In a couple of Indiana schools, he'd only registered for one or two semester classes. In three schools he had never been formally admitted. In two, however, Marjorie was able to trace his education toward a Bachelor of Liberal Arts degree. If Howland had ever demonstrated any unusual talents or activity of either a positive or destructive nature, she didn't see it. At this stage she didn't feel a need to penetrate too deeply into the records. She flagged some sites as interesting for future, more detailed examination.

Later in the afternoon, Marjorie helped the attending nurse change bandages on Lockem's leg and related to him what she had learned.

"I did find an interesting sort of pattern."

Lockem looked away from his bandaged leg to Marjorie. "What sort of pattern?" he asked.

"As you know, Martin Elliot married a girl who grew up in Rochester Minnesota, but he met Melissa at IU, wooed her and they married right after he was ordained. Now the interesting thing is that during her Junior year at IU she dated a college student from another college named"—here she took a breath—"named Trevor Howland."

"Well, how about that?" he said.

"That's according to a woman who told me she knew Melissa pretty well, in college. Nothing I found so far indicates the relationship was more than casual, but it could take some calls and deep dives to find out more. Anyway, Howland was a year behind Elliot in school and a year or so after Elliot graduated from divinity school, Howland married a woman from the

187

investment company where he worked. Her name is Elise. They are still married and have two children and live in a South Saint Paul neighborhood or village called Fish Lake. It's an upscale development."

"Good work." Lockem grimaced. "I wonder if there's a way to get some impressions from former classmates how the pastor and Mr. Howland got along during those years."

Marjorie smirked, "Oh sure, you wonder, Mr. Intelligence officer, Mr. former spy-master, if there's a way to," she paused, still smiling. "You wonder if I can dredge up some gossip, right? Well, for your information, I've already started. No responses yet. I have emailed a couple of people and we'll see what develops."

"I might have guessed. Good move."

"I think I have the school side of this period between Elliot and Howland covered as far as possible, right now. Any suggestions as to other leads I should cultivate?"

Lockem looked at Marjorie for a long silent moment. "Maybe your contacts will reveal new avenues or alley to examine. I would press the schools where Mr. Howland studied. I will follow his employment history."

Marjorie nodded her agreement and turned toward her office and her computer. When she signed on to her email she was surprised to see the screen filled three times with new messages all dated from just the past twenty-four hours. Scanning the list on the screen she determined that her query to Trevor Howland's college acquaintances had generated a surprising number of responses. She quickly discovered that her queries had been forwarded to other classmates, many of whom had responded, either to the classmate or directly to Marjorie. She shook her head and sat forward to read and categorize the messages.

It became abundantly clear that both Martin Elliot and Trevor Howland were well-known on the campus. Although Howland was a semester behind, the two of them seemed to have been considered close. They both lived in the same dormitory, at least until Elliot reached his senior year when he moved out.

Marjorie had emailed three women whose electronic addresses she acquired from school records. One had not responded, but it became clear, as she scrolled through the list, that that woman had forwarded Marjorie's email request to other former students and some of them had sent along comments or additional information.

She developed a list of names and contact information. It was not a long list.. Four women admitted to having dated both men while in college. Two claimed they had dated both boys to the same college Spring Dance. Either memories were fading or something rare and unusual had taken place that long-ago spring. Those women described the two men as charming, engaging and fun to be with. Marjorie talked at length by phone to one woman who seemed to have issues with Howland.

"I just don't feel right, talking about him," she'd murmured. "It was quite a while ago and I'm sure we've both gone on."

"I surely understand your feelings," Marjorie soothed, "but it would really help us resolve some of our questions if you would give me an indication of how you saw that relationship."

"Well," the woman sighed, "some people thought those two boys seemed awfully close. And, you know, that poor woman at the Spring Dance, somehow she hadn't realized her date was two men."

Marjorie tried for more, but sensed the woman was withdrawing as Marjorie pressed. They ended on a neutral note and when she turned again to the computer she saw language on the screen that might be interpreted as conveying discomfort. She flagged that message for possible follow-up at a later time.

Both men and women who reported some recollection of interactions with one or both men and the third list contained names of those who either had or had heard negative comments about either Martin or Trevor.

During the long afternoon she placed phone calls to a few of the women she felt might have something to share. Most of those calls were not very fruitful.

It was clear her queries had also touched some people who were resentful of being asked or had nothing to say, one way or the other. Her email In-box grew rapidly. Marjorie knew from activity lists for each man that some people were denying any useful knowledge, whether true or not. A couple of the messages were from relatives of the addressee, sadly illuminating damage from the passage of time.

It took her several intense hours to organize and pull the excerpts she felt might be relevant so lunch came and went unnoticed. She assumed, when she thought about it, their day attendant had managed to provide lunch for Lockem. Late in the afternoon she sat back from her keyboard feeling ready to report her preliminary findings.

CHAPTER 38

For the second time that afternoon, Marjorie waved a piece of typing paper in Lockem's face. "And this is the list of contacts that may be productive. I think the others are probably a waste of time."

Lockem nodded and stretched his arms overhead, bringing a slight twinge to his healing thigh and easing his lower back. "This is good work, my dear. Follow-up phone interviews are indicated and I can do some of that from my throne here."

"That will be much appreciated. Frankly, I'm a little discouraged with the information from the contacts I've already had. Other than two of the women I've talked to, it's been pretty non-productive, except for the growing list of possible contacts." Marjorie sighed. "It would help if somebody gave me a nugget of useful information. Maybe I should call the widow and just ask Melissa if she and Trevor Howland are getting together again!" She stopped abruptly, realizing she was raising her voice.

Lockem grinned knowingly. "Instead, why don't you take a break from college kids and call the mysterious Saint Paul cop, the one I talked to down at the station? See if he has any words of wisdom."

"Do you think he'll even talk to me? Your description was not very flattering."

"Try him. You never know." Another grin and he handed her a page he'd torn from a small tablet. The officer's number was scribbled across the paper.

Marjorie sketched a small salute with the hand holding the piece of paper and reached for the phone on Lockem's bedstand. The number rang once and was interrupted in the middle of the second ring.

"Yeah?"

"Inspector? My name is Marjorie. Marjorie Kane."

"So? You appear to be calling from a number associated with an investigator. One Alan Lockem?"

"That's correct, I—"

"You his secretary, right?"

"No, sir." Her voice became acerbic. "Mr. Lockem doesn't have a secretary. He does have a partner and that's me."

"Oh, the ex-stripper."

"Former dancer. Inspector, I want to ask you about some names. Anything you can give me about these people could be helpful."

"Dunno what I can tell you but go ahead and ask."

Carefully, pausing between each name to listen for the Inspector's possible reaction, she read the list of the known members of the motorcycle club. She wished she could have been looking at the Inspector's face to better judge his reaction. This was better than nothing, however. Inserted in the lists of motorcyclists, she had added three names, two were women the dead pastor had known in college and the third, his long-time buddy, Trevor Howland.

The unnamed police inspector asked her to spell the name of one of the women she'd included. Other than that, he had almost no verbal response except a terse goodbye.

"Well, that was –something." Marjorie replaced the phone on Lockem's bedside table. "I probably should have put him on speaker so you could hear him too."

"The speaker is so limited I doubt it would have helped. So, what's your read?" Lockem reached to the table and picked up the tall glass of water there.

"I thought his tone changed just slightly when I mentioned Trevor Howland. And he seemed to be getting impatient as the list went on. As if he wanted to be done after he heard all the useful information I had."

I'll play back the recording later and see if I can learn anything. I just wish we knew who that guy is and what he's doing there in relation to the murders."

Lockem scratched the edge of the dressing on his thigh. "That Saint Paul PD has an inspector assigned specifically to those motorcyclists tells us something, though. Doesn't it? There are a couple of possibilities.

192

One is that the Feds know about the group and for some reason, have an interest in following their activities."

"So, you think they may be doing bad things?"

"Bad federal things," Lockem nodded. "But the federal interest may be too tentative to open a case file so they asked the locals to take a look."

Marjorie shook her head. "I don't reject the idea, but it sure seems a stretch. A couple of possible bad actors, but most of them seem too young and unsophisticated."

He smiled. "I have the feeling your perceptions of young people may be a little dated. Who are your candidates?"

Marjorie got up and poured more coffee from the small thermal pot she'd brought from the kitchen. "If I have to choose candidates, I'm going with Obadiah and the Hamilton brothers. JJ and a couple of others are just too young for any serious lawbreaking."

"What about Kline?" asked Lockem. He's more mature than most of the others."

"He's interesting. They meet or congregate at Kline's, and he's obviously a mechanic who helps the cyclists with minor adjustments."

"Do we know anything about his background?"

"Mr. David Joel Kline is not a native Minnesotan. He moved to Saint Paul a few years ago, bought the house and installed his mother a year later. At least, I think that's his mother."

Lockem raised his eyebrows. "Interesting. Any reason to assume she isn't his mother?"

"Not really," Marjorie said. "But it's another possible avenue of inquiry."

"Just what we need," Lockem growled, "another avenue."

"My avenue of inquiry for the rest of the day is the other Ms. Cooper. I have a coffee date with the librarian, Edna Larson in about an hour. I'll drive to the library; park and we'll walk over to a little coffee shop near the lake."

"Sounds great," Lockem said. "Watch your back." They kissed and Marjorie drove to Uptown in Minneapolis. She parked near the library on Hennepin and found Edna Johnson waiting at the door.

Once seated in the café and ordering, Marjorie smiled at her companion and said, "I want to thank you again for agreeing to talk to me. This a very perplexing situation."

"I'm happy to talk with you, I'm just not sure what help I can be."

Marjorie nodded and fished a notebook out of her purse. Sipped her coffee which was excellent. "I know you had an interview with the Minneapolis police. And I know you had a relationship with Lorna Cooper. Tell me about that, please."

Mrs. Johnson smiled and shrugged, sipping her own cup of coffee. "I got to know Lorna Cooper about a year and a half ago. Perhaps even longer. She came in one evening and asked if we had any books on religious history. I directed her to our reference section and showed her our shelf of bibles and biblical reference materials. She was clearly disappointed a while later when we closed. I had to explain it was not possible for her to check out the reference texts and other materials."

"I expect that was because she had a day job and could only come to the library evenings or perhaps on weekends." Marjorie made a note.

"That's right. I never work on the weekends, but I did at one point ask one of the staff if Lorna Cooper ever came in on the weekends. Apparently she did not."

"Any reason given?"

Mrs. Johnson shook her head. "None that I know."

"And apparently in order to extend her time with the literature, she continued coming in the evenings?"

Mrs. Johnson nodded again. "Yes but there was no pattern I could see. She appeared early of an evening, went directly to the research cubical and stayed to closing. Usually three or four evenings a week."

Marjorie stared out the window toward the lake and then asked, "When did she start taking the books and other things out with her?"

"That was apparently in the last three weeks before we were notified she had died. You have to understand something. She always re-shelved the materials she was using. We checked, of course, and I told her she didn't need to do that. but Miss Cooper was very neat and careful. Now we realize she was concealing the fact that she was taking some Bibles and other materials home. She removed similar works from open shelves and placed them in the research section." She grimaced. "We've changed our policy so we have to check the shelves more frequently."

"Mrs. Johnson, do you have any idea why she stole those Bibles?"

Edna Johnson slowly shook her head. "Not the slightest. Only one of them was valuable and that was a gift from a local family. Its value is mostly to the family. We described it to a scholar and he estimated it might be worth a thousand dollars in the right sale, but it was undoubtedly more valuable to the family that donated it."

Marjorie scribbled furiously in her notebook. "Do you remember the name of the family that donated the Bible?"

Edna shook her head. "No, but I have a list of all the missing bibles and that one is on the list. The main library will have a list of donors as well so perhaps you can find out the name of the donor family."

The women finished their coffee and walked back to the library. Mrs. Johnson produced the list of missing bibles and Marjorie departed, wondering silently if there was a connection between the church and the missing bibles.

CHAPTER 39

Marjorie reported on her conversation with the librarian and gave Lockem the list of bibles and other documents Mrs. Johnson had provided. In the morning Lockem admitted his background in religious history and theology was probably deficient.

"I don't see anything on this list that suggests anything at all, except I probably don't want to read any of them." He grimaced and shifted his healing leg on the bed to a more comfortable position. "Standing briefly last night didn't result in any discomfort. I'm gonna try more maneuvering with my crutches today. I did have a thought about that list from the library.

"Glad your leg is improving. What about that list?"

"Take it to Ms Action. I won't be surprised if she can show you at least one or two bibles on that list."

Marjorie frowned.

Lockem smiled. "Maybe holding and looking at a book Ms. Cooper was interested in will suggest something helpful." He raised his eyebrows. She raised her eyebrows back at him.

Marjorie walked into the church office where Carolyn Action was sorting the mail and opening envelopes addressed to the deceased pastor Elliot. "Still getting mail for him?" she asked.

"Yep, our board wants me to sort out this stuff so they can get more folks involved. A temporary pastor is coming later this week.

Marjorie handed Carolyn the list of materials Delilah Cooper had apparently taken from the library in Minneapolis. Then she sat at the big office table, pulling the file from her copious briefcase. With the file a small folder of pictures came out. Marjorie had used various sources to collect portraits of those people involved in the case and made small prints. Ever since she had her smart phone broken by a suspect in a previous case when she showed him some pictures, she kept a separate file of pictures she thought might be important so she could protect her phone.

Carolyn returned with a large Bible she plopped on the table with a bang. "This is the only Bible we have that matches your list. The big Bible on the altar might match this one on the list, but it's too heavy to move. You can inspect it in the sanctuary." She looked down at the small folder of portraits.

"That's a nice snap of Delilah."

Marjorie glanced over. "No, I took that on my phone when we were talking to Lorna Cooper after the Pastor's funeral."

Carolyn shook her head. "I'm sorry. Except for the red hair, that looks exactly like Delilah." She stopped mouth slightly open. Stared at the picture. Marjorie looked at Carolyn, then at the picture and back to the head shot of the woman she knew as Lorna Cooper.

"Holy crap," Marjorie whispered. She grabbed her phone and called Lockem. He answered on the second buzz. "Alan, I just had a picture of Lorna Cooper identified as Delilah."

"What?" he shouted. Pause, then in a normal tone, "where are you? Who did it?"

"I'm at the church with Carolyn Action. She looked at the snap I took of Lorna at the restaurant after the Elliot funeral. She says the woman looks just like the dead woman, Delilah Cooper.

"Now there's a new element. Throws a lot of assumptions right out the window. My God!"

"I'll be home soon as I examine this bible. We can talk about it then." She severed the connection and turned a level gaze on Carolyn. "We need to talk about this." The women went over everything Carolyn knew about Delilah, which was little more than Lockem and Marjorie already had, until Marjorie was satisfied she knew everything Carolyn could tell her about the dead woman.

"I didn't get much more from Carolyn." Marjorie reported from the kitchen while she put together a quick light supper. Lockem eagerly awaited their discussion about the latest revelation concerning the Cooper women. Would this new development result in a major break in the case? They both hoped so.

"As far as we could determine, she only worked on three church projects. All were short term, like a weekend or a Saturday. They have no records, of course, how many times Delilah came to Sunday services. Never sang in the choir, so we really don't know if this was a planned deception or just a happening."

"Maybe we can set up an interview routine and talk to everybody who comes to services over the next whatever," Lockem mumbled over the food.

Marjorie looked at him. "You have any idea how long that would take and the cost?"

"I know. I know. Just thinking out loud. We have got to find out how those two Coopers are linked and what their target was."

"Is," corrected Marjorie. "We have no reason to assume the remaining Cooper will abandon their project. We do know Lorna Cooper is still in town, still working for that international marketing company."

"Do we know anybody who knows both women? It might be informative to talk with anyone who knows them both."

Marjorie squinted in thought. "Wasn't there an incident with the police at a bar? I seem to recall..." her voice trailed off. She turned to the file folder and began to rifle through the pages.

Lockem picked up his crutches and began a slow cautious maneuver down the hall toward the living room, the spaces he was using to regain his strength and mobility. Marjorie paused in her search to watch him go without comment.

Turning another page in the file she saw the copy of a police report. It related that one Lorna Cooper had been involved in a small altercation at a bar and her friend with the same last name, Delilah Cooper, came to the lockup and took her home. No charges had been filed so there was little useful information in the file. Two officers had initialed the report and Marjorie called to talk to the officer who had seen Lorna Cooper picked up by her friend.

"Did you notice anything about the friend who showed up to collect Lorna?"

"No," the woman said, after a pause. "They were impatient to get out of there. Not surprising. Oh, one of them called the other De."

"De. Maybe short for Delilah?"

"I guess. Except I have the impression it was the second woman who said it. Called the first woman De. But I could be mistaken. There were other people around, you know? Busy Friday night."

Marjorie agreed and then asked if the officer could describe the second woman, the one who came to collect Ms. Cooper.

"Not really. Casually dressed, loose jeans, tennies and a hoodie. Her face was sort of shadowed. But I do remember both women looked very similar. Build, what coloring I could see. They could have been sisters." Marjorie stared at the phone, thanked the officer, and sat down, her mind a wild turbulence of theories and possibilities.

"Alan?" She called.

"Shower," he bellowed back, having made his careful way up the short flight of stairs to their bedroom suite.

Marjorie smiled, went to the kitchen to pour cocktails, and put her thoughts in order.

CHAPTER 40

She heard Lockem coming down the stairs and went to watch him. He was seated on the steps, dragging his crutches beside him. Earlier in the week he'd tried to negotiate the stairs while standing on the crutches and had nearly fallen on his face. His home health aide had been close enough to grab him by the waist and keep him upright. Since, on the few times he tried stairs he navigated them on the seat of his pants.

Now he stood carefully on his good leg and set the crutches in his armpits. He smiled at his companion and took a few steps to stabilize his position. Then he looked over at Marjorie. "Something?" he said.

"Possibly. After Carolyn at the church miss-identified Delilah, I went back and found the police file on Lorna's detention for causing an incident at that bar on the East side. Remember that?"

Lockem nodded. He sat on his favorite chair and reached for the glass Marjorie held.

"A woman, we assume was Delilah, came to pick her up. I talked to the officer. She told me she couldn't identify the woman again but her impression was they were similar in build, and she's pretty sure she called the other woman De."

"De." You're telling me the woman taken in by the police, named Lorna Cooper in the file was called De by the woman who came to pick her up? As in short for Delilah?"

Marjorie nodded. "It's the only occasion *we* know the two of them were together in public. So suppose they are sisters, twins or look-alike cousins and play the switch game sometimes?"

"Something that started out as an innocent game may have morphed into something else, that's what you're thinking." Lockem's face revealed a variety of emotions.

"Exactly. For most of the time, I was sure the woman, Cooper, had been killed by mistake, collateral damage and we should concentrate on Elliot and his friends and family. Now, I'm changing my thinking."

"I'm with you there. I won't go so far as to believe Cooper was the real target, but there was definitely something going on with those two."

"So, I guess I better do some deeper background on Delila and Lorna," Marjorie smirked and wiggled her fingers, frantically typing on a mythical keyboard in front of her face.

"I have a suggestion," smiled Lockem. "Since I'm laid up, I'll do some deep diving using the computer. Why don't you do some deep interviews of people connected to the Cooper women's lives here in the Twin Cities?"

Frowning slightly, Marjorie agreed. "Well, okay. Shoot, I'd planned to spend the day in my sweats hanging here." She turned and went to her desk. She decided the deceased Cooper would be her target for the day. A call to XMR, the Saint Paul company where Delilah Cooper had worked as an executive, resulted in a reluctant afternoon appointment with a Mister Johnson.

When she reported to Lockem, his attention seemed tightly focused on the screen of his laptop. 'Yeah?"

"I have an appointment at Delilah's firm, XMR downtown."

He stopped typing and looked at Marjorie. "XMR. Huh. I don't think there was anybody from the firm at the service for her. In fact, the firm isn't even mentioned by name in the credits on the printed program. Odd."

"I'll say. Maybe I should ask when I meet Mister Johnson."

"Maybe you should." Lockem smiled and watched Marjorie head for their bedroom to get cleaned up and dressed for her appointment.

She was shown politely to a luxurious conference room on the fifteenth floor of the International Trade Building in downtown Saint Paul. One end of the room had a large window that provided a view of the east side of the downtown area toward the river. The other end of the room was an expensive panel of polished planks with a large monogram of the name of the company, XMR.

The receptionist had indicated to Marjorie there was hot coffee and tea on a sideboard. She sniffed the teapot and poured a small cup of Earl Grey. She sat across the table toward the end so she could view the doors to the room. A few minutes later a small fat man in a three-piece brown suit and a pale striped shirt bustled through the door and smiled at her.

"Ah, Ms Kane. A pleasure to make your acquaintance. Did Miss Maple validate your parking coupon?" He stepped to the table and thrust a meaty hand toward her. Marjorie stood and put out her own hand to grasp his fingers so he couldn't squeeze her fingers unnecessarily. I'm Arne Johnson. I was Ms. Cooper's superior. We were so sorry to lose her, an in such a violent and abrupt way. Has there been any progress finding the killer? We haven't had any word from the police in several days."

"I'm afraid you won't for some time. Law enforcement is almost always careful about what they can reveal during an ongoing investigation." She sipped her tea, watching him. "We feel the same way. It's important not to reveal too much for fear of alerting the perpetrator. I wonder, Mr. Johnson, if you can give me some background on Ms Cooper. Often, we can pick up helpful clues from background information."

Johnson nodded and opened the folder in front of him. "Yes, of course. We do want to cooperate with law enforcement. I'm afraid you may be disappointed. I wasn't with XMR when Ms Cooper was hired. Frankly, when I looked at her file, I learned it was pretty lean." He puffed out his cheeks and leaned back in the chair.

I think I'll have to chat with the chairman about modernizing our personnel records."

"I see you have a photograph. I wonder if I could have a copy," Marjorie asked?

"Yes, of course. I'll just have this scanned before you leave," he said.

"Can you tell me anything about her previous employment before she came to XMR? Oh and can you indulge me? What do the letters mean? Initials of the founder, perhaps?" She smiled and shrugged as if it was a purely casual question.

Johnson smiled. "As to the second question, I'm afraid I have no answer. Nobody seems to know if the letters stand for anything, so far as I can learn. XMR is pretty big and we have offices all over the world. Here." He handed Marjorie a glossy brochure. "We do private banking, you know, in addition to the information systems and certain financial services we offer.

"According to her file, Ms Cooper transferred here almost two years ago from our branch in Virginia. But I don't have any information on where she worked before that. She has a college degree, from MIT, and an accounting certificate from Wharton."

Johnson flipped some pages and frowned. "That's odd," he muttered. Then he looked up. "I'm afraid that's about it. The interviewer's page we use notes she came highly recommended and well thought of." He flipped the page around and placed it in front of Marjorie. She scanned it quickly, noting that the interviewer's name was missing. Only initials appeared in various places. She stared at several, committing them to memory as best she could.

Glancing up at the man across the table, she smiled, saying softly, "I don't suppose you could give me contact information for any of her clients, could you?"

"Oh, no," shaking his head vigorously. "We're very protective of our clients' privacy." He plucked the photograph of Delilah Cooper off the file and stood. "I'll just have this copied for you." He turned and started for the door. Then he stopped and turned back. With an apologetic glance, he picked up the file and went to the door. While she waited, Marjorie flipped a page in her notebook and tried to reproduce the initials she had seen on the interviewer's sheet. She glanced around the room, noting fixtures near the ceiling in several places that she thought might have been camera installations.

Arne Johnson reappeared in the doorway and handed her a computer copy of the photograph. She thanked him and slid the picture into her bag with her notebook. She and Arne exchanged insincere smiles and she exited sketching a small wave at the receptionist as she went by.

Chapter 41

Marjorie found her car in the ramp and took the freeway between the cities to drive promptly into the midway area of Saint Paul, near the new soccer stadium. She pulled off the freeway and parked across the street from the on ramp. She tapped an automatic keyed number.

Lockem answered immediately. "I have learned some background information that may illuminate things."

"Good. Tell. Then I'll tell what I've learned and why I'm going to Minneapolis instead of coming right home."

"Recorder is on," he said. "I think one or maybe both those Cooper ladies have had contact with either NSA or CIA. Maybe as contractors. I also had a call from a detective in the New York art theft unit. He suggested the church painting is a possible target of art thieves. He also told me to expect a call from somebody in the Italian art world."

"Fits," Marjorie nodded at the windshield. "Somehow I just knew that painting was going to be involved. We shall see. Now, XMR was pleasant, more accommodating than they might have been but basically not forthcoming. I did winkle a current HR picture of the woman they know as Delilah Cooper out of them. But I want to see if I can get into Worldwide for an informal interview before there's any deep communication with XMR."

"You think? I could call them, try to set it up."

"No," she said. "I'm making a cold call, seeking possible employment, don't you see."

"Got it. Good luck, stay safe and I'll see you later."

Marjorie closed the connection, reflecting that more obscure elements were unneeded at the moment. She drove back onto the west-bound freeway and went on to Minneapolis. She pulled into the parking lot of an electronics supply store two blocks off the freeway and bought a cheap flip phone. Sitting in her car she dumped some personal numbers into the memory and dropped it in her purse. Lastly she wrapped her regular phone in a plastic bag and placed it behind the spare tire. Then she drove into the commercial heart of the city and a commercial parking lot near International Specialties, employer of Lorna Cooper.

She parked beneath the office tower where the company had offices and sauntered into the main office on the fourth floor. "Excuse me, ma'am," to the lone woman. "I'm lookin' for the Personnel Office. Could you direct me?"

"Human Relations? Of course. They're one flight up, directly overhead," smiled the nice-looking young woman at the desk.

Up one flight Marjorie found a utilitarian Human Relations office with three unlabeled doors behind a lone desk and chair. She sensed an atmosphere of impermanence. The office was spare and devoid of decoration. She explained to another young woman at the desk that she was looking for employment, didn't have an appointment but would appreciate it if she could fill out an application.

The woman nodded and directed her to a table in the corner that held a laptop computer. The screen showed an application. Marjorie filled out the forms, being meticulous to put something in every box and on every line. Some of the information she inserted was the truth. She discovered the computer didn't allow her to switch to any other documents. She had decided before arriving that she would indicate she had been a chorus girl in Las Vegas but would avoid mentioning her headlining roles. The application was comprehensive and allowed her to demonstrate basic familiarity with computer skills. During her time at the computer she managed to open and lay out on the table, some of the materials from her purse.

When she asked to use the restroom, Marjorie left the materials from her purse at the terminal. When

206

she returned she saw immediately that the small pile of personal contents had been disturbed. The color picture of Delilah, now upside down, lay under the burner phone. She shoved everything back into her purse and finished the online application.

"Thanks for that," she said. I hope I get an interview soon."

"You're in luck, Ms Kane," the woman at the desk smiled at her. Our Personnel director is willing to see you in just a few minutes if you care to wait."

"Absolutely," in a delighted tone, Marjorie agreed. "Thank you so much." She sat down again in a hard chair, wondering if the picture of a dead woman had triggered the unusual access. Five minutes later, a chime sounded at the desk, a door lock clicked and the woman directed Marjorie into a short hallway where a second woman stood beside an office door a few yards away. Approaching the only door on the dim and narrow corridor, she wondered why the hall door had been locked. A woman appeared at the door, smiled and beckoned. Marjorie walked toward her and smiled as well.

"Right this way." The woman, Marjorie guessed, was about forty or forty-five years old, stood erect on short heels and dressed in a dark well-cut business suit over a cream-colored blouse. A pin that might have been diamonds adorned her left lapel. She gestured Marjorie to a casual chair beside her desk. "Ellen Huss," she said tersely.

Marjorie gently clasped the offered hand. "I'm Marjorie Kane. Thank you for seeing me so promptly." She sat in the indicated chair and neatly crossed her ankles.

Huss sat and peered at the computer screen on her desk. "It's quite unusual, but frankly, I was intrigued by your background. I see you were a chorus girl in Las Vegas."

"Yes. I'm still a pretty good dancer and it turned out to be a fun couple of years. Traveling overseas was interesting and some of the big metropolitan venues

207

were—interesting. But, you know, there's no real future in it, unless you hook up with a wealthy guy who's unmarried." She shrugged. "I wasn't interested."

Huss nodded once and said, "I assume your chorus work gave you some social skills, mingling with the crowd, giving the club a positive reputation, and you do have a variety of typical office skills. This division of the company is growing and looking for someone who can handle basic computing and work with the public from time to time. How did you happen to appear here? I'm not aware of any personnel job or career promotions from the company just yet."

"No, I was in the area and I've been applying at various companies. Yes, I know about job centers and state services. I just prefer to try on my own and follow private contacts." Marjorie sketched a brief twitch of her lips that might have been a smile. She knew that the combination of that remark and the picture she carried of a known employee might send tremors through some offices. How strong the tremors, which offices, and what the results might be were the unknowns. She'd made a contact, however tenuous.

After a few more casual questions and comments, the Huss woman stood and said, "You have a solid resume and if we develop a need in the next few weeks, I'll probably give you a call."

Together with the pro forma smile, Marjorie was shown the door.

She left the office and walked sedately toward the elevator. A tall younger man—most of the men she encountered these days were younger—in a well-fitting dark blue suit appeared from a door across the corridor as she passed. She thought his assessing glance was a tad longer than it should have been. They rode together in the elevator to the ground floor where the man left the cage after another quick glance in her direction.

Marjorie continued in the elevator to the below-ground parking area and then walked back up to street level and to her car. Several visual scans of the area didn't reveal anything untoward. She entered her car and drove home.

Chapter 42

"Here's what I think," Marjorie said, concluding her report to Alan. She looked him in the face, carefully. He was used to her often-penetrating scrutiny. "Lorna and Delilah worked together doing some kind of deal. Scam? Not sure. But the people at Worldwide were quickly interested after they saw the picture of Delila, the picture I so cleverly left exposed from my purse while I visited their restroom."

"Why do you suppose it's called a "rest room," Alan muttered. Marjorie could tell he was paying attention and at the same time curious about a minor oddity.

"You men wouldn't understand, I suppose. Sometimes called retiring rooms, a hundred years ago, women didn't use public toilets. At all. So comfortable chairs or lounges were installed in suites to help entice women to department stores."

Alan nodded. "Moving on, you now think the two women were engaged in possibly illegal activity associated with that painting. I agree with you. Let me propose a scenario. I've been thinking about this mostly all day.

"The two Cooper women came to the cities to examine and possibly steal or otherwise acquire that painting at the church. They followed a trail from the sales history and research in various texts, in this case Bibles, until they discovered the location of the painting. If they were still alive, I bet the original owners of the painting, the couple who donated it, could tell us more of its history."

"Okay, and now the two women are here, working, exploring the landscape, possibly working out how to acquire the painting." Marjorie scratched her nose. "Okay, that works. If Delilah was not the target, was the pastor killed to somehow make the painting more accessible. Humm. Seems far-fetched."

"It does," Alan agreed. "Suppose the pastor was the primary target and Delilah was collateral?" He stopped and watched Marjorie carefully. After a moment he could almost see her rearranging facts and questions in her mind.

"Oh. That's an interesting idea. That would mean the killer of the pastor encountered Delilah and murdered her to avoid detection, after he shot the pastor." She nodded, looking thoughtful. "Okay, and that scruffy band of cyclists is involved in some way we haven't yet unearthed."

"If the women came here focused on the painting, their employment must somehow be linked." Alan scratched his messy hair.

"That could mean the two companies are linked. I didn't see anything,' said Marjorie. "Wasn't looking for it. And World Wide has been here for at least five or perhaps six years. But I have profiles of both companies on my computer. I'll run some comparisons after dinner."

And so she did. Sometime later, while Alan stared at the news program on the small TV, Marjorie came to his bedside with a single sheet of paper, what looked like a stats worksheet. It had two vertical columns one labeled XMR the other World-Wide. Down the left side were a series of partial words, indicating a lot of the usual corporate intel, such as incorporation date and places, branch locations, numbers of employees and similar stuff.

Allan took the offered sheet of paper and scanned it, nodding. "Very comprehensive. Learn anything that might help us?

"I'm not sure, but there is one intriguing fact. Trevor Howland worked for an XMR satellite office during and right after Pastor Elliot graduated from Divinity school."

Alan's eyebrows shot up. "What? Really?"

"There's more. A man on the maintenance crew at XMR in Saint Paul is named David Klein." Marjorie smiled with satisfaction.

"Connections. Connections! Threads to follow. Good work, my love."

"You looked at those pictures I snapped of the guys at the garage, right?"

"Yes," Alan nodded. "I made digital copies and sent them to the FBI and the PD. I don't expect anything soon from the FBI, but it's been a couple of days and nothing from the locals. I better make a follow-up call." He turned to the phone on his table and looked at the small clock beside it. "Probably too late to call today." The telephone chimed and he picked up the instrument.

The voice he heard was not only distorted, but it also seemed to be cutting in and out, the way mobile phones used to do all the time in the early era of mobiles. "I'm sorry, I can barely hear you and the signal is terribly distorted. Repeat, please?" He glanced at Marjorie who reached for her phone to hitchhike on the call. Alan shook his head, afraid of degrading the signal further.

"Please speak louder and slower." He realized the caller was not a natural English speaker. She refused to give a name or her location, but Alan began to understand the woman was Italian and probably did not want to be discovered at her end of the connection. He grabbed a pen and tablet and made notes, nodding, occasionally grunting. After several minutes, the connection was terminated and Alan set his phone down, rubbed his ear and smiled.

"Well, that was interesting. Best I can make it out, she is an art curator in some city in southern Italy. That art theft detective I talked to asked her to contact me. She knew of the sale of a certain painting to an American couple many years ago. She was obviously referring to Sins of Odom, the painting hanging at the church." He stopped and took a drink from his water glass. Then he continued.

"She called with a warning. International art thieves have hired two young women *duo sorelle gemelle,* she said several times, to find and steal the

212

painting for a client. Apparently, according to my New York source, there is a kind of network of different groups that steal on contract. Inerestingly, in the case of already stolen art, the same people have been helpful in efforts to retrieve stolen art to return it to rightful owners."

"I've read about that," Marjorie said. "I read a book about a big heist at a Boston gallery years ago. Most of that art has never been found, apparently. Sorelle gemelle, she muttered and rapidly tapped the screen of her phone. "Here it is. It's Italian for twin sisters."

"Aha." Alan smiled. "Out of the blue, a warning. I wonder why. What that confirms for us is that the Cooper cousins, not sisters but nearly identical even so, are here with a specific target. We don't have actionable proof, and Delilah's death may upset their plans, but we can at least alert the authorities."

"And this could explain the theft of the Bibles and other texts from the library. One of those women wanted to do some research, probably to be sure as they could they were looking at the right painting. She may have been afraid of exposure if she spent too much time at the library." A look of satisfaction crossed Marjorie's face and she licked her lips. "I wonder if the local riders are or were somehow involved with the Cooper girls."

Alan yawned and swung his injured leg around with a grimace so he could rearrange the blanket and sheet and settle down for the evening. Marjorie leaned in to give him a kiss and then went off to her lonely bed.

Chapter 43

It was three AM in a dark moonless night when Marjorie's bedside phone chimed. She awoke, reached for an absent Alan, cursed under her breath and fumbled for the phone.

"Yes?" Her tone was sharper than she usually allowed. She took a breath and said, "sorry, I'm not quite awake. Who is this?"

No response, other than a faint breath or sigh.

"C'mon. You called me, unless this is a mistake," she murmured.

"How's Lockem doing?" The question and the scratchy, distorted voice in her ear surprised her. Traveling days long gone she was not used to imperfect overseas telephone calls.

"Who is this? What do you want? Why are you calling at this hour?" She spoke rapidly in a normal tone. No response, but listening carefully she sensed or heard rhythms of a live human.

After several seconds of relative silence, there came a rustle and a low voice said, "I need to talk to you." Some of the distortion had apparently been removed.

"All right. You want to come here in the morning?"

"No. That's too exposed for me." Not unexpected.

"All right. What's this about? Where do you want to meet?"

"Be at Peterson's Coffee Place on Payne Avenue at ten. Take one of the booths on the south wall and sit facing the street. The main entrance. Ten A.M. It's important to your case." Whoever was calling clicked off and the connection died.

Marjorie dropped the instrument on the bed beside her. Grabbed a pen to scribble a note. Then she remembered that all incoming calls were automatically rcorded,whether answered or not. She replaced the pen, switched off the light and fell back in bed witb a soft explitive.

Morning came too soon and she was up working in the kitchen when she heard the rattle of a crutch against the door jam and Alan poked his head through. "Hey," she said, "you're mobile."

"Just," he growled. "Took near an hour to get outa bed, to the bathroom and then five steps to the kitchen door." Slowly he maneuvered himself across the room to stand beside the kitchen table. He stood on his good foot, slid a chair out and sank down, letting go of his crutches which clattered to the tile floor. His encased leg stuck out in front of him. He slowly lowered it to rest his heel on the floor.

"Good to see you up and around," Marjorie smiled at him and slid a plate of bacon and two fried eggs to the table in front of him. "We had a call early this morning. Some unnamed male caller asked how you were doing."

"Huh," Alan snorted. "Anybody calling in the middle of the night can't be offering good thoughts."

"He wants to see me. To talk, he said."

"I'll bet he won't come here, will he."

Marjorie shook her head again. "No he asked me to meet him at ten this morning at a coffee shop over on Payne Avenue. Peterson's?"

"I've never heard of it. Did you look it up?"

"Yep. They have a web site with their menu and a picture of the front of the building. I think I'll go."

Alan frowned, opened his mouth to protest and closed it again. He knew Marjorie was not likely to go precipiously and blindly into a dangerous situation. "It could be a really dangerous situation," he finally said.

She looked at him with a neutral expresssion.

"Yes, yes, you know that. Wear your pistol," he said. She nodded in response.

Their landline phone rang. She picked up the instrument. "Hello. This is Marjorie Kane."

"When you get to Peterson's ask for the second booth on the south wall. Sit facing the front door and be sure you are alone."

Marjorie twisted her mouth when the call abruptly ended. "Guy just gave me specific directions on where to sit." She repeated the caller's words. "I may have heard his voice before. Met him, maybe."

"Dangerous situation, I still don't like it," Alan frowned again.

She checked her watch and reached to pat Alan's hand. "I'll be fine," she said. "And very careful. Why would anybody want to harm me?"

"Because you are about to expose something or someone?"

"I just think this is about giving up something or exposing someone, not attacking us. I've had that feeling from the first call."

"Instincts," Lockem growled with a half-smile.

***

Half an hour later she was dressed and ready to leave, her Pico snugly secured to her waist under a loose caftan. It was sunny and warm enough she didn't need a coat. She smiled at Alan and went to the garage, secure in knowing he'd been on the phone probably arranging a security escort to be at the coffee shop.

She arrived fifteen minutes early, parked on the street just up the block and entered the pleasant-appearing shop. The tables were about half filled with the loudest conversation coming from a crowded table of oldsters. She recognized two former legislators among the group. One she knew had been a regular patron of a Minneapolis gentleman's club where she had headlined many years ago.

One of the booths in the designated area was empty and she slid into the wide faded red naugahyde booth seat. The seats had high padded backs, topped with a shiny aluminum strip securing the fabric.

Marjorie slid to the wall happy that her holstered pistol was on her right side, protected against unintentional exposure by the building wall. Then she decided to protect herself more by not leaving the left seat open. She slid back to the left side of the bench.

A waitress approached with a big white earthenware mug which she clunked on the table. "Coffee?" she asked.

"Thanks. Black, please. An acquaintence is joining me in a few."

The woman nodded as if she was aware and said, "Blossoms are really good today."

Marjorie, with no clue as to the waitress's meaning said, "Sure, thanks." Moments later she returned with a steaming coffee server and a plate displaying a baked pastry roll cleverly shaped like a flower bloom. It seemed apparent that one was expected to eat the cinnimon-flavored roll with one's fingers. Marjorie tore off a piece of the pastry and placed it on her tongue. The crispy bit immediately dissolved in intense sugary taste. She took a sip of strong excellent coffee and reached for another piece of pastry.

There was a clunk of another mug landing on the table and the booth seemed to shift slightly as a figure in a dark closed hoodie slid into the seat across from her. She raised her head slightly, eyes on her fingers removing a whole leaf from the pastry. She smoothly placed the leaf between her lips and chewed slowly, letting the intense sweetness infiltrate her taste buds.

"You should try a blossom," she said. "They are wonderful."

"I have," he growled.

The voice cemented her belief that the figure across the table was David Klein. "So, why did you want to see me?" She decided not to reveal she knew her companion.

"Your investigation is messing with mine. I need you to stop."

"Suppose I told you we don't have a conflicting investigation of you., or your biker gang."

Klein sighed. "Okay, so you recognize me. Look, I'm undercover and we are getting really close to a major bust. I can't have you messing about with these people right now."

Marjorie smiled gently at David. "Do you have any indications that any of them are involved with the murder of the pastor?"

Klein sighed and shook his head. "No, none. All of the active members can be accounted for. Look, I know you took pictures when you came to the house." He gestured at her. "Can I see them?"

Marjorie knew that undedrcover officers often felt threatened by cameras. Inadvertent snapshots had resulted in exposure of more than one officer. "Somebody saw me using my camera phone from my car?"

"Yeah," he said.

She slipped her phone from her bag and opened the digital album. Klein thumbed quickly through the pictures to verify her assertion that the only image of him was a rear shot where he still leaned over the engine compartment of the old truck.

"Do you know who was driving the truck that tried to murder Alan Lockem?" Her tone had sharpened and she leaned forward.

"No, I don't. The hood shook. I can account for most of the members that morning, but none of them are experienced enough to try that trick."

"Except you."

"Yeah, but it wasn't me."

"I'm almost inclined to believe you," Marjorie growled. "You say you're a cop. Maybe a fed. I don't see any ID."

"Look, none of this group has any interest or involvement in those killings. None of us tried to run your guy off the road. That's it. You just have to trust me and stay the hell away. I'm too close to wrapping this thing up."

"And what thing is that?" Marjorie asked sweetly.

An exasperated grunt came from the hood across the table. "Look, I can get you run off this whole thing if I have to."

"Threats now?"

"No, a promise."

Marjorie relaxed her shoulders and nodded, blank faced. She had been persuaded the guy was real. "Okay. We'll back off, at least for now. But here's a gentle warning: if we find something that directly pings one of those guys, we'll be back in your face."

"Thanks." Hoodie nodded, slid out of the seat, leaving his mug of coffee untouched and disappeared into the kitchen, presumably to the rear door.

Marjorie drank her coffee, thought back over the conversation and dropped money on the table. Then she too slipped out of the naugahyde seat, waved at the waitress and exited the coffee shop.

Chapter 44

"I called Saint Paul PD while you were out," Alan greeted Marjorie with a substantial hug when she entered the house. "I actually talked to that inspector I encountered earlier, remember him?"

"Yes, Mr. Unforthcoming."

"Right. He was actually forthcoming. Sorta. He agreed the biker group is being watched and might have been infiltrated."

"So, we can pretty well rule Mr. Klein out of suspicion for the murder attempt on your life." Marjorie was seated at her desk. She glanced at Alan, now dressed, while he stomped around on his crutches. She felt a certain pride and amazement at how rapidly Alan was recuperating from his injury.

"Do you feel secure?" he asked abruptly. "Here?"

"Yes. Of course. Why do you ask?" She frowned up at him.

"Nothing specific. It's from my service days. We got in the habit from time to time during action-absent times of checking ourselves so we didn't lose our alertness." He shrugged and grinned.

She grinned back, shaking her head.

"Now, we've effectively eliminated the cycle gang from the murders, along with the murdered Cooper woman."

"Unless there were two guns, two killers," said Marjorie, staring at her computer screen.

"Wait. What?" exclaimed Alan, spinning back toward her on his good leg.

"I've been thinking, always dangerous, right?. Suppose there were two shooters?"

Alan shook his head. Then turned his laser stare on her, another technique he'd learned and developed in the Army. "I've never once questioned the police interpretation of the crime scene." He stopped. "We haven't seen anything about the weapons, have we?"

"There is that," Marjorie agreed. "Try this. That bullet hole high up in the organ pipe bothers me. Suppose Delilah Cooper shoots Pastor Elliot, then gets shot by another person who can't afford to be seen there and in dying, fires an errant bullet into the pipes?"

Lockem considered her question for several seconds, playing back scenarios in his mind. "Huh. Kill the pastor, discover a third party who is a better shot, shoot the ceiling and die. But what's that other shooter doing at the church?"

"Searching for something relating to the painting? Trying to eliminate Pastor Elliot?"

"Seems far-fetched. Maybe it was an errant shot by the same person who killed both the Pastor and Delilah."

Marjorie shrugged and smiled. She and Lockem often played at odds when knotty questions about sequences or motivations arose. They enjoyed their debates and often discovered the truth resting at the edges of their discussions. But this puzzle seemed more intricate and darker than most they had encountered.

Silence ensued as the partners considered the elements of the case from their individual positions. Lockem then raised another question. "We haven't really examined motive, have we?"

"No, and in fact, I don't think we have a motive, or motives to examine. Do we?"

She knew the answer and so did he. "One of the problems," Lockem muttered. "There are multiple possibilities. We are pretty sure the Coopers came looking for that damn painting."

"True, Marjorie said, "but we can't prove it—yet."

"We now also know that at least some members of the motorcyclists are involved in something illegal. Possibly drug smuggling?" Lockem frowned at the wall.

"I think we may now have some suspicions that there are connections between the widow Elliot and

221

Mr. Trevor Howland." Marjorie paged swiftly through her file notes on her computer. "I still have to review and enter some of my notes on Howland, but I see a pattern."

"Trevor Howland," said Lockem, "He's the guy who showed up when we were making our condolence call to the widow, right? Do you suppose he's connected to the drug smuggling?"

"My impression is no," said Marjorie. "I think he's been a little or a lot jealous of Elliot since their high school days. I will not be surprised to learn he thought Melissa should have been his wife."

Lockem raised his eyebrows. "Do you think he's jealous enough to have committed murder?"

"Killing the pastor? I—gosh, that would mean he also killed Delilah. I think that's a bridge too far."

"While you were off chatting with your undercover pal, we had a visitor, sort of. A motorcycle rider drove into the cul de sac. He—I assume it was a he from what I could see of him—stopped on the west side and looked us over. It was only for a few seconds because the security van appeared and he cycled off. Or motored off."

"Let's suppose," said Marjorie. "Suppose the Coopers came here on the trail of that painting. They encounter a fraught situation in which the pastor, Michael Elliot is under attack from his old high school buddy, Trevor Howland. Maybe he, Elliot, doesn't know Howland's motive. Maybe Melissa does."

"Hell," interposed Lockem, "maybe she and Howland are already having an affair."

"Possible but I don't think so," said Marjorie. I think her obvious attraction to Trevor really began to show after her husband was killed. I agree, I suspect if we looked deep enough we'd find evidence of an attraction going back several years."

"You saw that attraction recently," said Lockem.

"I watched her reaction when he showed up the day we were their house. And I noted her reactions when I interviewed her. Until now, she might not even be aware she's sending signals. If she is."

"Can we use that somehow?"

"It might open a crack in her defenses, but I don't have a sense that she feels guilty—about anything. I doubt Melissa had as much interest in socializing with the motorcycle group as her husband, but I'll bet Howland is playing on her bereavement."

"That might be a way in."

Marjorie said, "Yes, but I'm not at all persuaded she had anything to do with the murders except as a bystander. Think about it. She didn't know either Delilah or Lorna. She seems to have little to no interest in the painting. I asked her if she recalled it, and unless she's a really good actress, it looked to me like a dead end."

"What more do we know about Mr. Howland?"

"Ah, well, we have a pretty good background file until we get to the Elliot's move to the Twin Cities. Education. We know he shadowed Elliot around the Midwest until Elliot went to a church on the East Coast."

"Do you think we need to contact that church?" Lockem asked.

"Probably not. At that time, Howland was employed by an employment company that was absorbed into a larger company." She paused.

"And," he prodded.

"The larger company is named Worldwide—"

"No shit!" Lockem exclaimed. "The circle tightens. Or it's just another coincidence? I'm wondering if the killer was aiming to murder Elliot because he wanted access to Melissa Elliot and Cooper was unfortunate collateral."

"Coming back full circle, aren't we? That's where we were at the edge of this swamp. Let me ask you something."

"Of course," said Lockem.

"When you went to Delilah Cooper's apartment you discovered empty shelves, right? And we assume

223

she'd been storing stolen Bibles and other research materials in those spaces. And we talked to that Librarian about her interactions with Ms. Cooper. But has she seen a picture of the real Delilah? Or the real Lorna? Do we know who did the actual research?"

"We don't, Lockem admitted, shaking his head. I'm not sure if it matters,"

"True," Marjorie agreed, "Unless Lorna Cooper was the shooter." She smiled at the look that passed over Lockem's face. "Maybe a mistake, maybe deliberate."

Lockem tilted his head back. After several seconds of silence he said, "That could work. The women came to Minnesota to look into the painting. For reasons unknown, they split and one saw the opportunity to eliminate her cousin, not realizing the pastor was in the robing room. Cousin A hears or sees Cousin B coming with a pistol, pulls her own, gets shot and while falling shoots the organ pipe. Reverend Elliot rushes to the door and is shot by Cousin B who then departs the scene."

"That works," Marjorie agreed softly. "That certainly works."

CHAPTER 45

"The medical exam found no evidence that the dead woman had recently handled a weapon." Alan set down the copy of the medical report on Delilah Cooper. He picked up a second report, the medical officer's finding on Pastor Elliot. "There were no weapons found at the scene and Mr. Elliot hadn't recently held a weapon, either. So it could have happened the way you suggested except that the third person, the killer, took away a weapon he found on Delilah."

"Why would he—or she—take the weapon?"

"Dunno." Lockem shook his head. "Maybe just to confuse us. Do Saint Paul police have any evidence of a third person at the scene? Maybe I have to pull in some favors. I'll call my FBI contact and see if he can help."

"Before you do that, call that Saint Paul officer in charge of the case. Direct contact might be better in this case."

Lockem smiled and reached for the phone. Listening to Lockem's side, Marjorie thought the call went pretty much as expected. But then in mid-sentence, Lockem stopped and frowned. "What's—" then he shrugged, frowned more deeply, and terminated the call.

"Something happen?" Marjorie asked.

"Apparently. You heard me ask him about the church and he started to answer then I heard a shout in the background and he hung up." He grabbed the phone and dialed the number. After several rings it went to voice mail.

"I'll call him again later. Now, I think we can assume Trevor Howland has been pursuing Elliot or his wife for several years."

Marjorie nodded. "Yes, you just put into words something I've felt since we first met her at their home after the funeral. Remember? Howland was there and seemed to me to be quite comfortable, almost at home, as it were."

"An affair with Melissa?"

Marjorie shook her head. "Not then. My impression is she was grateful for his support at that terrible time. Close, but not intimate."

The phone on Lockem's bedside table buzzed. He leaned over and plucked the instrument off its cradle. "The is Alan Lockem."

"Lieutenant Gage here, Roseville Police."

Lockem responded to the crisp, official tone. "Yessir. How can I help?"

"Our Intelligence Officer asked me to reach out to you." Lockem knew Roseville wasn't large enough to have an independent intelligence office, so it was a signal that he, Gage, was not alone.

"You have been watching that motorcycle group from Saint Paul. There's been a break in that case. The FBI and DEA have been tracking drug running and our undercover was blown yesterday. Some of the gang are being chased through southern Minnesota but there's a standoff with a SWAT team at a home on the hill. We thought Marjorie might be able to help with negotiations because one of the group mentioned her name."

A flush of perspiration rose in a tidal wave through Lockem's body. Negotiations between police and hostage-takers were never entirely safe and the emotional toll on participants sometimes lasted a long time, regardless of the outcome. Now the authorities were asking for Marjorie's presence and possible assistance. A comfortable afternoon had suddenly turned.

Lockem took the phone away from his head and looked at Marjorie. He explained the situation and request in a few short sentences, ending with "You can refuse, you know."

"Of course, I'll go. How?"

"Lieutenant?" questioned Lockem.

"A squad will there in a few minutes. Thanks."

Marjorie nodded and raced to change to a comfortable pair of shoes. When she returned to Lockem, the doorbell rang and they saw the outline of a uniformed officer through the glass of the front door. Marjorie grabbed her coat, gave Alan a quick kiss on the cheek and ran to the door.

"Be safe," he called and the door slammed behind her. Almost immediately the siren sounded and grew faint. Lockem let out a huge puff of air and lay back on his bed.

Five minutes went by while Lockem stared at the ceiling in his room. His telephone chimed. Lockem rolled to his side, winced at the twinge in his injured thigh and glared at the readout. He didn't recognize the number and hesitated to answer the call. After the fifth chime he reluctantly opened the channel.

"I would have called again, and again until you picked up," came the voice Lockem recognized. Lieutenant Gage.

"Thanks. What can you tell me now?"

"I've stepped into the bathroom here. Two of the gang are on the run somewhere in the southeast. As I told you earlier, J.J. and somebody we don't know, probably their drug contact from the border are likely in the house. There are at least two women in the house, the older one with a rifle or shotgun. All the rest of them, including our undercover, David Kline, are apparently barricaded in different rooms. We don't know who's armed and who's on which side."

"Who asked for Marjorie?"

"We think it was Kline, but nobody knows for sure. The plan was to get an officer into the front door with a warrant for a different address. But she was recognized by one of them. She saw a lot of weapons just lying around. Then one of them named her and reached for a weapon. She bolted and was only grazed by the shot."

"So, now I suppose it's a standoff, because Kline is in the house."

"Yeah, Kline and the unknown girl and maybe a baby," said Gage.

"How soon will Marjorie get to the house?" Lockem looked at his hand resting on his thigh. No movement. Good, but inside, in his gut, it was much different. He knew there was a chance Marjorie could become more entangled in the situation than just talking by phone to somebody inside the house. That was more likely because David Klein, an undercover federal agent, had asked for her.

"Have the people in the house asked for anything?"

"Apparently not. They just said to stay out or they'll blow up the place with everybody in it."

"Great."

Gage sighed.

"How many people are inside?" asked Lockem.

"We're not sure, but there are at least three of the motorcyclists, two women and a baby. There may be another female but that could have been a repeat sighting."

"Is there a plan?"

Gage grunted something unintelligible. Then he said, "I haven't tried to insert myself in the active business with Saint Paul PD. They'll tell me eventually whatever they want me to know. What I do know is it's a stalemate right now and they're hoping Marjorie can resolve things peacefully. I expect the commander at the scene is a bit unhappy with Marjorie being there. I know I would be, even knowing her. If it were me, I'd prefer to use a known, experienced negotiator."

"I appreciate that," Lockem responded, not reassured.

"I'm gonna try to persuade our chief to talk to Saint Paul to get them to put you in the loop as long as Marjorie's involved. Your background might be useful."

"Thanks, I'll hope for a call soon." What he didn't tell Gage was that Marjorie had taken a cheap

228

cell phone with her. They could possibly communicate privately should it become desirable.

CHAPTER 46

Alan shifted his weight off the hip on his injured side and swore at the sharp brief pain that lanced through him. He reached and pulled the extension phone instrument for the landline onto the bed beside him. He eased back against the mounded pillows at the head of the bed and sighed noisily. In southeast Asia he'd frequently sent agents and small squads of reconnaissance fighters into dangerous circumstances on scouting missions. It had always been a time of tension and worry until the men returned, something he'd always been able to force to a private place in his mind during the operation.

Now those emotions flooded back in his concern for Marjorie. He knew, practically, that she faced little or no danger. There was no conceivable scenario in which the local PD would put her in any danger at all but worry still intruded. And he knew Marjorie. Hostage situations could be volatile and she...

"What's the situation?" Marjorie asked from the rear seat of the squad. The patrol officers glanced at each other.

"We really don't know, ma'am," said the female officer looking back at her. "We just got urgently routed to pick you up and take you to an address in the city."

Marjorie frowned, the siren and flashing lights slightly distracting her. It was apparent she had more current information than her escorts. She sat back and tried to relax while the driver expertly worked the squad through neighborhood traffic to a main artery and onto the freeway. In what she would recall later as taking only seconds, but was actually almost fifteen minutes, the squad pulled up beside another police vehicle in the middle of the street, just a car length beyond the intersection where she had parked to observe the activity at the group's home a week earlier.

Several patrol cars, lights flashing, filled the street in front of the target house. In front of her stood a dark blue vehicle resembling a recreational vehicle. It appeared more substantial with smaller windows.

The Roseville officer opened the rear door of the squad and Marjorie stepped out almost directly into the arms of a large man in civilian dress and wearing a protective ballistic vest with a big semi-automatic pistol strapped in a holster outside his jacket.

"Ms Kane." His voice told her this was the officer she had spoken to on the phone days earlier. "We have a seat for you in the com van."

"Thank you, Officer..."

"Colonel," he corrected her firmly, his body movements pushing her toward the door to the long vehicle.

Three uniforms nodded to her when she entered the van and then promptly returned to their tasks. One was scanning a bank of three small color monitors being fed by cameras focused on the house from separate directions. One had a medium shot of the same upstairs window where Marjorie saw movement of the curtain when she was there previously. The other two had different angle views of the front door. She sat in a comfortable chair at a small desk with a telephone attached to the writing surface.

The colonel in plain clothes who'd met her at the car sat beside her on a stool he fished out from a recess below the window. "We're going to try to establish a phone link so you can talk to the man who asked for you."

"Who is that? And who's in the house?"

He held up one hand to interrupt her questions. "Normally, involving a civilian in situations like this is never done. Normally. But one of the men inside, perhaps the undercover officer, insisted your presence could help defuse things."

"We don't know for sure who is inside. One of the officers saw or thinks he saw a young boy peeking from that upstairs window when we arrived. He pointed at the same front window where she'd seen the curtains move when she'd been there before. He blew out a gust of breath in what sounded like a high level of frustration.

"All right, I'm here," Marjorie said in a low firm voice. "What do you want me to do?"

"Talk to the man in the house. The one who asked for you." He pointed at the instrument on the table. "Don't agree to anything. Just try to find a way to defuse the situation."

She picked up the telephone hand piece, looked over at the officer sitting at a console of lights and switches and small wave monitors. She nodded. The officer's fingers flashed over the keyboard and connected the line.

Marjorie heard the ring in her ear. After three rings, like an old-fashioned dial phone, somebody picked up.

"Yeah?

She thought she recognized the voice. "Hoodie?"

Long pause and for a moment she thought she'd lost him. "It's Marjorie. Marjorie Kane." She'd never been in this kind of situation before and she didn't know what to say.

"Are you alone?"

"No. Of course not."

"Where you at?"

"I'm in the police van, parked in the street just down the block."

"Just follow your instincts," whispered the policeman beside her. "Be a mother."

Marjorie rolled her eyes. Mother was a label she'd never wanted and never had been.

"Joel?" she spoke softly into the mouthpiece. "Or is this David?"

Big sigh in her ear. "Okay, you got me. "Obi— Obadiah is here in the house but I don't think he wants to talk to you. Not right now."

232

She heard a click and a dial tone. "He hung up on me." She frowned.

"That's okay. He didn't sound angry." The colonel unhooked an earpiece. The com officer nodded and smiled at Marjorie.

"Sometimes it takes a while to establish real communication," she murmured. "Like some coffee?"

"A diet Seven-up or something similar would be better," Marjorie flicked a quick smile back at the woman and pulled out a handkerchief to wipe the moisture from the phone. A trickle of sweat ran down the back of her ear. "I don't think I'm cut out to be a negotiator in situations like this." She waved at the window where a member of the SWAT team, armed and intent-appearing stalked past the van.

"Give them five minutes and place a call," said the Colonel.

At the four-minute mark the phone chimed. Marjorie looked at the Colonel and he nodded. She reached for the phone and noticed a slight tremor in her fingers. Frowning., she grasped the instrument harder and said, more abruptly than she'd intended, "Hello? This is Marjorie Kane. Who's this?"

The colonel beside her winced and she silently mouthed sorry at him.

"Mizz Kane. Obadiah here. You 'member me?"

"Apologies, Obadiah, I didn't mean to sound so impatient. Yes, of course I remember you. Alan and I met you at the Widow Elliot's home on the sad day of his funeral."

"Yeah. Okay, dat's right. I'm Obi."

"Obadiah, I'm not going to call you Obi, even if that's what you like your guys to call you. I know better about you. I looked you up at school. Use your education, use proper English."

The colonel frowned and raised a hand as if in protest of her assertiveness. She shook her head at him.

"Okay, Ms Kane. Yes, ma'am. You got me there." Obadiah sighed tiredly through the connection. My

233

guy, Judah, he said I should talk to you. I guess he and you had some connection. That right?"

"Judah? The man at the garage? I wouldn't call it exactly a connection, but yes, we have talked." Marjorie crossed her fingers, hoping he'd think of her appearance a few days ago at the garage of this home. Was that a street name for Klein?

"Yeah. He said you smart. He say you pretty sexy, too."

"Obadiah. Stop. Let's talk about getting you out of there safely. Do you have a child with you?"

He sighed again in her ear. "Yeah, my boy. An' his granny. 'Nother girl and her kid, too."

"Where's his mother? Your son's? Isn't she there?"

"No. She dead."

"Oh. Obadiah, I'm so sorry."

"S'all right. She turned no good. Long time ago. Lissen. There be seven, eight in here. Me, Joe Kline, both Hamilton brothers, Jody, he's my kid and his-- Junie's ma. Granny."

Marjorie noticed all three cops in the van were listening intently and scribbling notes. "Okay, Obadiah, got that. Where are—" there was a sudden bang as a weapon discharged somewhere in the house. "Obadiah! What was that?"

Everyone in the van flinched.

"No worries. No worries! JJ just tripped and his rifle went off."

"All right. Obadiah, we need to get you out of there before something worse happens. How can we do that?"

"Look. The cops think we killed the pastor, Elliot, and that girl—woman. At the church? We didn't have nothing to do with that! You hear what I'm sayin'?"

"I hear you. In fact, I believe you." Marjorie glanced at the colonel. He looked back, expressionless. "Our investigation is still going on and we are sure your group was not involved in those murders. Now,

234

can we end this without somebody getting shot?" She heard a rattle and a different voice hit her ear.

"Ms. Kane? David Kline here. Obadiah wants me to bring the kids and Jody's grandma to the front door. Can somebody take them?" His voice betrayed tension and maybe fear.

"Yes. Of course, David. Will you come too?"

"No. I'll stay with my boys." He severed the connection.

Marjorie lunged out of her chair. "I'm going up there."

"Wait. No. We can't allow that." The cops in the van were all of one mind. She was a civilian and couldn't go anywhere near that house.

Marjorie stared at the woman closest to the door. The female officer stared back at Marjorie and slowly removed her headphones.

"Look." Marjorie raised her voice. "You got me down here. I think they trust me. At least, Obadiah does." The female officer nodded. "I think she can do it."

Already on her feet, Marjorie went to the door and stepped down to the street. Behind her she heard the colonel bark "Jesus! Put a vest on her."

An older, grizzled officer who had obviously been around the block a few times, turned and nodded at her. "I'm gonna be your escort, ma'm." A young patrolman trotted up from down the street holding a Kevlar vest. He helped her put it on.

"Okay" she said. "Let's go." Together they stalked along the sidewalk and started up the steps.

"Don't try to engage," he grunted. "Just take the people that offer to go with you. Those that come to the door. And do not go inside." She glanced up at the house and saw a small face at the upstairs window. She waved and the face disappeared.

They stepped up on the small front porch, making no attempt to conceal their approach. The cop patted her shoulder and stepped back down the walk, turning his back on the house in a deliberate manner.

235

"Obadiah! Joel!" she shouted. "Come out. It's Marjorie Kane."

She reached to rap on the door when it swung open. She stepped back to the edge of the porch. An older, bent gray-haired woman appeared holding tight one hand of a small boy. "His daddy's back there with a gun," said the old woman in a low hoarse voice. Marjorie's stomach clenched.

"Jody?" cried Marjorie in a loud voice. "Is that you? Come here, baby."

The boy grimaced. He apparently didn't like being called baby. But he stepped forward and held up his arms. Without thinking about it, Marjorie took a long step to the door and swept the little boy into her arms. He was clearly frightened. The old woman glanced back over her shoulder and quickly followed. "The other boy's coming. Buddy. C'm on. Gotta go."

Marjorie stepped off the porch and bellowed back over her shoulder, "Obadiah! This is stupid. There's a hundred armed cops out here. Get your guys to drop their guns and come out of there. You want to see your son grow up, right?"

Marjorie held the little boy more tightly and ran down the steps. With the cop and grandma and the second boy a step behind her, she carried Jody, now quiet in her arms, down the walk and toward an ambulance that had drawn closer in the street. Behind her, she sensed officers with riot shields moving to protect her back. She deposited Jody into the ambulance and the care of an EMT and turned to the woman. She boosted the other little boy into the ambulance.

"Are you all right? Can I get you anything?" The woman, crying, shook her head and the other EMT took her gently by the arm and led her to a seat in the ambulance.

The cop patted Marjorie's shoulder smiled into her face and sent her back to the communications van after helping her out of the vest.

CHAPTER 47

"Good job, Ms. Kane," said the officer at the desk in the communications van. She accepted the smiles and nods of congratulation from other com van staff and a cup of steaming hot coffee into still trembling fingers. She took a call from Lockem and related a sharply condensed version of the rescue of the children and Obadiah's grandmother. An uneventful hour passed.

Members of the SWAT team were preparing to storm the residence as afternoon light began to fade. In spite of advice not to call, Marjorie called the house. The call went unanswered. Raised voices could be heard from the open windows. The argument seemed to move about the house and upstairs, then back down to the main level.

The ambulance took its occupants to nearby Regions Hospital Emergency Department.

Marjorie began to lose patience. She didn't want to watch SWAT officers storm the house. She didn't want to see shooting and loss of life. She jumped up and stormed out of the com van to find the SWAT team leader.

"Give me a bull horn," she insisted. "I'll try to talk them out of there." The SWAT commander looked at her intently for a long silent moment. Finally, apparently recalling her earlier success, he agreed. She took the bullhorn, walked to the end of the sidewalk at the curbside in plain sight and howled at the house. "Obadiah! Joel! Stop being so pig-headed! You know there's no escape. Be smart. Please put down your guns and come out of there."

She used every female argument she could remember against male recalcitrance . Behind her, beside a vehicle, she heard the police commander chuckling.

She paused for breath and to organize her thoughts and a single gunshot from the house rang out. "WAIT. Wait, she shouted. Stop. Obadiah? Joel?"

"It's okay," came a voice. "We're coming out. Just give us a minute." More officers moved up beside the house toward the front door.

Two of the youngest members, the Hamilton brothers, appeared in the doorway, hands raised overhead. When they reached the bottom step they were grabbed by officers and hustled off to the side, behind a shield and a tree.

Two more figures appeared in the doorway. One was holding the other up. Slowly, David Kline maneuvered a wounded Obadiah down the steps. His left side was dark with blood. Halfway down the steps, Obadiah's legs gave way and he and Kline tumbled to the sidewalk. Officers and an EMT jumped forward and pinned both men. Offering no resistance, both were quickly shackled. Other officers hurried into the house to secure the premises. Marjorie set down the loudspeaker and slumped to the bumper of a police vehicle. This crisis was over.

The Colonel walked to her side and put out a hand. "Thank you," he said. "Probably saved lives today. Some of these boys were running drugs up from the southern border. We monitored them pretty close and I couldn't ever see how they were involved in those murders at that church. I wish I could have told you sooner."

She nodded understanding. "Look at it this way. If you had, I wouldn't have been here today."

A Saint Paul officer trotted up. "Ms Kane? I'm to give you a ride home if you're ready?" She looked at the Colonel.

"Sure. Go home with our thanks. There'll be some follow-up, of course, but we'll call when we need you to report.." They shook hands again. She turned toward her ride and noticed that members of the cycle gang were already out of sight, in custody.

The ride home was silent, except for the occasional crackle of the radio. She sat quietly, eyes half closed, unwinding from the tension of the event. So much could have gone wrong, yet everybody involved seemed to have moved carefully to avoid exploding the situation. The attitudes and actions of the police had impressed her. She left the car and watched the officer exit the cul de sac. Lights blazed from every window and the front door swung open to the smiling face of Roseville PD Lieutenant Gage.

"Congratulations, hero," he said, squeezing her briefly in a tight embrace. "I had a call while you were in transit. Saint Paul is impressed and happy with your performance."

"I'm glad they're happy. I'm happy no one got killed, including yours truly. How's my guy?"

"I'm right here," Alan boomed from the doorway to his room, "and so pleased to have you home and safe."

Marjorie smiled broadly at the tall figure framed in the doorway and strode quickly across the room. She wound her arms around Lockem and pressed her face into his chest. She felt his arms slide smoothly over her shoulders and press her to his body. She noticed a slight tremble as he adjusted his stance and loosened her grip, not wanting to put pressure on his injuries.

"I remembered what you said once," she murmured. "Be calm, careful and centered."

"I was both terribly worried and absolutely sure you would handle things." He kissed the top of her head and eased back out of her embrace to sit on the edge of the bed.

"Well, the police had the scene under control so I really didn't have time to be afraid. I just didn't want anybody to get shot." Marjorie went on to briefly relate what had gone down at the biker house in Saint Paul.

Lockem turned with one arm around her shoulders and pulled her gently around so they sat together at the tiny table beside his bed. He smiled at her and said, "I think we need a small drink to

239

celebrate. This feels to me like we have not only saved a good guy, your undercover friend, but helped bust up a drug traffic ring."

"Really?" Marjorie raised her eyebrows in a question. "I did hear a bit about drug running."

"Yep, Gage explained while we were waiting for you to return. Some of the bikers were going back and forth between Minnesota and the Mexican border, carrying packages of cash and drugs. It's possible some of them didn't even know for sure what they were carrying."

"Interesting. How would they not know? I'm glad I was able to help them get David Kline out of there. And those boys. That's a piece of the murder case we can eliminate from inquiry going forward."

"Yep. I also think that the Cooper cousins are another timing coincidence. I'll bet we're going to learn they've been involved in some shady deals elsewhere in the world and they came here on the trail of that painting."

"Really? How strange. That leaves us with an almost empty cupboard of suspects for a double murder." She shook her head, looked up at her companion. "Weird. We do get a lot of strange cases but look-alike-twins in business chasing art scams around the world takes the cake."

"Or maybe the pie."

CHAPTER 48

"So, where are we, Madam sleuth?" Lockem's voice from the bathroom near the offices and living room and kitchen where he had been moved while his leg wound healed, boomed off the hard tile walls and bounced to Marjorie in the kitchen. She shook her head and continued to concentrate on softly scrambling the eggs to her companion's favorite texture.

"Madam sleuth is occupied with other matters at the moment. Just wait your turn," she called back.

When she heard him stump out of the lavatory, the sound of his crutch told her he was relying less and less on the metal brace. Recovery was more rapid than they had hoped even in their mutual optimism. "Sit. Sit," she commanded, pointing at the chair where she dished scrambled eggs and fresh toasted bagel. Two links of gently browned pork sausage added their aroma to the kitchen air.

Marjorie dished up the rest of the eggs, sausage and toast and took her own chair. She eyed her companion's ratty bathrobe. "I think it's time to move back up to our big bedroom," he remarked after a forkful of eggs and a slug of strong coffee. "I've been practicing that short flight of stairs. I only stumbled and fell once," he said, grinning.

She looked at him in brief alarm, then realized Lockem was kidding. "I think we have a clinic visit today, don't we?" she murmured.

"Correct. I'll get to demonstrate my dance steps for the good doc. But let's review. We got a few nuggets from the small number of former classmates of Elliot and Howland, but nothing that raised questions, right?"

She nodded.

"My trip to that gallery in Minnetonka revealed nothing. Your clandestine breakfast meeting with the undercover fed came up empty and we're waiting for anything useful from your successful hostage resolution."

Marjorie cleaned her plate and swallowed some coffee. "We're also still waiting for an expert report on the painting, we've discovered that the Cooper cousins are look-alikes who have been implicated but never arrested in some art thefts elsewhere. And I gently point out that discovering nothing in a particular area of a case is frequently something."

Lockem threw up his head and laughed. "Right you are." He sat back from the table smiling "And you've developed a chunk of information about the Bible thefts from the library in Minneapolis, by one of those Coopers. You know, I think we have enough evidence, backed by suspicions, to ask somebody to detain Ms Lorna Cooper for questioning, don't you think?"

Marjorie shook her head. "I'm not so sure. If the Coopers came to the Twin Cities to assess and possibly buy or steal that painting, there must be a client out there somewhere. But we haven't a clue. Arresting Lorna might just drive the client away."

"And that'd make you unhappy, right?"

"Yes."

"Remember, murders are neatly tied up in books, not in real life."

The landline telephone rang. Marjorie walked swiftly to the office and picked up. "Hello, Marjorie Kane here. Can I help you?"

"Hello, Marjorie. Amanda here. From MIA? I did the analysis of that painting in the church office. Remember?"

"Of course. How are you?"

"Fine. Listen, we found something that I wanted to share with you. It may not mean anything, but I thought you should know."

"Thank you, Amanda. What have you got?"

"Analysis of the paint turned up significant traces of copper ore." Amanda paused, as if she had made a big revelation.

After a moment to breathe, Marjorie said, "I'm sorry, Amanda, but what does that mean? Is copper ore common in artists' paints?"

"Sorry. Not this kind. It's a sulfide and it is extremely old. It pre-dates the Christian era. This is one way we can date artists paint, by the chemicals in the painting. It probably proves that the artist used paint from that region and at the time. In ancient times it was called Edom."

"Really! Wow."

"Yes. Really. I'd say it proves the provenance of the painting. There's been a good deal of archeological research in that area of Jordan in recent years. There have been some interesting discoveries. I won't bore you with the details, Marjorie, but the Kingdom of Edom, five or six thousand years ago was a big source of copper, and it predates the rise of the Iron Age."

Marjorie could tell Amanda was excited about the discovery and she was pleased the painting's provenance had been validated. The church membership would be happy with the information and the rise in value. The price had been high. Reverend Elliot had been their pastor for a relatively short time, but he was fast becoming a fixture in their lives when he was murdered.

Marjorie had more to think about. She relayed the new information to Lockem.

"It wouldn't be too surprising to learn the cousins Cooper had some prior intel about the painting. You know, we haven't got any intel on that apartment in Saint Anthony Park, have we?"

Marjorie stared away for a moment. "You're right. I better call Saint Paul."

"Get an investigator to go let you in," Lockem said. "I bet they've already processed the place, but it won't hurt for you to have a look-see."

The Saint Paul detective assigned to the double murder case gave Marjorie the name and number for the building supervisor. Marjorie accepted his offer to call the man to be sure there's be no problems letting her have access to the apartment. It was a five-minute drive and she was able to park on the street directly across from the three-story beige brick building on a corner lot.

It was an ordinary-looking rectangular brick structure, taking up all of the front and sides of the lot, with a broad concrete staircase that led directly to the front door. The windows were evenly spaced on all three floors with red-painted frames. She walked up the side street to cross the tiny, graveled parking area at the back. As she approached the rear door, it opened with a bang and an old man in a neat overall appeared.

"Ms. Kane?" he enquired.

She nodded, smiling. "That would be me."

"Saw you comin' up the walk. Guess you the investigator working on the church murders, right?"

"Yes, that would be me. Marjorie Kane, of Lockem and Kane. Pleasure to meet you, Mr. Edwin."

"Well, you just c'mon with me. That young lady had the smallest apartment in the building. One bedroom." Edwin led Marjorie up the well-lit carpeted staircase to the second floor. She noted that although the building had been constructed in the early part of the Twentieth Century, it looked clean and well-kept.

"Yep. We put new hall an' stair carpeting in a few years ago. Like to keep things nice, you know. Most of the tenants are long timers. In the two buildings," he waved at the south wall, "we got only three tenants less than three years. Here we are." He stopped, pulled out a ring of keys and unlocked the door. "You just shut the door when you're done. I'll prolly be in the basement if you need me." Edwin pushed the door open wide, stepped aside, smiled at her and went back down the hall the way they had come.

The air in the apartment was musty. Marjorie considered leaving the door ajar or opening a window but decided against it. She stood just inside the door, looked slowly around, and concluded almost instantly that this was likely a waste of time. Still, she would not stint in her examination of the apartment in the hope of learning something to help them identify the shooter.

244

Minimal furnishings, a small sofa, two armchairs a small desk and chair and a bookshelf of three levels made up the room. The bathroom contained a tub, stool, shower head and ratty curtain. The medicine cabinet was empty. A thin film of dust coated the radiator and just about every horizontal surface.

In the bedroom she found a bare mattress on a double bed frame, an empty two-drawer bureau, and a closet, also empty of all except a single black wire hanger. Closer examination of the closet walls door and floor led Marjorie to the conclusion that the apartment occupant had kept few if any clothes in the place.

The kitchen and living room, in contrast bore evidence of recent use. The electric stove and oven needed cleaning, there was a single glass on the drainboard and a mixed assortment of stainless utensils in the drawers. Under the sink, no wastebasket. All of the cabinets next to the empty refrigerator were also devoid of the usual sorts of containers of dry foods, condiments, and small tools, like a mixer. Marjorie suspected the police had either taken the missing items or the renter had not actually lived in the apartment.

Back in the living room, she opened the desk drawer. Like the rest of the place, empty, except for a single piece of narrow note paper lying in the center of the lap drawer. Scribbled on the paper was a list of words. Marjorie found tiny pieces of old tape attached to each end. Her questing fingers on the underside of the desk top detected residue of adhesive. She surmised the list had been carefully taped to the underside of the top of the desk, missed by the police and had fallen into the drawer. She took a small tweezer from her tool kit in her purse and slid the list into a plastic envelope, placed back in her purse. She spared a few more minutes to look for possible hiding places and found none. She left the apartment, called goodbye to Edwin, and drove home.

CHAPTER 49

Typing more notes into the computer file, Marjorie finished and then sat at her desk and just stared out the nearby window at the lawn. Lockem limped in. He'd graduated to a single crutch and was rapidly learning to maneuver without straining his injured leg. He looked at her for a few moments and then said, softly,

"Problems?"

"What? Oh, no. There was nothing at the apartment in Saint Paul of any use except this." She fished out the plastic envelope with the list she'd found in the desk drawer. "But I was just thinking. Melissa Elliot asked me about a bracelet her husband owned. She said it was a favorite and he always wore it. It's apparently gone missing."

"Right. I remember his wife mentioned it when we talked to her. The police report doesn't list it," Lockem said. "You haven't come across it. I don't know what else we can do."

"The question is, is it significant?"

Lockem leaned against the door jamb to take more weight off his injured leg. "Everything is potentially significant. Potentially. It's possible somebody in the case lifted it, but that would be highly unusual. What may be seriously significant is why the bracelet is missing and who has it."

Marjorie smiled, frowned, and then puffed out a breath. "I'm going to call the widow." She tapped in the number. Melissa Elliot answered promptly.

"Marjorie Kane., Mrs. Elliot. Just a couple of questions if you have a few minutes."

"Of course. I haven't had any news recently from the police about their investigation. Have you?"

"Mrs. Elliot, you have to be patient. The authorities are not inclined to talk to anyone about their investigations until they make arrests and request charges from the County Attorney. I have little knowledge about their progress with the case, but you might wish to know that the painting in the church office is authentic. We brought in some experts from the MIA and their tests and research conclude the painting is true, not a modern forgery. The scene is the desert south of Israel near the location of an ancient kingdom called Edom."

"I see." Marjorie got an impression Melissa Elliot didn't care whole lot about the painting.

"Mrs. Elliot. You asked me about a bracelet you say your husband wore. Do I remember that correctly?"

"Yes. It was a favorite. He wore it almost all the time."

"I couldn't locate a listing for it in the police files. Could you describe it for me?"

"It's a solid metal band, about an inch wide. Smooth with some kind of raised symbols down the middle. Must be about nine or ten little symbols around the whole circle. Martin told me he received it from a favorite teacher in graduate school when he graduated. He told me the symbols were religious but I didn't recognize them."

"Polished? Dull surface? What color is it?"

"Umm. Burnished, I'd say. It didn't have a mirror surface, you know, but sometimes it flashed light. The symbols were outlined in black, mostly, I think. He never took it off. Well, almost never. Wore it in the shower."

Marjorie could tell talking about the bracelet was hard for her and she decided to quit while Melissa still held herself together. "Just a couple more. What color? Was it silver?"

"Oh, no, it was a rosy kind of tan or brown. Martin didn't think it was valuable, except personally to him, you know."

"Could you call it copper colored? A copper bracelet?" Marjorie paused and took a breath. "Was he wearing it the day he died?" she asked more softly.

247

"Yes," Melissa affirmed. Her voice quivered. "He was. You would call it a copper bracelet. Is that all? I do have to go."

Marjorie nodded as if Melissa could see her. "Thank you, very much. Again, I am so sorry for your loss. Take care." She closed the call and transferred her scribbled notes to the computer file. A copper bracelet. A painting showing a scene near a pre-Christian copper mine. What a development. But how relevant?

She and Lockem had borrowed two family albums from the widow and digitized all the pictures they found of the murdered man. Now Marjorie began to go through the folder, looking for a picture that included the missing bracelet on Martin Elliot's wrist.

Search programs in her computer resulted in nothing, even though she employed some complex and very powerful processing programs. So Marjorie began a careful, visual scan of pictures in the file. After an hour of staring at sloppily framed, often out-of-focus shots of the Pastor and his family, she hit the mother lode.

There, in sequence, were a series of pictures from a family lakeside outing on a warm summer day. In three of the photographs she saw a bracelet on Elliot's left wrist. It was a narrow band that was obviously just large enough to slip over his compressed hand. In one fuzzy shot he'd slid it part-way up his forearm. She could see symbols on the band just below the ridge of squeezed flesh. One other shot sharp and crisp of he and his wife, she copied to the color printer and then enlarged and enhanced the image as much as their equipment allowed to make another color print, this one of the dead pastor's wrist from hand to elbow.

It was fortunate that the original camera had been in steady hands and was apparently a good quality lens. Even after her manipulation of the selected image, the wrist and circling bracelet were crisp and well-defined. Marjorie was sure she'd be able to recognize it if she came across it.

She placed a call to an acquaintance Alan had developed at the city morgue. He promised he'd check the container of effects removed from the body. While they were on the phone, he had scanned the list of effects. No bracelet was listed. No jewelry of any kind was listed.

When she appeared at the door to Lockem's temporary bedroom, he was deeply engrossed in a large book he'd retrieved from the bookshelf in his office. He was holding it open, resting it on the cast that still protected his damaged thigh.

"What have we here?" She inquired.

"Reading up on the Middle East," he smiled. You have news?

"More like more mystery. Turns out Elliot always—emphasis on always—wore a small copper bracelet. But there was no bracelet on the body when he went to the morgue."

"So it's possible somebody, like a killer, removed it after shooting Elliot. Copper, you say?" His voice sharpened more than he probably intended. "That could be important. We need to find it."

Marjorie stood in the doorway, silent. Obviously, Alan thought the bracelet was important. She opened her mouth to say something, but Alan continued, "Sorry, I've just been reading about that ancient area, the Kingdom of Edom. That's the place that painting might be illustrating. The people there became the principal sellers, world-wide, of copper ingots."

"No shit!" she exclaimed. A rare expletive. "That's what Elliot's bracelet is made of. Coincidence? Oh, I don't think so."

"He might have known of the kingdom. It was in Old Testament writings and studied in the early years of the Twentieth Century. But the copper ore lode wasn't seen as so important until just a few years ago." He waved the magazine he'd been reading. "Apparently scientists believe the copper ingot production came from sophisticated operations by skilled, well-paid workers. Huge. Large."

"What does that, fascinating as it is, have to do with our murders?"

249

"Probably nothing directly," Lockem nodded, grinning. "Except. As you sort of noted, it's a coincidence revealed to help us solve the murders."

"Huh," she grunted. "I have to admit, on rare occasions, something happens or there is an odd reveal to help us along the winding pathway to truth."

Chapter 50

Heat sent shimmers of dusty air across the
street and yard. Marjorie stood by the front bumper of
her car, looking up at the Elliot home. The yard looked
untended. She saw a curtain askew in an upstairs
window, a reminder of another upstairs window and a
small face peering down.

She walked briskly up the steps to the front door,
wondering if Trevor Howland was present. He seemed to
show up frequently and not wanted. When she'd called
to ask to see Melissa Elliot, she'd gotten a fleeting
impression of another adult in the room. She couldn't
have said why she felt that way; there'd been no
hesitation in Melissa's voice when she agreed to see
Marjorie, it had just been a feeling, a faint sense of
unease. There had been nothing in their brief
conversation that gave Marjorie pause; perhaps she'd
just been listening or hoping for something, anything,
that would be a clue. But a clue to what? She ground
her teeth in frustration and banged on the door. She'd
already learned that the Elliots had a dysfunctional
doorbell.

Melissa Elliot opened the door to Marjorie with a
small smile on her lips. Her welcome was soft and to the
point. "Come in, Ms Kane." It was apparent she would
tolerate this visit with a minimum of enthusiasm. When
they entered the back sunroom, there sat Trevor
Howland. Marjorie instantly rearranged her questions in
her mind. She'd intended to gently disarm Melissa Elliot
into revealing more about her relationships and social
activities outside the marriage and the church. She'd
planned to gradually lead into her relationship,
whatever it might be, with Trevor Howland. Now,
however, with her principal target present, she'd deviate
from her original plan.

"Hello. Ms. Kane, isn't it?" Howland stood and
extended his hand. Marjorie nodded in acknowledgment
and they briefly shook. Howland's hand was soft and

251

she didn't detect any calluses. His grip was almost non-existent, as if his fingers had no muscles.

"Would you like tea? We're having tea," Melissa asked. She sounded a little nervous.

"Thank you. That would be nice," Marjorie said. "Well, Mr. Howland, how are you getting along? I imagine experiencing such a shocking death of a long-time friend, must be unsettling at the very least."

"It is, it is," he nodded. "But things are moving along. My company wants to move me to Chicago as soon as I can get away. It's a nice promotion." He smiled in a way Marjorie interpreted as almost a self-satisfied smirk. She didn't like Trevor Howland, she reflected silently, watching Melissa bring the teapot and another cup. She hadn't liked him the first time they met, but she didn't know why. Her reaction apparently came from the same part of her psyche she used to evaluate men she met when working in strip joints in her past.

She watched Melissa pour the tea and savored the sweet aroma. She took the cup and held it on her lap. Melissa sat across from her on the sofa next to Trevor. "I just need to verify a few things. How are the children doing?"

Melissa smiled. "Right now they are at the neighbors. They seem to be doing all right, probably better than I am." She glanced at Howland who didn't seem to react.

"I wondered if you have had any recollections since last we talked as to any contacts you might have had with Delilah Cooper? When we last spoke you said you hadn't. It's just that we found some indications at the church that Mr. Elliot may have known her."

"Sure," Howland spoke up. "I'm pretty sure he did. I remember him mentioning a pretty woman new to the congregation that he was counseling."

Melissa glanced at him with a bit of a frown and Howland's voice faltered and he stopped talking. Melissa appeared to shake her head slightly. Marjorie sensed this might be a sensitive topic.

252

"I believe you told me you would be selling this house and moving with the children to the Chicago area. Do I have that right?"

Melissa nodded. "Yes, I believe so, although the lack of a resolution to the case is apparently slowing things down." She grimaced. "Our real estate agent told me we might have to cut the asking price."

Marjorie nodded. She'd encountered this barrier before. A crime associated with a property frequently delayed or reduced the price. "Have you had any recent communication from any of the boys in that motorcycle group?"

"Oh, yes," Melissa smiled. "Obadiah calls every week. So does David Klein. I think they miss their sessions with Martin."

"I notice you never refer to him as Marty. Is that just a non-habit?"

Melissa smiled. "He didn't like Marty. I guess some people called him Marty when he was in school somehow disparaging him."

Howland smirked. "Oh yeah. When he did stuff in high school, there was a certain group. Jocks, you know? Marty, Marty, Marty. Like a chant. In college, in Indiana, I could jack him up a little if I called him that."

Marjorie sent him her most insincere smile, the smile she had developed long ago when she'd be pestered in the clubs where she danced in revealing costumes by aggressively amorous male spectators who figured, wrongly, that she was available to anyone who could afford the tariff.

"Trevor, I noticed you went to some of the same colleges after your two graduated from high school. Were you really close?"

"Well, yeah. I mean we were best buds last three years at White Bear. So after he told me he'd been accepted to that little college in Illinois, I just decided to try there too." He shrugged. "I mean, I didn't really care where I went. My folks just pressured me to get a college degree. So I went."

"What did you major in?" Marjorie asked.

"Marketing and sales. I eventually got my BA from the U in Minneapolis. At the time they had a distance learning program and took all my credits from Illinois. I didn't want to go to Divinity school. So I came back home and got a job and my B.S. Now I work for XMR. Good job." Trevor smiled.

"XMR?" He hadn't told Marjorie anything she didn't already know but here was a small opening. "What does XMR stand for?"

Howard stared past her for a moment. "You know, I don't know. I don't think I've ever heard it."

Marjorie turned her attention to the widow. "I know it's difficult and painful, but could you tell me again about that day, the day your husband was found?

"Oh." Melissa's hand holding the teacup stopped halfway to her mouth and Marjorie felt her toes tense, waiting for a splash of liquid to the carpet. A noticeable tremor disturbed the surface of the tea and Melissa carefully bent forward and placed the cup and saucer on the table beside her. "I guess—I suppose I can go over it again. You know I was interviewed extensively by a detective from Saint Paul."

Marjorie inclined he head once. "Yes, I am aware." She didn't go on to say she had found the written report to be spare and unhelpful. "Please start with your morning, if you don't mind." She noticed Howland glancing at Melissa before turning his gaze once more in her direction.

As Marjorie worked her way through a series of prepared questions, her attention registered the tension that seemed to flow occasionally between Melissa and Trevor Howard. Was it just his effort to support her in her bereavement, which was apparent sometimes, or did his attention run deeper? If he was, in effect, romancing the widow, did her apparent discomfort have to do with Marjorie's presence or something else? At one point in her mis-jointed, sometimes rambling, narrative of her day up to the explosion of the police appearance to tell her of her husband's death, Howland's hand had crawled across the space between them on the cushion of the sofa and he touched her hand. When Melissa snatched her fingers away into her lap without looking at Howland, Marjorie thought she might have detected a look of disappointment.

Chapter 51

In a deliberately unstructured appearing way, Marjorie led Melissa through her day. Occasionally she accommodated Trevor Howard's intense appearing interest with a quick question to him as well.

"Mr. Howard, were you at work the whole day? That day?"

"Oh, sure. Sometimes I visit a client. You know, part of my job involves client evaluation. Our insurance people often want an independent impression of a new client. XMR is particular about who we insure."

"Really? That's interesting." Marjorie turned back to Melissa to follow up on when she'd left home to pick up the children from their day school.

"The school is a few blocks north of us. I usually have one of the cars, but that day, one was in the shop. It was a nice day, so I walked. When I got back, police were here." Tears leaked down her cheeks.

"If you'd called, I could have picked you up," Howland said.

"You were in Minnetonka, at work, you said."

"Well, yeah, but I would have come. You know that." He glanced at Marjorie as if to see if she was following the conversation. She had her head bent so her gaze appeared to be on the notebook in her lap.

'When do you plan to move back home?" Marjorie kept her voice calm, her pen at the ready.

Melissa frowned and pursed her lips. "I don't know, anymore. Originally I thought we could go almost right away after the lawyers and—and the po—police wrapped up the case."

Marjorie could see she was near tears. "I'm sorry. I know this is difficult."

"Cops have been sniffing around for a long time. I think it's pretty clear one of those women did it. One of those cousins." Howland's voice was harsh. Marjorie opened her mouth to say something but Melissa raised a hand toward Howland as if to protest or calm him.

"Well, it's true! Those women showed up and caused all sorts of trouble! Mel, I think we ought to get the girls out of school and move to Chicago. Put all this behind us."

Marjorie could see agitation and perhaps some embarrassment growing in Melissa. She began to wonder anew about their relationship. It seemed clear to her that Trevor Howland was continuing to press his relationship with the dead pastor's wife, whose cheeks now blossomed with a rosy hue.

"Trevor?" Her voice quavered and she stared rigidly at the cushion between them.

He jumped to his feet and pointed an accusing finger at Marjorie. "And it's your fault. Coming around. Stickin' your noses in. It's too bad that truck on the river road didn't do a better—" he stopped suddenly, mouth gaping.

"How do you know about that?" Marjorie was on her feet, hard stare stabbing at Howland. "We never said a word about that. How do you know about Alan's accident?"

"I—I don't—it must have been in the newspaper. I don't exactly remember. Anyway," he waved his arms, "what difference does it make? Why can't you just` butt out and let us alone?"

Howland spun around and Marjorie could see his shoulders trembling.

"Trev? What's she talking about?" Melissa Elliot had also risen to her feet.

"Oh, screw this," he shouted and jumped for the door to the kitchen. Moments later the back door slammed as he tore out of the house.

Melissa shook her head and said softly, "I'm sorry. He sometimes just goes up like that. Temper tantrums. His wife left him recently."

"I want to know how he knows about the accident." Marjorie's voice rose as she got up from the settee. "I think I'll leave now, but you have to do some serious thinking about your relationship with that man." A window across the room splintered and the

257

settee shuddered. Marjorie flinched and lunged at the other woman when a second shot crashed into the room. Melissa Elliot cried out and grabbed her left side as Marjorie crashed into her and sent both of them sprawling to the floor.

An automobile engine wailed a loud careening whine from the back yard where Howland had parked and quickly faded. From her prone position on the carpet, Marjorie twisted her head to locate her purse and her holstered Pico. It lay on a straight chair cross the room. She started to crawl toward it when she heard Melissa whimper and start to cry softly. She looked and saw Melissa's shirt staining red with more blood seeping through the fabric.

"He shot me," Melissa whimpered. "It hurts."

Marjorie crawled to her and yanked the tail of the other woman's shirt out of her skirt. She found a short furrow just above Melissa's hip where the bullet had broken the skin as it went by. She pulled the tail of Melissa's shirt around and stuffed it over the wound. Then she slithered across the floor and grabbed her cell. The 911 operator responded on the second ring and instantly related she was dispatching a police unit and an ambulance. Marjorie stayed on the line to reassure the operator that she and the wounded woman were in no immediate danger.

The welcome sound of an approaching siren, doors slamming and heavy footsteps pounding closer, screen doors flung open, and shouted commands prompted Marjorie to replace her pistol in her bag. She put a hand over Melissa's wound and sat up with her back against the settee.

Two uniformed officers burst into the room guns drawn. In terse language Marjorie explained the situation and one officer exited immediately through the door to the back yard to confirm the shooter had left the yard.

An ambulance arrived and the attendants took Melissa to the hospital after she called to have her girls sheltered. An hour of interrogation and explanations ensued but as the sun faded into the horizon behind the cities, Marjorie and the police officers took leave and Marjorie drove home to Roseville. She took her time and carefully surveyed the vehicles around her at every stop sign and traffic light. Trevor Howland hadn't been located and while she hadn't seen him with a pistol, Marjorie knew he had been the shooter. Saint Paul police were treating the fugitive as armed and dangerous.

Exiting the garage up into the living room, she discovered two police officers in the house with Alan. He mumbled and kissed her on both cheeks. "Lieutenant Gage is busy but he sent a patrol unit to meet you."

"That was nice of him, but I'm fine."

"Sure. I think he just wants to be prepared if Howland comes after you."

Marjorie frowned. "I think he'll run away." She looked up at Alan. "Melissa was understandably upset but just before the ambulance took her to the hospital she muttered something about Howland's arm. I didn't pay much attention but now I wonder if she didn't see the missing bracelet on his wrist."

Lockem stared at her. "Would he be that arrogant? Or careless?"

She shrugged slowly. "Can't say, obviously."

Chapter 52

Hours later, after the police squad left their home Lieutenant Gage showed up at the door with a large brown paper sack containing several containers of appetizer food from a local restaurant. While he laid out the containers on the dining room table he announced that he had invited a guest to join them.

"Justine?" queried Lockem in his "told you so," tone to Marjorie.

Gage paused laying out tableware and cast a stern look at his host. "Yes, if it's any of your business."

"Since it's my home, I guess it is, sort of. Not that I'm suggesting I should disapprove—or necessarily approve of your, um, love life."

Gage shook his head and grinned.

"Boys, boys. Play nice or I'll send you to your rooms," came a voice from the kitchen where Marjorie was wrestling a large pot of water onto the biggest burner. Spaghetti and meatballs with a home-made sauce she'd developed over years of experimentation would be the main course.

The doorbell chimed and Gage turned to greet the newcomer. He flung open the door and an enthusiastic welcome died on his lips. Standing on the step, Justine Temple, hands at her sides didn't look happy. She looked deeply concerned.

"Inside," said the man almost hiding close behind her. He prodded her in the back. Gage shifted to one side and recognized a pistol Trevor Howland pressed to the small of Temple's back. He raised his hands in surrender and backed slowly into the entryway.

In the kitchen, Marjorie raised her head to call a welcome, when her gaze fastened on Lockem. His rigid stance and arm and hand pointing rigidly toward the floor behind his thigh told her something was amiss. She slid sideways to conceal herself as Howland forced Gage and Justine Temple and then Lockem ahead of him toward the living room.

"Go, he snarled, "into that room. Don't even think of it," he raged at Gage. "If you try for your gun I'll shoot you right now. I don't care anymore. My life is ruined. Where's your wife?" He snarled at Lockem and pushed Temple hard into Gage's arms, sending them both sprawling onto a couch.

"Upstairs," Lockem said, "Getting dressed."

"Call her. Get her down here."

"Marjorie?"

"Just a minute, hon." Her muffled voice came from somewhere closer, but Howard wouldn't know that.

"Get down here," Howard suddenly shouted. He stepped away from Justine's feet and his finger flexed. The pistol he held fired a bullet into the ceiling with a boom, and everybody flinched. The room went quiet. Then Howard began to snarl and curse, hurling obscenities and threats at everyone while he waited impatiently for Marjorie to appear.

An empty saucepan flew into the room and landed on the carpet with a soft thump. Howard's attention and his gun hand followed the arc of the pan. As he turned back toward the kitchen entry, Marjorie stepped into sight, swinging a heavy iron frying pan with all her might. The pan met Howard's gun hand with a loud clang. The collision sent the pistol flying. Howard screamed in pain and grabbed his wrist. Gage and Temple flung themselves at the intruder and brought him down in a tangle of shouts and a smashed table lamp. Marjorie came around, ready to flail out again with the frying pan. Lockem speared the fallen pistol with his crutch and bent to grab it.

Clutching the pistol he swung toward Howard. "Stop!" He roared. "I'll shoot you." He thumbed off the safety, pointed the weapon at the wall just above Trevor Howard's head and everyone froze again. After what seemed a long minute, Justine Temple rolled off the floor, grabbed handcuffs from her bag. Howard heaved a deep ragged breath and seemed to gather himself for a leap at Lockem. Justine rolled over onto

261

Howard's splayed legs and back and cuffed his hands behind him. She hauled him up by one shoulder and shoved him roughly to a chair.

Lieutenant Gage picked up his cell and called 911. Within minutes a squad arrived along with two detectives from Roseville. The squad took Trevor Howard into custody and the two detectives efficiently went about taking statements.

Deputy Sergeant Justine Temple spent the most time with a detective relating how Howard had accosted her just outside and forced her into the house at gunpoint.

Marjorie gave the shortest response to detective's questions. "He came past the kitchen entrance. He had a gun. I hit his hand with the frying pan."

A couple of hours later, the two couples sat together in the living room. Marjorie eyed Gage and Temple, holding hands on the couch and said, "Well, children, the snacks are gone, but I can still make spaghetti. If anybody is hungry."

"What about you?" asked Gage. "You're the civilian here," resulting in snorts of relieved laughter around the room. Tension over the dangerous intrusion continued to dissipate.

"I think Marjorie deserves at least an honorary badge," Temple grinned. "Or maybe a contract with the Twins. That was quite a swing."

Marjorie rose and went to cook the spaghetti, secure in the warm smile Lockem sent with her.

Sometime later, after a fine supper and exclamations and jokes over Lieutenant Gage's fumbled announcement of his engagement to Justine Temple, and her announcement that she had been promoted by the Washington County sheriff's department to Commander of the Investigations Division, Marjorie said,

"Trevor Howland was wearing Elliot's missing bracelet tonight."

"I noticed that," acknowledged Lockem. "Another nail, you might say, in the man's coffin. The police have been alerted to the significance of the bracelet and will no doubt pin down its ownership and travels."

"Looks like all is secure," murmured Gage, obviously more interested in his companion than in the ratty tail-end of the case of the two murders in the church.

"I am still not sure I understand what pushed Trevor Howard off the cliff."

Lockem looked up from his plate. "We know that ever since they hooked up in high school, Howard has been chasing Elliot. Their rivalry wasn't ever heated, even when they went to the same colleges in Indiana. And it appears from all we learned, that he gave up for a while on Melissa. He split from Elliot, got married and began to develop a career."

"That's right," Marjorie chimed in. "He and his former wife were having marriage issues when Pastor Elliot and Melissa showed up in the Twin Cities. That apparently roused all Trevor's old issues and he set out to seduce Melissa and take her away from Elliot."

"That's so sad," chimed in Justine, shaking her head slowly. "He probably could have been saved with some counseling."

"Lorna Cooper told the police she was pretty sure her cousin planned to go to the church to get a closer look at the painting the day she was murdered." Marjorie frowned. "They are such smart, talented women. It's a shame they turned to crime. Howard apparently went to the church intending to kill Martin Elliot and after he shot him, discovered Delilah in the sanctuary."

Gage roused himself to sit straighter and said, "Now that Howard is in custody, I guess the thing is wrapped up, yes?"

"The thing?" Marjorie teased. "I do believe "the thing" as you put it, is completed. The remaining cousin is in custody as is our killer."

"I don't get it all, I guess," murmured Justine. "Pardon my inquisitiveness. How are the Coopers involved in this business?"

"It turns out they've been working for years as a team. They're suspected of scams involving illegal acquisition of art objects from collectors and even companies all over the world. Apparently they came to the Twin Cities after learning about that painting." Marjorie shook her head. "The painting has been authenticated and the historian thinks the scene may be close to the entrance to the ancient kingdom of Edom. Remember, that's where all the copper ore came from back then."

"Only one or two holes that may never be filled," smiled Lockem. "We still don't know who ran me off the road, or why, and there's that mysterious hole in the organ pipe in church and—" he hesitated, glanced at Marjorie and picked up a plastic envelope. "And this."

Justine came more alert and leaned forward out of Gage's arm over her shoulder. "This? What's that?"

"Oh, I am not sure," said Marjorie. "I discovered this list of names or places or something in that empty apartment the cousins rented in Saint Anthony Park. Pure fluke."

"You did? Huh." Justine plucked the plastic bag from Marjorie's fingers and stared closely at it. "What do you think it means? The cops missed this?"

"It was well-hidden, taped under a desk drawer. The tape gave up when I opened the drawer." Marjorie smiled.

"I think it is time for us to depart," said Gage, glancing at his wrist watch.

Lockem, crutch firmly under one arm walked the couple to the door and bussed Justine on her cheek as they left. "Another day another clue, another puzzle."

Books by Carl Brookins

TRACES A Senior Sleuth crime novel
GRAND LAC A Senior Sleuth crime novel
THE CASE OF THE GREEDY LAWYERS
A LAKE SUPERIOR MYSTERY
THE INSIDE PASSAGE
THE CASE OF THE YELLOW DIAMOND
RED SKY
REUNION